INTO THE LAWLESS LAND...

When Sam T. entered the low-ceilinged adobe structure, he immediately noted the two men at the bar. They stopped drinking and eyed him suspiciously.

"What's your business here?" the taller one demanded. Sam T. realized that, even drunk, these men would be deadly. He calculated that Jesus and Too-Gut had enough time to be in place.

A woman shouted from the back of the cantina. The men whirled and drew their guns.

Sam T. dropped to his knees, the .45 in his hand. His gun kicked and the roar of pistols blasted the room. Sam's bullet caught the taller outlaw in the chest and sent him sprawling backward onto a table. The shorter one headed for the back, but Too-Gut's rifle cut him down before he reached the rear doorway . . .

"Action explodes on the opening page in Dusty Richards' account of Arizona lawlessness, and the pace does not let up until the last outlaw has been salted away—and there are plenty of them."

—Elmer Kelton, author of *The Bitter Trail* and *The Time It Never Rained*

THE
LAWLESS
LAND

DUSTY RICHARDS

St. Martin's Paperbacks

This is a work of fiction. All of the characters, organizations, and events portrayed in this novel are either products of the author's imagination or are used fictitiously.

THE LAWLESS LAND

Copyright © 2000 by Dusty Richards.

All rights reserved.

For information address St. Martin's Press, 175 Fifth Avenue, New York, NY 10010.

ISBN: 978-1-250-09195-6

Our books may be purchased in bulk for promotional, educational, or business use. Please contact your local bookseller or the Macmillan Corporate and Premium Sales Department at 1-800-221-7945, ext. 5442, or by e-mail at MacmillanSpecialMarkets@macmillan.com.

Printed in the United States of America

St. Martin's Paperbacks edition / May 2000

St. Martin's Paperbacks are published by St. Martin's Press, 175 Fifth Avenue, New York, NY 10010.

10 9 8 7 6 5 4 3 2

ACKNOWLEDGMENTS

There are books where worthy supporters must be acknowledged; this series about the Territorial Marshals has more than the usual amount of people to be recognized. First, Jory Sherman, the dean of western writers, gave me a blueprint many years ago for these books. For him and his sage advice I am most grateful. Dr. Frank Reuter, my teacher in fiction. Then my writer's group: Velda Brotherton, a.k.a. Samantha Lee; Judy Ballard; and Charlé Pierson, who were great mentors. To Linda Qualls, who typed the first drafts and always believed. A kind thanks to Lynn Carney and Louise Goodman, who helped. To all my great friends in Western Writers of America, Oklahoma Writers Federation, Ozark Writers League, and the Eureka Springs Creative Writers Conference. To Dan, Peggy Eoff and Linda Heddon at the National Chuckwagon Racing Championship in Clinton, Arkansas, where each Labor Day Weekend I share the announcing chores with Danny Newland. To all my great rodeo and western friends who have helped, supplied ideas and sources to find things. To the Cherry Weiner Literary Agency, which never once gave up, and

Marc Resnick, my editor, who allowed me the opportunity to bring the Arizona territorial days alive again. And to my wife Pat, who has supported my writing since the first day, before the first rejection, and still shares my enthusiasm for it. And you, the reader—God bless you all, and thanks.

—Dusty Richards

PROLOGUE

MAY 25TH, 1880

MAY 25TH, 1880
Beneath the hot midday sun, Diego Fernandez and five gang members rode up to the isolated mine office. They reined their sweaty horses to a stop before the hitch rail and Diego prepared to dismount. A tall hombre emerged from the doorway. Dressed in a dark brown suit, he wore a bowler hat cocked to the side. He stepped into the sunshine on the porch under the sign announcing HALLELU-JAH MINING COMPANY. Suspicious of this gringo, Diego remained in the saddle and carefully studied the big man.

A pained expression of impatience and contempt was written on the gringo's face, like he wondered why he even bothered to come outside for the likes of them. Then he spat off the platform and in a big voice said, "We ain't hiring today. Come back next week."

"You stupid *bastardo*, we ain't looking for no work!" Diego drew his Navy cap and ball .44 and shot him through his stomach. A crimson spray left droplets of blood on the office wall as the man crumpled to the wooden floor. With a wave of Diego's pistol as their cue, the others dismounted with noisy cheers. The outlaws rushed past the prone body, charged inside the office and, in a boiling hell of sulfurous gun smoke, mowed down a bookkeeper wearing a green visor cap, Neptune Allen; the president of the company, J. C. Fremont; and the mine superintendent, Able Drumright.

Finding the doors to the tall green safe unlocked, Diego allowed a smile of relief to cross his face. He swung the doors back and told the others to start filling up the stack of canvas bags. The men holstered their weapons and hauled the packets of rich gold ore outside.

From the window Diego could see Black, the tall Texan on horseback, and the three large red mules with panniers hung on their crossbuck saddles. The men filled them with the heavy canvas bags from the safe. Meanwhile, the youngest gang member, Raphael, stripped the bodies and put the booty in a large sack. The youth's job completed, Diego looked around one last time, satisfying himself they had taken everything of value. He followed Raphael outside.

"Burn it!" Black ordered and indicated for Diego to do so.

He rushed back in the office, began to smash the coaloil lamps, and spread their greasy contents over everything: desks, papers, ledgers and even the bodies. In a minute, this place would be ablaze and they'd be gone with the gold. He smiled to himself at the ease with which they completed their deadly task.

A gunshot outside shattered his confidence. The glass globe he was holding slipped from his fingers and broke on the floor. Filled with concern, he rushed to the doorway in time to watch the others pouring bullets into a downed man's body on the porch. His clothes smoldered from so many shots at close range. A derringer was still grasped in his outstretched hand. Diego blinked through the bitter haze of smoke and saw Jose Ruiz holding his wounded brother Raphael on the ground.

"Next time, you be damn sure they're dead," Black said. "Load him up. We ain't got all day."

"But he will die if we move him," Jose protested.

"He'll die anyway. Load up! Lamas said to clear out, and that means now! Get in there and burn that sumbitch down!"

"*Sí.*" Saddened by the shooting of the young man, Diego went back inside and struck a match on the desktop; then, holding some important-looking papers in a wad, he lit them. With his torch, he set the oil afire in a flash and ran out to his horse.

The others had already loaded Raphael on his mount and one rode on each side to steady him. Black told them to split up and how they were to be at the next meeting place in three days.

A few miles from the mine office, they halted to care for the wounded man. Diego looked back. Black smoke from the burning building rose like a great beast in the azure sky. Would it draw the authorities down on them? With a head shake for the unknown, he bounded off his horse to do what he could about the wounded man.

"I—am—gut—shot and dying," Raphael moaned when they laid him gently on the ground. "Someone shoot me. Please?"

Blood rushed from between the man's fingers where he clutched his stomach. Diego was forced to draw in his breath. The men looked at each other, for who would answer the dying man's wishes? The only sounds were the *whit-woo* calls of quail off in the chaparral.

"You can't die, my brother—" Jose began to cry.

They could not stay there all day. *God forgive me.*

Diego stepped before the man, drew his pistol and mercifully shot him between the eyes. Raphael's head slumped to the side.

"Put him over his horse. We will bury him someplace

away from here," Diego said, then he tried to swallow the great knot in his throat. He never minded killing rich gringos like that surly one back at the mine—but his own kind was much harder. Holy, blessed Virgin Mary, forgive me . . .

At dark, they buried Raphael under a pile of rocks in a lonesome canyon, then used switches of pungent greasewood to wipe out their tracks in the soft places. In somber silence, they split up again. Somewhere out in the night, a red Mexican wolf bitch sang a sorrowful requiem for Raphael.

MAY 29TH, 1880

Diego lay on his belly, overlooking a dry wash. He raised the new oily-smelling .44/.40 Winchester to his shoulder. Greasewood branches and tall dry grass rustled around him. A creosote odor hung in the hot air. He could look up and study the peaks of Mount Lemmon to his left. It would be much cooler high up there. Hot sunshine glinted off the deep sand in the crossing and forced him to squint.

A wagon was coming. He could hear it and the drum of horse hooves. He looked down the barrel through the buckthorn sight at the tiny brass bead, then eased the hammer back with a click.

Two people in a buckboard, a man and a woman. The man driving, and he reined the two sweaty buckskins down to a walk as they started to cross the wash. Fine horses, they danced on their front legs, snorted and breathed hard from running. Diego drew aim and shot the near one. It crumpled; the other one reared in fright and Diego's second bullet sent it over backward in the traces. The horses screamed in pain. The woman was spilled off on the ground and the gang's cross fire cut down the hatless, gray-headed man before he could fully draw his six-gun.

"No! No!" she screamed hysterically.

Diego rose to his feet. Lamas rode up on his shiny bay horse. Such a handsome man, his features were Castillian and Diego envied his leader's good looks. Even dressed as peon for this robbery, Lamas looked more like a *generale* to Diego. Lamas gave him a nod of approval for good shooting. Filled with pride, Diego rushed down the steep bank to help the others. More gang members hurried in on horseback. Near the buckboard, wide-eyed with a mixture of rage and fear, the woman charged Diego. He used his rifle as a ram and shoved her down. Stupid bitch. For a moment, she blinked at him in disbelief; then, as if realizing the danger she was in, she moved crablike away on her butt. He sneered at the horse-faced old hag, too ugly for him to even bother with, and went on.

Benito caught her by the hair and jerked her up.

"You know what I am going to do to you, woman?" the outlaw asked. Then, grinning, he drug her to the edge of the wash, with her yelling, "Oh, no. God, no!"

Black pushed his stout roan in close to the rig, where some of the gang members stripped the dead man's body. They were taking handfuls of money from the man's pockets. The big Texan held out the canvas sack for them to fill.

Diego picked up the dead man's pistol. Using his sleeve, he tried to brush away the dust and grit from the blue metal parts. A good new .45.

"Keep it," Black said to him.

Diego grinned gratefully at the tall man and stuck the Colt in his waistband. He could use a new-model revolver. Some of the others were already having a time with the long-toothed white woman, whose kicking bare legs flashed in the sunlight while they pinned her down on her back. He overheard them say they would have "turns." Hernandez dropped his pants. His bare butt shone in the sun, then he went down on top of her. A loud cheer went up from the men.

"Tell them to meet us at the crossing on the Santa Cruz above Tubac in three days," Black said with a disgusted look and shook his head at all the commotion going on over the woman.

"And remind them that everyone rides in alone or Lamas will be angry. And Diego, you take his holster too. You made some great shots on those horses." Then the big man rode off to join Lamas.

"*Sí.*" Diego hurried to strip the fine holster off the dead man and tell the others where they must meet at next.

JUNE 5TH, 1880

Diego sprawled on his belly in the deep cover for a long while and waited for the mine payroll to arrive. A good wind helped ease the stifling heat, but it rattled the willows and tall grass stems around him. Noisy mockingbirds chattered in the cottonwoods. Beside the sound of the river's rush, it was hard for him to hear well. He would be glad when the payroll wagon finally got there.

At last, two guards with rifles appeared across the shallow ford on their horses. They stopped, stood up in their stirrups, viewed the crossing. Seeing nothing out of place, they started across the shallow Santa Cruz River. Behind them, the light wagon with a driver and shotgun rider on the spring seat entered the stream.

When the rig reached midstream, Diego squeezed off a round at the nearest horse in the team. The black fell like a rock into the water. In a deafening roar, each guard and his horse were struck down in a barrage of bullets from the other gang members.

Diego rose to his knees and aimed at the flushed-faced

wagon guard, who was too shocked to do anything. The
.44/.40 belched gun smoke and doled out a full serving
of death as the rider's shotgun went off into the air. Hard
hit, he pitched off the seat. To save his life, the driver
dove into the shallow stream. He came up dripping, and
in a hail of bullets that ripped through his torso, he was
sent flying back into the scarlet water.

"Good work," Don Lamas said and rode his dancing
bay horse down the bank into the river. He wore an expensive brocade coat and fancy sombrero. A handsome
man. Diego really liked him. He was a *mucho* good hombre for a poor man like Diego, who had only a small ranch
in Sonora. And Lamas was smart, too. He knew when
the money was moving, where the good horses were to
steal and he paid all of his men well. May God always
bless Don Lamas, may he live forever.

Diego went for his horse. When he returned, the payroll was loaded and Lamas on his prancing bay was
speaking to the gang.

"There is a ranch on the border, with many fine horses.
It belongs to a very rich man in Tucson. He doesn't need
those horses," he said to them. "Who needs them?"

"We do!" came the chorus.

Diego noticed the gang member they called Sarge
standing at the side. The one with the "dead" eyes.
Dressed in a tattered U.S. Army uniform, the man sent
shivers up Diego's back—this hombre was more than a
killer. Diego knew that look and he didn't like it.

JUNE 10TH, 1880
In the darkness of night, Diego rushed with the others
toward the ranch house. Before sundown, Lamas's Yaqui
tracker Sanchez had drawn them a map in the sand. The

vaqueros who worked at the ranch all slept in the right wing of the house. The gang was to kill all of them. Sanchez and Sarge would take care of the ranch manager and his wife.

No witnesses. Nobody would ever identify them, because they left no one alive to talk. Every man who rode with Lamas took an oath of silence. Anyone who snitched on the gang would have his tongue cut out. If any man allowed a potential witness to escape, he would be killed for his neglect.

Diego's fist closed around the new Colt's red wooden grips; he had so meticulously cleaned the works of any sand. He hurried to the open doorway. Pedro ignited a coal-oil-soaked rag and tossed it into the room for light. They stepped in, each taking a side, and emptied their six-guns into the half-awake vaqueros.

The stinking, billowing gun smoke made Diego's eyes water, but he waited to be sure none of them moved. Then he went outside and reloaded his revolver. He was about to say to the others they should go back in and check to be certain they were all dead when Benito dragged a screaming naked girl out of the main house.

"Come on!" he shouted. "This one is pretty!"

Not yet; Diego still had work to do. There would be time later for him to have some of her—or there would be another. He went back in the room. The raw smell of spent powder and burning coal oil filled his nose. He holstered his pistol and drew out his skinning knife. On his thumb, he tested the edge of the knife. It was important for him to keep a keen blade when there were throats to cut. Enough light came from the still-burning rag for him to see. It cast his shadow like that of a great bear on the wall. He stepped toward a moaning, wounded vaquero in a hammock.

Slash.

JUNE 15TH, 1880

Before dawn, north of the border in the Peloncillo Mountains, they struck a camp of silver smugglers. As Diego descended the slope, his rifle issued an orange flame with each round. In the dim light, he could see the men in the camp surrendering. Fine, the outlaws could shoot them later.

"Catch a horse and round up their mules," Black ordered, charging about on his roan.

Diego rushed to obey the man. With the gray light of predawn coming over the horizon, he hurried through the junipers on the hillside and reached his horse. He bounded into the saddle and spurred the horse downhill. They would need those pack animals for the panniers full of bars of silver. He spotted two loose mules and sent his mount after them. The pair crowded into each other. Diego quickly rode in and snatched their leads.

"Good man," Lamas said when Diego rode into the camp with the pair.

"*Gracias*, Don Lamas."

"You are one of my best workers, Diego."

The leader's words filled him with pride. Quickly he handed the mules' lead ropes to Anton and rode after more.

JUNE 20TH, 1880

The intense heat in the narrow canyon made streams of sweat run from under his straw sombrero's hatband and down Diego's face. It was damned hot. The gang had been waiting for the noon stage from Silver City, New Mexico. At last, the rattle of wheels and four horses came from the top of the canyon and entered the confines of the rock walls. Overhead, turkey vultures rode the updraft as if they knew there would soon be a meal for them.

When the charging horses came into sight, Diego shot the near leader and the bay horse dropped in its harness. The second team piled into the downed horse. Their impact caused the driver to be thrown hard from the seat into the boulders. He never got up. The shotgun guard lost his balance and realized the situation. He tossed his greener aside, threw up his arms and climbed down. Two men in suits, their eyes full of fear, came from the coach with their hands high.

Methodically, the gang forced the three captives to kneel. One of the passengers was very vocal and told of his importance. It made no difference. Sarge went around and shot each one of them in the back of the head. Juan quickly emptied the dead men's pockets, while the strongbox full of gold was removed and placed on a pack mule.

The gang split up as usual, but they were to rejoin in three days. Diego was anxious to meet with Lamas in the woodcutters' camp deep in the Dragoons. Lamas promised to pay them there and give them some leave time to return home to their families. Diego looked forward to seeing his wife, Consuela, and sharing her bed again. He missed his young children, but with what he made in these four weeks, they could eat very well again for a long time. It would be a good reunion. *Tequila, mescal* would flow, much *cabrito* and, *oh, si,* a roast pig—ah, *fiesta time.*

Close to dark, he scouted a familiar spring in a deep side canyon. Thirsty, but still cautious, he wanted to be sure no bronco Apache waited in ambush. Most of the Chirichua Apaches were up at the San Carlos Reservation, but they were like the wind and could be anywhere.

He dismounted and listened to the noisy grasshoppers. Some topknot quails gave their *whit-woo* whistle off in the junipers and pancake cactus on the steep canyon sides. Good, no moccasin tracks. A deer or two, maybe. He knelt down to cup himself a handful of water.

Something sprang at him from the boulders beside the small pool. His horse bolted back with a snort, but too late for Diego. The sidewinder's fangs dug deep into the flesh of his cheek. He jumped to his feet, and with both hands he tore the muscular, squirming serpent from its hold. Then, in a fit of rage, he flailed the rattler to death on the rocks.

Shaking with fear, he drew out his knife and, using his reflection in the water, sliced open where the two puncture holes in his face oozed red drops. Holy Mother of God . . . Stunned by his misfortune, Diego sat back on his butt. Blood like thick rainwater ran down his cheek and dripped on his shirt. The growing numbness in the side of his face told him enough.

He, Diego Fernandez, would die horribly at this place—in this canyon, where the coyotes and buzzards would feast on his bones, without even the benefit of a priest or the last rites. No one would be there to tell his poor wife, Consuela, and his children, of his bad luck. It would not be an easy death either. He swallowed hard, lifted up, drew the .45 out of the fine hand-carved, silver-mounted holster and opened his mouth.

A few minutes later, two purple doves alighted and drank. Their soft cooing was the only sound above the dry wind.

CHAPTER 1

"Vicious criminals are ravaging the southern half of this territory. They've got to be stopped." With a scowl of disgust written on his bearded face, Governor John Sterling replaced the cork stopper on the cut-glass decanter. He handed the fresh drink across to Major Gerald Bowen.

Tumbler in hand, Bowen sat back on the captain's chair in front of the long mahogany desk cluttered with documents and considered his place in this matter. Dressed in civilian clothing, he felt less powerful than he had in uniform. He still had to make a lot of adjustments to civilian life. Sterling sounded a little more than upset, but sitting there, Bowen felt uncertain what he could do to solve the man's problems.

"Right here, I have three newspapers complaining about the Border Gang. That's what they call them. This bunch of killers made headlines in Yuma, Tucson and some rag printed in Casa Grande." Sterling stacked the copies on the front of his desk for Bowen to look at.

"Who are they?" Bowen asked, glancing at the front pages.

"Damned if I know, and I'm not getting any answers either. I wired Durwood Allen, the chief U.S. marshal in Tucson, and he sent me back a moronic telegram about how he would investigate the reports. Investigate, hell! Why, the damned newspaper in that town knows more about them than the federal law does down there."

Bowen watched the tall, bearded man in his three-button suit pace the office floor like a trapped animal. He knew full well that Sterling's first six months as President Hayes's appointee to the territorial governorship had been hectic. Earlier in the year, the Arizona "Machine" voted down his request to the legislature for a troop of rangers to enforce law statewide. Bowen clearly recalled how the whole thing unfolded. With nine of the ten county sheriffs in the capitol that entire week openly campaigning against the act on the legislature floor, it was doomed to failure from the start. After the ranger issue went down in solid defeat, the legislature promptly adjourned for the day. They all jubilantly retired to the Palace Bar on Whiskey Row and the sheriffs bought rounds of drinks for all of them until the wee hours. Their bar bill alone must have run over a thousand bucks.

"Those scalawags told me that the county sheriffs could handle anything," Sterling continued. "But all they have to say is, 'They aren't in my county and that relieves me of any responsibility.'" He tossed down his own drink and set the crystal glass back on the tray with a deep sigh. "Talk to me, Gerald."

"Hire a few tough men."

"A few? My gawd, this Border Gang alone must have fifty members. What could one or two men do against them?"

"It's obvious that the legislature isn't going to write you an à la carte law enforcement program."

"They won't do anything. This county-by-county sheriff deal is so sweet and such a political plum, they won't dare to change it. Why, from their percentage take of the tax collections alone, these sheriffs earn thousands upon thousands of dollars a year, then they have the nerve to claim they don't have the personnel to chase down these criminals."

"You need a strike force. Not a posse."

"And how do I get that?"

Bowen felt cornered by the man's question. The two of them were boxed in by the territory's most powerful politicians from solving Arizona's law enforcement needs. His experience was military, not keeping civilians happy, but perhaps like what George Crook did to combat the Apaches would work in this instance. Sterling needed a lightning-fast team of experienced lawmen and without many rules to hamper them. They would need good trackers as well. The formula incomplete in his mind, he speculated out loud.

"What about hiring a few tough men to locate the outlaws and then let the local law have all the glory of making the arrest?"

"It sounds awfully far-fetched. That bunch of mealy-mouthed legislators from Senator Green on down is going to scream like a stuck pig if they learn I've done anything like that."

"They'll do that anyway." Bowen sipped on his whiskey. Sooner or later, Sterling was either going to bite the bullet and buck the politicians or let the outlaws rule.

"You're right, they won't like anything I do. Tomorrow morning, Supreme Court Judge Nelson Tripp will be here from Tucson to confer with me about this matter. Would you meet with us and go over some of your ideas with him?" Sterling made a wry face as if another distasteful notion had struck him and rapped his knuckles on the newspapers. "If any of those headlines ever get out of the territory, the telegraph wires between here and Washington will burn down."

"They will," Bowen said to grimly reassure him.

"I wish you and George Crook could handle it like you did the Apache deal."

"Remember the latest thing on posse comitatus? The use of federal forces to combat lawlessness is null and void these days."

"That doesn't mean it's not a good idea to call out the army and round up all these hoodlums."

"I'm certain the president does not want to call a state of emergency for the Arizona Territory."

"Heavens, no! He wants a much lower profile than that."

"I best be going. I promised my wife I'd be home to handle a few details."

"Retirement suits you?"

"No. But with the sorry state the military is in these days, I belong in civilian life."

"I understand. Give my regards to the wife."

"I will, John. Ten tomorrow morning?" Bowen asked.

"Yes, that will be fine. Then maybe the three of us can devise a way to bring law and order to the territory."

Bowen agreed and picked up his hat. He quickly tossed down the whiskey and handed the glass back. The man served good liquor. Maybe with the judge there they could figure out a solution. Sterling was in a hot seat and from the sounds of things, he needed some action and quickly.

"Tomorrow," they repeated to each other and Bowen headed for the front door.

Half a block away, Ella Devereaux paused while dressing and used her long index finger to move the lace curtain aside enough to see better from the second-story window of her apartment. Who was coming out of the governor's mansion? Well, it was Major Gerald Bowen. My, my, what was that ex-military man doing up there talking to the governor?

"I swear, Sassy," she said to her black servant girl. "What do you reckon that Major Bowen wants with our governor?"

"A job?" Sassy moved toward the curtain to see who she meant and Ella stuck out her hand to stop her.

"Here, stay back. He don't need to know we're peeking at him, does he?"

"No, ma'am."

"Haven't you got some kinfolks who work over there at the mansion?"

"Yous knows I do."

"After you help me into this dress, why don't you take that cousin of yours around to the back door of the drugstore? You knock real nice and you ask Mr. Harvey or his boy, whoever comes back there, to fix each of you a bowl of ice cream."

"Sure will do it, Missy." Her lips peeled back and exposed her large white teeth in a smile.

Ella let her finger fall from the curtain, then quickly spun around and pointed it at the girl. "And you learn everything she knows about what that major was talking to the governor about this afternoon."

"What if shes don't know nothing, Missy?"

"Then she better find out something or I ain't spending no more damn dimes on her eating ice cream. Is that clear?"

"I'll tells her." Sassy made a worried face and held the stiff green dress up to place it over Ella's head

"Just a minute, don't rush me." Ella pulled the corset higher to make certain shifts and adjustments so her ample cleavage looked about to spill out of it. Then she raised her hands up for Sassy to dress her.

"Your cousin's name is Daisy, right?"

"Yes, ma'am, Daisy B. Boudean."

"What's the *B* stand for?"

"I never knowed. Her mama always called her Daisy B. Boudean, all her life." Sassy moved in and began to fasten the hook and eyes up the back that drew the stiff dress in around Ella's mature figure. Anyway, Ella considered her shape mature. Why, half the fifteen-year-olds who worked for her were skinny as deer. Luckily for her, different men liked different forms of women.

She arranged the front of the dress before the tall mirror until she was satisfied with her appearance. A last shift of the waist and she went to the dresser and drew two dimes from her change purse. This better be a good investment.

At a distance she held out the two silver coins like bait. "I want information about that meeting they had today."

"I's knows that."

"Be off and don't be gone all day. And Sassy!" she commanded with such sharpness the girl stopped in her tracks, turned around and faced her.

"Don't you screw none of those boys at the stable in those clothes."

"I never—"

Ella shook her head to dismiss Sassy's lying. She knew damn good and well what that little fantail did with those boys at the stables every chance she got. "You better hear me. You get Daisy B. and go right over there to get that ice cream and you come right back here to me with what she knows. You can do that whoring around on your day off. Hear me?"

"Yes, ma'am." Sassy made a curtsy.

"And find out something."

"I will. I sure will." Sassy ran off down the hallway.

Ella went back to the window and stared at the traffic in the street. A few clouds were gathering. There might be an afternoon thundershower. She watched twenty-three-year-old Tommy Dean drive by in a buckboard. Just married to that Nichols girl. They wouldn't see him back at the Harrington House for several weeks—he'd been a regular customer up until the nuptials. Oh, that horny boy would be around to see her again. He liked to do kinky things with one of her girls that his little virgin bride would never do for him.

The Harrington House was a wonderful place for gentlemen to relax. Many of the most successful businessmen in the territory dropped by when they were in the capital and she knew them well. Discretion, clean girls, the latest-model billiard table right from St. Louis, a concert-grade piano and lots of services to please the individual. Nothing in all of Prescott even matched the decor or the elegance of her place. Besides, she paid some debts, like keeping the right people informed about what was happening. This new governor, John Sterling, along with being too damn pious to even come into her place for a simple drink, was a thorn in the side of many of the territory's leading citizens and legislators. People whom she must keep informed of his actions.

She started down the quiet hallway. At this time of day her girls would all be napping in their rooms. They would need to get their rest because business started just before six o'clock. Some customers, however, never showed up until dark. This helped cover their entrance into the courtyard, where they could stable their horses or teams in the great barn, hidden from prying eyes. The kitchen help was her next thing to check on. They were always a problem for her.

"Where's that Sassy be going in the middle of the

day?" Abraham asked from the foot of the stairs. The towering ex-slave had anger in his bloodshot eyes over something when she came down to the entranceway.

"I sent her on an errand. It's all right. But I warned her not to screw any stableboys this time. She's finding out for me something that just happened over at the governor's mansion."

"She done told me that. If she'd-a been lying to me, I was going to bust her ass a good one."

"No, she's working."

"Good. All I needs to know." Abraham was her man for everything. He kept the yard, cleaned the stables and gave her horses good care. He chauffeured her around in the two-seater when she or the girls wanted to go anywhere. If anyone became too rowdy in the house, Abraham would subdue them. He even disposed of corpses. There had been a few of those during her three-year tenure in Prescott. Two of the girls overdosed on laudanum; the other was strangled in her bed, but the matter was tastefully handled and the young man who was responsible for it came from a very wealthy family and was promptly sent off to school back East. A case of perhaps a little drunken rage at his own impotency, but with all the consideration shown and her discretion, she managed to keep the whole matter quiet and left herself in good stead with the prominent men of the city.

The big ex-slave from Mississippi came with her to Arizona from Westport. Indispensible to her, he looked after her business around the clock.

She stood with her hands on her hips in the doorway to the kitchen and startled the help so badly they jumped at her words.

"What in the hell's going on in here?"

"Oh, nothing, señora."

"That's what I thought." She began giving orders and

clapping her hands for the three Mexican girls to get busy fixing supper. Sassy and that meeting were still on her mind; she wondered what the girl would learn from her cousin.

A saucy blue jay scolded him from the limbs of the pine tree; Lamas sat on a crude stool behind the rough table. Around him, the peaks of the blood-red Dragoon Mountains towered over the deep canyon filled with tall ponderosas. Lamas liked this place. Few people knew about it. Water from a good spring gurgled down the creek bed. There was plenty of grass for their tired horses. With Cochise and his Chirichuas marched off to the San Carlos Reservation, this mountain location made a good stronghold for his men to meet at.

His job under the warm sun was to pay off his soldiers. In four weeks, they had robbed the mine near Silver City, New Mexico, taken a mine payroll, rustled a great herd of horses and sold them below the border and robbed another stage with a gold shipment. The various scenes of their many crimes were vivid in Lamas's mind. Like the rancher in the buckboard returning from selling his cattle to the army and his long-toothed ugly wife. He could even recall her screams. This had been a wonderfully successful raid due to his careful planning and good informers, whom he paid well. His men's efforts had filled Lamas's pockets with much money and gold. He would pay them well for their loyalty and bravery. It was time to let them go home. These were the husbands and brothers who came from the small villages in Sonora to ride with him. Good but simple people. He called out their names one at a time, then each man came forward with sombrero in hand to receive his pay. He issued each of them fifty silver cartwheels. That way it felt like they got more money than to pay a small pile of thin gold coins.

His fancy black sombrero on his shoulders, the expensive brocade coat brown with dust, Lamas casually counted the money out on the tabletop, reaching down into the small chest beside him for more to finish the sum.

"Jose Ruiz!"

From the line of a half dozen men, the young man hurried forward with a grim look on his face.

"I am sorry your brother, Raphael, was killed. Will you take this money to his widow and tell her we all cried for him?"

"*Sí, señor.*" Jose nodded soberly he would do so.

"Jose." Lamas reached over and placed his hand on the man's arm gathering up the cartwheels. "You will be sure that the poor woman gets all this money, won't you?"

Their brown eyes met. Jose swallowed hard and said, "Oh, yes, I will."

"Good man. Now I will count your money."

"*Gracias, Don Lamas.*"

He liked the *Don Lamas* part. Silver dollars filtered out the ends of his fingers until fifty were stacked for Jose. The young man quickly scooped them up and joined the others.

"Where is Diego Fernandez?" His absence bothered Lamas. One of his best men had not shown up. The head shakes in the line told him enough; no one had seen the man since the stage robbery. Had some bronco Apache gotten him?

"Who will take this money to his wife?"

"I will, Don Lamas," Benito said with a sly grin as he hurried forward.

"If you don't deliver it to her . . ." Lamas held the money in his fingers.

"He will deliver it," someone catcalled. "She's got big tits." They all laughed. Lamas paid the man and then he stood up to give them their instructions.

"All of you must take different ways home from here and I will send word when I need you again."

The men raised their rifles and shouted, "*Viva Don Lamas!*"

He nodded politely at them, but his attention was upon the big Texan Ezra Black, who stood beside the heavily laden packhorse. The panniers bulged with sacks of gold dust and booty from their month-long raid. With what he stashed in secret places and carried on that horse, Lamas was a very rich man.

At the sounds of hoofbeats, Lamas looked up sharply. A familiar rider charged into camp and everyone who had their hands on their gun butts let them relax. It was Sanchez, his Yaqui tracker. The rat-faced man jumped off his lathered horse and rushed up to Lamas.

"Two prospectors coming off the ridge trail. They look dirty and tired." He tossed his head to indicate where they were at.

"They're coming out?" Lamas asked, then he smiled at the man's nod. "Good job, Sanchez."

"All the rest of you head for your homes by different ways." Lamas waved the men away. "Sarge, you and the kid go with Sanchez. He has a surprise for us."

"*Muchas gracias*," one of the departing men said to him, then mounted his horse and rode away after the others.

Lamas waved after him and watched them file out. Once away from the mountains, they would scatter like dust to the winds and go their separate ways back to their *casas*. Time to go see about this new find. He dropped the lid down on the chest half full of silver and stood. His back muscles felt stiff from sleeping on the ground so much. He carried the small strongbox in both hands. Black unflapped a canvas lid for him to place it inside the pannier on the horse.

"You've got them all paid and sent home. What did Sanchez find?" Black motioned toward the mountain.

"Two prospectors anxious to be robbed."

Black nodded his approval, recovered the pannier's straps and set it up straight on the crossbuck.

"What about the kid?" Black asked. "You haven't paid him yet."

"I will pay all of you back at the ranchero, even him." Lamas made a face at his discovery that the boy still sat there. "Stupid boy anyway. Why didn't he ride out to help the others capture those two?"

Black shrugged.

"Jimmy! Get off your lazy ass and go help them!" Lamas pointed up the canyon.

The lanky boy blinked, bewildered, then scrambled to his feet and hurried for his horse. In an instant, he was gone.

"Black, bring the big horse along," Lamas said over his shoulder. The Texan made the best guard for it; he couldn't be separated from that packhorse. Lamas knew Ezra Black lived without fear. Nothing ever shook the big man. Then Lamas smiled to himself. His own portion from the four weeks of hard work made him a very wealthy man.

At the mouth of the canyon, Lamas stopped his dark bay horse on a high spot. He could see that Sanchez, Sarge and the kid already had the two men captured. Black rode up cradling the .44/.40 in his arm and leading the sorrel.

"How rich are they?" Lamas asked him.

"How in the hell should I know?" The Texan scowled.

"You always say that, Black. But you know."

"Looks of them from up here, they've been working a claim or some diggings for a while. If they found anything, they're wearing it."

"My thoughts exactly." Filled with newfound pleasure at the prospect of getting more gold, Lamas spurred the horse from under the pine trees. It went stiffly down the steep grade. The two prospectors stood on the trail, floured with dust from their uncut hair and beards to the tip of their caked boots, hands raised over their heads. Lamas's three men held their guns on them.

He rode up close to the taller one.

"I want your gold."

"Ain't got none." The man shook his head with a sour grimace on his face. His eyes were bloodshot from all the dust and grit. He seemed drawn and tired from his labors.

Lamas took a hard look at the two men. They were on their way out of the mountains. Prospectors went in with supplies and came out with gold. Lamas seldom bothered any going in; he knew the difference.

"Open your mouth," Lamas ordered and booted his horse closer to him. "Wider. Open it wider."

He drew his Colt, cocked the hammer and stuck the muzzle inside the man's mouth. Then he pulled the trigger. In a burst of gun smoke and a spray of blood and bone, the man flew over backward, a portion of his head blown away. He lay on the trail, kicking his right boot in the last spasm of death.

"I believe you are next," he said to the other prospector. Then he glanced down at the dark spot in the man's crotch that began to drip.

"You piss in your pants?" he asked the man in disbelief.

The man nodded woodenly, still looking wide-eyed in disbelief at his dead comrade, then back at Lamas. The other outlaws snickered and motioned to each other at the man's accident.

"When Lamas asked for his gold, what did this dead man say?"

"Nothing—he said he had none."

"That was a lie, wasn't it?"

"Yes—"

"But he was stupid. You are not stupid, are you? No." Lamas shook his head at the man as if to dismiss his concern. "Where is your gold?"

"Here." The man hastily ripped out a leather pouch from inside his worn shirt, secured by a leather string looped around his neck. He took it off and offered it to Lamas.

"Thank you. Is that all the gold you have?" Lamas weighed it in his palm.

"Yes."

"Where is his gold?"

"Around his waist."

"Sanchez, come here."

Dressed in the filthy white clothing of a peon, a wide-brimmed palm-frond hat and bearing a rifle, the Yaqui stepped forward. His rat like face looked up at his boss for his next command.

"Get the money belt off that dead one and check him over good for any more." Lamas holstered his gun and watched the Yaqui unbuckle the belt and pull it free from the dead man's waist. It felt heavy when he handed it up to him

Carefully Lamas examined it. Dull yellow gold dust and plenty of it in each individual pouch around the canvas belt. He closed it and nodded in approval. With care he opened the flap on his saddlebags and shoved the belt deep inside it. Then, politely, he smiled at the prospector. "*Gracias, amigo.*"

A wave of relief spread over the man's blanched face. He began breathing deep and grinning. "Oh, thank you, señor. Yes, thank you."

"You three know where to meet us?" Lamas scanned the gang members but glared at the kid most of all.

"Yes," came the chorus. Good, they knew the place on the border. His method of dispersing his gang and having them join up again drew less attention from the law. So far it had worked perfectly. He drew a deep breath of the turpentine-smelling air through his nose and reined the impatient gelding around. Time to go.

"Sanchez, you, Sarge and the Kid all head for that cantina on the border near Clanton's. Wait there. I may have more work for you three." Lamas checked his impatient horse, made sure his men understood what he expected of them, then half-grinned at the paleface prospector. "Kill him and make it look like the Apaches did it."

"Nooo!" the man cried, but by then Lamas was headed back up the slope to where the tall Texan sat aboard his thick-built roan and held the lead on the sorrel packhorse.

"Let's ride. We must meet with Old Man Clanton tonight. I want to make a deal to sell him some more cattle. He is expecting us."

"You know where the cattle are yet?" Black asked, not turning back toward the prospector's desperate pleading that echoed off the canyon's walls.

"We will take them from whoever has them rounded up."

"Makes it easy enough. I just hate giving that old man all the profit."

"All the profit. You and I can't sell them to the army or the Indian agents. We have to have that old goat."

"I don't have to like him."

"No, Ezra, you don't have to like him," Lamas said as the two riders spurred their horses up the canyon. He knew the big Texan wanted to be called Black; no one else dared to call him Ezra. He did it to bait him.

They came to the pass at the head of the canyon. A fresh wind swept Lamas's sweaty face and cooled him. He gazed across the yellow-brown grassland that spread from the base of the Dragoon Mountains far south into Mexico and Old Man Clanton's place. They had many miles to travel if they wished to speak to the old man that night.

The prospector's cries reverberated through the mountain pass. He was tougher than Lamas thought he would be. Lamas's spurs urged the horse to go faster. He wanted to sleep in a bed at Clanton's compound this night, instead of on the hard ground.

CHAPTER 2

In the fresh pine-smelling air, Gerald Bowen stopped and surveyed the capital. Several blocks of Prescott were simply empty staked-off lots. Others bristled with everything from cottages to fancy mansions. Hammers rang in the morning air and the sawmill's scream indicated there soon would be more lumber to build with. A city in flux, where livestock still roamed on the free range and a smelly goat liked his wife's flowers. A good place to be. Things would happen here. There were fortunes to be made and to be lost. The nearby Bradshaw mining district intrigued Bowen even more as an investment than the urban real estate.

He headed for Mahoney's Saloon on the end of Whiskey Row to buy a fine cigar on his way to the mansion. He liked the exercise of walking the hilly streets of the territorial capital, and besides, it was the coolest time of the day. He parted the batwing doors and entered the empty barroom. The former army noncom came from the back, wearing his white apron with a broad grin beneath a well-trained handlebar mustache.

"Good morning, Major, sir. What brings yeah out so early this fine morning?"

"A good cigar for a meeting, Mahoney."

"Be glad to furnish you with one." Mahoney brought the glass humidor to the polished bartop, set it before him and removed the lid.

Bowen dismissed the generosity and grinned at the man, drawing out a long stogie. "More to smoke in this one."

"Oh, it must be going to be a long meeting." Mahoney laughed and offered him another. But Bowen shook his head and Mahoney put them back.

Bowen put a nickel on the bar to pay for the cigar. The Irishman nodded in approval.

"Yeah ever hear from me captain, Sam T.?"

"Yes. He's in Denver, working for a large detective agency." Earlier that morning Bowen had thought hard about Sam T. Mayes. Mayes was one of the men he planned to recommend for Sterling's force. Strange that Mahoney would mention him.

"I can remember he was some officer. We rode up and down that Old Wire Road with our company trying to keep them Rebs from cutting and rolling up the dang telegraph wire from Cassville to Fort Smith. Had him a temper, oh, he'd fistfight you if you made him mad. But he was smart too; he could out figure those guerrillas and outsmarted them many times."

"He didn't always do it by the rules, but Sam T. got lots done," Bowen agreed.

"He didn't ever let some silly regulations keep him from doing his job."

"That too. Those were fine days, Mahoney, and you were a top sergeant."

"Yeah, but it ain't the same, is it? The military, I mean."

"No, we had a war to win back then. Now they don't need us."

"Wonder if Sam T. ever got over that pretty girl." Mahoney reached for a bottle of whiskey, held it up to offer some to Bowen.

He declined the offer. Enough whiskey would flow across the governor's desk at the meeting. He didn't need any to start the day with. The man replaced it on the shelf.

"Her name was Sharon . . ." Mahoney shook his head as if he had forgotten the rest and then patted down his freshly oiled hair, parted in the middle and recently cut.

"It was Rose of Sharon McCarty."

"That's it. He met her on a raid we made up the White River. He sure had a bad case for her."

"Yes, he did." Bowen recalled Mayes, his junior officer at the time, explaining to him about the beautiful daughter of guerrilla captain Latton McCarty and how he had been so struck by her. Obviously she and Sam T. had met several times in secret.

"He finally broke up with her. Afraid that she was a spy and then right after that she was killed by bushwhackers." A look of pain filled Mahoney's blue eyes. "Oh, me Lord, she was a beautiful girl."

"Yes, and I always wondered if those six men found hung near Goshen, Arkansas, was the work of guerrillas or my own men."

"Ah, Major Bowen, some things are better left that way. Untold."

"So I can go on wondering?"

"So you ain't bothered with the truth." After a pause, Mahoney smiled. "I always keep those best cigars on hand and love to talk a few words about the old days." Mahoney shrugged. "They're usually cheery."

"Yes, they usually are. I'll be back. We had some good

times." Bowen waved good-bye and pushed his way through the swinging doors into the bright sunshine.

When he arrived at the governor's mansion, a sparkling landau with two fancy black horses sat parked in front. Must be the judge's rig, he decided.

"Good day," he said to the black driver in passing.

"Oh, good day, sah." The man tipped his top hat to Bowen.

"I guess you must be the judge's man?"

"Yes, sah. He's inside."

"You get hungry or thirsty, slip down the alley. They'll sure feed you a big plate at the back door of Molly's place. She has great tea too."

"Thank you, sah, but there's some good people here at the mansion usually remembers me." The man laughed freely.

"Fine, I didn't want you to go hungry out here."

"No, sahree, and I sure thanks you."

Bowen knocked on the front door and waited. On his past visits, he'd noticed the black servants working in the mansion. That must be who the driver meant would feed him. Good enough. The butler John Howdy, an English gentleman, showed him inside and to the office. Bowen shook hands with Sterling and met the justice, Nelson Tripp.

They took chairs around a polished circular conference table and exchanged niceties over coffee and sweet rolls delivered by a young black girl. Tripp appeared anxious to hear about Bowen's past involvement with Crook and the Apache Campaign.

"So you have your military service behind you?" Tripp asked after the chat.

The girl refilled his coffee cup from an ornate ceramic pot; Bowen nodded to her. "That's behind me, I hope."

"Once a soldier, always one, they tell me."

"I doubt I will ever put on another uniform."

"Someone better put something on," Sterling said and stood. "That's good enough. You may leave now, Daisy." He followed her to the double doors and closed them.

Bowen leaned over and asked the judge, "What do you know about the Border Gang?"

"Merciless killers." Tripp's voice filled with rage. "For weeks they've been killing and plundering all over southern Arizona. They shot and robbed a good friend of my family, Bart Lambert, and his wife, north of Tucson three weeks ago. They ravaged her before doing such despicable things to her body I won't even mention them." He dropped his gaze and sat silently until Bowen's question broke his reverie.

"Border Gang did this to her?"

"Yes. The best we know." Tripp shrugged as if too pained to continue. "Bart had sold a large herd of steers to the quartermaster at Fort Lowell. Like so many ranchers, he didn't believe in banks, so he had the cash with him."

"At the current rate of bank failures, who can blame him?" Sterling added, pulling up his chair to join them.

"They struck Bart in a deep sandy dry wash about ten miles north of Tucson. How did they know he even had the money or would be passing there? This was not by chance; no, they had spies. Just a few days later, they robbed an armed party with a mine payroll south of Tucson and left no one alive." Tripp shook his head in disgust.

"Who leads them?"

"Good question. They don't leave any witnesses alive. Their butchery is worse than . . . yes, even worse than Apaches. Some swear they're renegade Apaches doing this, except we know they've struck down in Mexico too. The authorities down there call them the 'Ones of Death.'"

"Are they Apaches?" Bowen considered the notion, though it sounded far-fetched.

"No, I don't think so. They ride shod horses. They all use .44/.40 ammunition with shiny new brass cartridges."

"Anyone try to track them?" Bowen asked.

"Can't. They split up and disappear. Some Papago trackers followed one for two days and lost him. They're ghostlike." Tripp made a hard face. "There may be as many as twenty men in this gang. No, if they were Apaches, someone would have seen that many bucks off the reservation and reported them."

"They have to be stopped," Sterling said, folding his hands on top of the table. "And the current established law enforcement won't or is unable to handle the matter."

"I agree. Recently I was in Bob Baylor's office. He's the Pima County sheriff," Tripp explained. "I talked to him about this very thing. He threw up his hands. Says they're out of his jurisdiction. Do you know what his deputies are out doing?"

"No."

"They're going out counting cattle so they can collect the taxes on them."

"That's where the money is," Sterling said and shook his head in disapproval. Then he glanced at Bowen. "Tell him what you think will work."

"Gentlemen," Bowen began. With his knees spread apart, he placed a hand on each leg and leaned forward. "If you want real law in Arizona you are going to need a tough, lightning force of men to strike at these outlaws wherever they're hiding."

"But how? You know what the damn legislature did to me about rangers."

"Call them marshals!" Bowen realized he was way too loud and dropped his voice. "It doesn't matter what you call them, you need men that are tough and have one job. That's to keep the law, regardless of boundaries."

Sterling held his hand to his forehead. "Gerald, you don't know my problems with that."

"Yes, I do. I sat right here and listened to those lawmakers get stone drunk over on Whiskey Row that night celebrating, the defeat of your ranger bill."

"We either do what Bowen here recommends or we can kiss this territory good-bye." Tripp rubbed his small mustache and gave a shudder of his shoulders under the suit coat. "These rampant lawbreakers will ruin us. It is anarchy and the Border Gang is only a part of it. Outlaws are coming into this territory like flies to a cow-butchering. They know the law isn't being enforced. When things get too hot, all they do is skip over into another county and get away."

Bowen sat back, agreed with Tripp's interpretation, then he began. "You realize most of these outlaws won't stand for being arrested. This won't be like arresting some jubilent drunk in the street." Bowen paused. More than anything, he wanted Tripp to understand they shouldn't ask a man to risk his life over a worthless outlaw. "There's going to be many of these criminals not live to see a courtroom."

Tripp nodded his head as if in deep thought. "I stand for the law, but I know what you say. It's down to us or them, who is going to rule this territory. We will never be approved for statehood under this reign of lawlessness."

"Gerald thinks a few men could handle this." Sterling squeezed his chin and flattened his beard.

"The right ones—maybe."

"They could," Bowen said. "I had all night to think on this matter. A few experienced men with packhorses could cover lots of ground. They would need money to pay snitches, and with a free hand, they could make a big difference."

"Make them officers of the court," Tripp said. "I can talk to my colleagues and they'll back a plan like this. Both Bob Wallace and Martin Burl are as upset as I am. Sterling, don't you have funds from the federal government for the operation and needs of the territorial courts?"

"Right, I do—but—" Sterling stammered.

"Then use it to finance the marshals," Tripp insisted with a sharp frown at the governor.

Bowen agreed with the judge's plan; good idea.

"Gentlemen, there is no way to reason with the legislative committee or Senator Green." Sterling shook his head and looked glum.

"Sterling, I wouldn't tell them a damn thing," Tripp insisted. "You have the authority and access to that federal money for court business. Use it for financing the marshals."

"The judge has a point," Bowen said. If they didn't get Sterling off that business about what the "Machine" liked and disliked, they would never get anything accomplished.

"The minute I send a marshal—"

"Wait," Tripp interrupted him and pointed at Bowen. "Let's let the major handle the marshals. Obviously it will all have to be secret. So you two will have to keep it that way so their spies can't hear about them. I know they have them all over. We'll let Bowen handle it."

"What do you think?" Sterling asked, looking hard at Bowen.

"If you want an arm of the law, I'll do my best to make it work. Who hires them?"

"You," both men said and then smiled at each other.

"Bowen, you've worked with plenty of good men in your career. Can you get some of them to be marshals?" Sterling asked.

"Yes, but they won't be cheap."

"What's 'not cheap'?" Sterling asked.

"At least a hundred fifty a month and expenses."

"That's not a bad price for a good man," Tripp replied. "Go ahead."

"Who will you hire first?" Sterling asked.

"The man I want to go after the Border Gang is Sam T. Mayes, gentlemen. He's a former captain in the U.S. Cavalry. He was my next in command at the end of the war. He understands guerrilla fighting."

"But one man?" Sterling shook his head. "Does he even know anything about Arizona?"

"No, but I also plan to hire some deputies to help him, two ex-Army scouts, trackers who can show him where the outlaws went and how to get there."

Tripp rose, clapped Sterling on the shoulders. "Sounds great to me. I have to use the facilities." He opened the outer door and turned back. "Listen to the man, Sterling. He has it all figured out."

Sterling went and closed the door. He turned back and raised his eyebrows. "One man and two scouts. Aren't you taking a big risk?"

"You don't know Sam T. Mayes. He can handle them."

"But Papago trackers couldn't—"

"Couldn't find their own ass in a dust storm. Excuse my language, but Crook tried them all, Papagos, Navajos. He found if you want a crack tracker get an Apache. The rest were worthless."

"And this Mayes?"

"Stop worrying. You don't know Sam T. Mayes, but

you have my personal guarantee he's a man of many at-
tributes, and being steel-tough is one of them."

Sterling nodded, satisfied with Bowen's guarantee,
then excused himself and went into the outer office.
Bowen sat back, blew out a long breath and considered
what he must do next. He heard the governor tell the girl
Daisy to get his whiskey and three glasses. The deal must
be settled; Bowen drew out the aromatic-smelling cigar
from his vest. He licked the body of it with the tip of his
tongue, used a small jackknife to cut off the butt. Then
he struck a parlor torpedo match on the underside of the
polished table and lit it up. Wedged back in the captain's
chair, he drew deep, thinking about the things he must
do. Then, in a pencil-thin stream, he sent the smoke out.
This marshal business might prove interesting before
it was over.

The black girl delivered the cut-glass decanter and
three crystal glasses on a tray and set them down on the
table.

"He need something else?" she asked, looking around
for the governor, who no doubt had gone to join Tripp in
the facilities.

"No, that's all he needs, Daisy."

"Hows you know my name?" she asked, drawing back
her head wrapped in the red cloth and standing straighter.

"Why, the governor told me. He said that Daisy is the
best worker in the mansion."

"Oh, mercy." She held her hands up to her small bust-
line and wrung her long fingers fretfully. "He never done
told me a thing like that."

"Well, I did. You may go, my dear."

"Oh, thank yeah, thank yeah, Mister Major. Thank
yeah." She left skipping and about collided with the governor and Tripp, who were returning.

"Sorry, sah," she said and was gone.

"What's she so excited about?" Sterling frowned after her.

"I told her she was so good you were giving her a big raise."

Sterling shook his head and closed the door. He turned in time to see the hilarity that Bowen could no longer contain. All three men laughed; Sterling still looked uncertain and poured their drinks.

"Here's to starting the Arizona Territorial Marshals!" Tripp shouted and they raised their glasses.

"To the Territorial Marshals!"

Clink.

Ella Devereaux again spread the newspapers out on the bed. She looked wryly at Strawberry, who stood before the lace-curtained window in her underwear.

"Get over here," she demanded. No reason for that little slut to stand there in the half nude. Besides, someone might see her and there would be an uproar about her advertising in broad daylight, though the girl wasn't ugly to look at. Had a cute butt on her, no breasts, but the men liked her anyhow.

"Yes, Missy." Strawberry made a displeased face at her. "Oh, not those damn dumb newspapers again. I told you I read them twenty times and didn't learn a thing about the governor."

"What did you read in them?"

"A man hit his wife over the head and he got ten days in the Pima County Jail. Hogs are cheaper in Chicago and are expected to keep falling in price. Banks're failing all over the country."

"What else?"

"They sell an elixir that you can drink and makes you ten years younger and folks can go to Eureka

Springs, Arkansas, and take baths and get cured of cancer."

"What else?"

"That Border Gang killed some big-deal rancher north of Tucson. They killed and ravished his wife. That means the whole bunch screwed her, huh?"

"Watch your language. This ain't some damn cheap whorehouse. Do you want to work in one of those places?"

"No, Missy."

"Then quit talking like some back-alley slut. What does it say about the military?"

"Some company at Fort Apache is being transferred to Fort Grant."

"No, that ain't it." Ella inhaled deeply. Nothing to help her figure out what they were up to. "Go back to your room and get some rest. It may be be a busy night. Harris sent word there's some bankers in town."

Strawberry wrinkled her freckled pug nose in disgust. "Hope they tip better than the last ones. They were cheap."

"Get out of here and send Sassy up before you lay down."

"Yes, Missy."

From the window, Ella watched the judge leaving the mansion. At last. Justice Tripp, Major Bowen and Sterling had been in a meeting all morning. They were up to something no good and she needed to know what. Bowen climbed in the landau with Tripp, and his driver went out the driveway. She could see the men's cigar smoke leave a wispy trail.

What were they up to?

"You needed me, Missy?" Sassy asked, rushing in the doorway.

"I wouldn't have sent for you if I hadn't needed you."

"Yes, ma'am." She made a curtsy.

"As soon as your cousin, Daisy B. Boudean, gets through with her lunch duties, you take her for an ice cream at the drugstore's back door. Then you bring her over here by the back alley. You tell her I want to reward her good."

"She smuggled them newspapers like I asked her to do."

"That's why I wanted to reward her. What did you think I was going to do?"

"Aw, nothing, Missy"

"But if you mess up and don't bring her to me . . ." Ella stopped and looked hard at the girl. Sassy's hands slid protectively behind her backside and she straightened. That's right, girl, Abraham will bust your ass a good one for me, Ella thought.

"She be here," Sassy promised. "But it be near two o'clock."

"Fine, just so she comes." She gave Sassy the coins for the ice cream.

Ella had plenty of time to reread the newspapers. The reason she made Strawberry read them, was that she knew the girl had a good education from attending a high-class boarding school in St. Louis for several years. One night, she climbed over the fence and ran off out West with a slick-talking tinhorn. He made her do prostitution for his gambling money, which he lost every night. She left him and showed up in Prescott on the back-door steps of the Harrington House looking for work. She lied about her age when she came, said she was eighteen, but Ella was convinced she was closer to fifteen then.

But with all her fancy education, even Strawberry found nothing more than she did about what the governor and Bowen were talking about in those newspapers. If she could believe what Sassy relayed from Daisy B., very little had taken place. Somehow that wasn't right.

That girl had to know something more after this latest meeting. Those three men must have talked for hours. In disgust, Ella threw down the newspaper on the brocade spread. It was useless to keep going over them. Border Gang did this, Border Gang did that. It looked like she needed that Border Gang to come spend some of their robbery money with her at the Harrington House.

At two o'clock on the grandfather clock in the hall, Ella intercepted the two girls in the kitchen and took them quickly in the parlor. She shut all the doors and turned to the lanky Daisy B., who was busy licking the spoon with her long tongue, her hatchet butt rested against the billiard table. She better not get one drop of that sticky cream on the new green velvet—but Ella cut off those words before she spoke them.

"What did they talk about today?"

"They said real loud, 'Marshals.' "

"What marshals?" Ella could not fathom what the men must be going over. The Prescott Police Department called themselves marshals. Did they plan to hire new marshals? Every week, she paid her fair share of the cost of the city police force. Maybe they planned to hire new ones and run her out of town?

"They started talking and done shut them doors." Daisy lowered her face and looked up at Ella.

"That Judge Tip—"

"Tripp."

"Yeah, that's him. He was talking to the major about 'crook'?"

"General Crook?" Ella frowned at the girl.

Daisy B. turned up her empty hand and showed the white palm. "He say, 'crook.' "

"What else?"

"Once I hear that major say real loud, 'Marshals.' "

"What else did you hear?"

"Big voice shouted once, 'Call them marshals.' "

"Daisy B., you did real good. You go back and listen very close for what those men are up to and you tell Sassy here what you hear every time."

"I don't know, Missy. That major he say that the governor, he really likes me." The girl in the red bandanna ran her tongue over her teeth under her lips and then grinned.

"What do you think that governor's going to do about it?"

Daisy B. wrung her hands and ducked her head like she couldn't say it, then blurted out, "He likes me enough he may jump my bones."

"You want that, Daisy B.?"

"Being in his bed be a lot better than sleeping on them corn cobs."

"You'd tell me if he ever does that, won't you, Daisy B.? Because Missy is all the time buying you ice cream," said Ella.

Daisy B. rubbed her sticky palms on the front of her print dress. "Maybe I would and maybe I wouldn't."

Ella bit off her anger at the girl's sass. A smile pasted on her face, she put her arm around Daisy's shoulder. "Don't you worry about that. You listen for this marshal talk and let Sassy know all about it."

"Oh, I'll do that, Missy. It's fun."

Thank God. The girl would tell Sassy if she knew anything. She liked the ice cream too well not to. If Sterling was going to hire new marshals and then close the Harrington House down, she better get busy and talk to some of her influential friends. One thing she knew was how to fight fire with fire.

But what could she tell Senator Green when he came

by? The potbellied little man was due by the capital any day and always had a million questions to ask her about the governor and what he was up to. Ella felt herself being watched and realized that Sassy was still standing behind her. Daisy had left minutes before.

"Yes, Sassy?"

"She told you all she knew." Then Sassy shot her fist up to her mouth to suppress her giggling. "But . . . if that governor jumps her bones, he's pretty hard up, ain't he, Missy?"

"You never can tell about men and what they like, dear."

Sassy laughed and then tried to contain herself. "Why, she's so skinny, be like him getting on a fence post with a woodpecker hole in it."

"Enough of that talk. You keep checking on her."

"I will." And she went off laughing about her joke.

Ella frowned. It wouldn't be so funny for any of them if Sterling closed down the Harrington House. No, sir, she better get to talking to her friends.

CHAPTER 3

Sam T. Mayes sat with his butt planted upon the small board platform between the heavy ceiling trusses over the Keaton Brothers' warehouse. Darkness long before had closed in on the building. At six o'clock, everyone in the building left work. With his passkey, Sam slipped inside, climbed the ladder to the loft, then made his way through the huge wooden trusses until he stationed himself where he could look down and easily see the row of dock doors.

He listened to the cooing pigeons that had stolen in earlier and roosted close by. Sit and wait . . . a detective did lots of that in his line of work. Someone was stealing large amounts of merchandise from the company's warehouse and while he felt the job was being done by insiders, he had no proof. This stakeout might require weeks of sitting up there at night. His back pressed against the rough-cut four-by-four that went slantwise to the roof, he tried to think about something more interesting.

About this time of day Shirley McKenzie, the love interest in his life, would be sitting down to her supper. He could be there with her sipping on good wine and preparing to feast on some delicious dish. The dark-haired widow would be much better company than those moaning pigeons.

Suddenly something dropped.

He turned his ear to listen. It was only a rat scurrying around down below. The rats he sought were larger ones than that.

False alarm; he settled back again. By this time of night, he could also be having a friendly drink in the Elephant Bar with some of his detective friends and marshals from the Denver police force. Why hadn't he brought something to drink? It would only have made him need to get down and piss that much sooner. No, he would give them a few more hours to show up.

The old wound in his hip made him squirm around. He still carried a minié ball from a bushwhacker's rifle. One of his many treasures of war. The sharp discomfort of it was his reminder of the days he spent in uniform, when he and his company patrolled the Old Wire Road in southern Missouri and northern Arkansas, a part of the original Butterfield Stage route from St. Louis to San Francisco. By the end of the war, most of the guerrilla leaders who kept him so busy were dead. Ingrahmn, Buck Brown, Smith, McCardy and even Sharon.

He closed his eyes and began thinking about the beautiful hill girl. She still haunted him, even after all these years. The glaring hatred in her defiant gaze the first day he and his command surrounded her home searching for her father. Those looks of hers would have killed him had they been loaded with ammunition. All those secret places where they later met. He could recall kissing her under a towering grove of walnut trees that filtered the moonlight. Her lithe body in his arms—

Damn, what was that scraping sound? He looked off

the edge of the platform. Someone whispered down below and came inside the warehouse. Too dark to see them. Maybe they would light a lamp. He hoped so, at once feeling better about the whole thing, His suspicions were correct. The intruders had a key to the place. Insiders, who no doubt worked here.

Then the glow from a lamp shone up in the cross network of trusses. He wouldn't dare risk looking over at them for a while. They might be suspicious and searching to be sure they were alone.

"What's the game?"

"Five-card stud. You feeling lucky, Herb?"

They were going to play cards? He made a sour face at the discovery. He hated—detested—gambling, in any shape or form. In the first six months of his service he had been fleeced by card sharks and gamblers until he couldn't stand even the mention of cards or dice. So they were using the company warehouse for a poker den— damn. How long would they play? All night? He hoped not. He couldn't give himself away by coming down. Then his cover would be blown.

"Ralston, you seen that new girl over at Hattie's?"

"The brunette?"

"Yeah, calls herself Hurricane." The ruffle of cards being shuffled was audible.

"I like the china dolls at Susie's."

"Raise you two bits. When're them guys going to get here?"

"Hell, you know they have to borrow a team and wagon from the livery. Some teamster has to leave them for the night, then they use them for free. And it has to be all clear."

Sam T. looked over the edge and smiled; his bladder could wait a little while longer. So they even used a team without the owner's permission to haul off the goods.

Some poor teamster got up the next morning and couldn't figure why his rested animals weren't pulling like they should. He took out a pad and pencil, licked the lead and wrote *Herbie* and *Ralston*. There was a bald-headed man without a cap and the other guy had on a bowler and wore overalls.

"I'm going to take my money this weekend and throw me a helluva time at Marie's cathouse."

"Them prettier?"

"Yeah, they sure are, and expensive."

"Cost yeah what? Hey, I raise fifty cents."

"Well, gawdamn, you must have a royal flush."

"Hey, I hear horses."

"Yeah, they're here now. Close this game down. And Fennie said no damn horseshoes this time. He's got four barrels of them that he can't sell."

Who was Fennie? Sam T. caught movement out of the corner of his eyes. He half turned to see a large warehouse rat heading down the beam toward him. Rats made his skin crawl. Go away! He reached inside his coat and drew out his .30-caliber Colt.

If he shot the fuzzy critter, they'd sure know he was up there and might start shooting at him. Go away! The rat advanced, baring his teeth. You come much closer, I'll bean you with this gun barrel. He tried to decide where the men were down below. Oh, damn, what a time for a rat to challenge him. Must be a thirty-foot fall to the crates and boxes.

"About time you got here. What've you been doing?"

"Hell, we had to find some horses and a wagon. This old boy owned this team like to never have left the stables."

"Get this hardware and kegs of nails on the wagon. We ain't got all night."

The rat started for him. Sam raised the pistol. One

chance would be all he had to hit it. Sam T. waited until the last moment, then made a swipe and connected. The angry rat was hurled off in space. Quickly, Sam T. drew back and huddled on his small platform after the smack of the critter hitting below.

"What was that?"

"A gawdamn rat. It's raining rats in here."

"He fall off from up there?"

"Unless he had wings, by God, he did."

"I never heard of a rat falling off nothing."

Now you did. Sam T. closed his fist on the Colt and held his breath. Close call, and it wasn't over yet. He wished they'd finish stealing and get out so he could climb down and empty his bladder.

"That's enough. Fennie says you load it too full, you draw suspicion. Besides, these horses are really tired; he must have drove them hard today."

"Yeah, see you next Thursday night."

Sam T. thought to himself, You crooks will see each other, all right—next Thursday and the one after that. Because, gentlemen, you will be in Denver City's finest jail, getting ready for some long stretches in the state pen. He holstered his Colt in the shoulder harness.

"Yeah, sure. We'll be here. You don't be so damn late coming next time."

"We going to play some more cards?"

Sam T.'s heart stopped. He looked at the ceiling for divine help. No more gambling.

"Naw, my old lady's pissed about me being gone so much."

"The rest of you?"

"No. Not tonight."

"See you, Curly."

The light went out below and Sam T. stretched his arms over his head. Give them a few more minutes to get away from the building, and he would pick his way across the trusses and down the ladder.

Detective work was supposed to be interesting. Of late, it had lost most of its charm for him. In the winter months it was even worse, freezing to death out in the snow during a stakeout, combing the slums for some wanted person. He had a bellyful of city life. He could recall loping his mount in the clear air of the Ozarks, no sooty smoke or stinking garbage piled all over.

Outside in the moonlight at last, he vented his distressed bladder and watched the rats scurrying about the alley in the starlight. That one probably survived his blow and the fall. They were hard to kill. Good thing he didn't need to share the beam again with him. Next time, Mr. Rat might bite him.

He pulled out his pencil and added *Curly* and *Fennie* to his list. Still had the police to contact. Old Man Keaton would sure be shocked that his long-term employees were the ones looting his warehouse. Oh, well, the rats were on the inside as well as the outside. His appetite whetted for some food, Sam T. hurried off for the Elephant Bar.

By midmorning the next day, Sam T. oversaw two of Denver's finest as they escorted the four Keaton employees out into the wagon parked at the back docks.

"I can't believe it. Those men have worked for me for years. Why, Herbie's been here over ten years," the short man in the tailor-made suit said with a wag of his head.

"Probably been stealing that long too," Sam T. added. The police had them loaded. Time to move to the next place. "You will excuse me, Mr. Keaton. I'm going over with these officers to the warehouse where Curly said the goods were being stashed. We have a search warrant."

"You've done a very excellent job, Mayes."

"Thanks. Great Western Detective likes to serve our customers."

"Oh, I'll tell my friends."

At the next warehouse, Sam T. recognized the voices of the two from the night before, who, under some pressure, admitted to their guilt. With the pair in cuffs, he was about to leave, when a tall, well-dressed man entered and walked over to speak to him.

"What's going on here?" the man asked rather stoically.

Sam T. looked him up and down. "Your name Fennie?"

"Yes."

"Good. Fennie, you're under arrest. Officer, here is the ringleader." He waved one of the patrolmen over.

"You can't do this to me!" Fennie protested. "I know the mayor, the councilmen—"

"Yeah, and maybe they'll mail you cookies in the state pen too." Sam T. looked around, satisfied the police had things under control, then went outside and caught a cab to the office.

In the bright midday sun, he dug out the money to pay the driver. The sparkling red-brick, three-story building looked like a shrine except for the gaudy yellow letters, THE GREAT WESTERN DETECTIVE AGENCY smeared across the front like a circus sign. He entered the main office, waved at the various clerks busy at their desks and headed for his own cubbyhole.

"Morning, Mr. Mayes. Getting to work kinda late, ain't yeah?" The office boy shoved a telegram at him.

Sam T. ignored his mouth, thanked him and pocketed the envelope. He planned to deal with the message later. Less than three hours of sleep; he had been up more than half the night. On his desk was a memo; he had to make a preliminary court appearance in a few hours.

He checked the large clock on the wall—in two hours he needed to be in court. After not having a bath in two days, the odor of the musty warehouse clung to him.

"That wire might be important," the boy shouted after him.

Oh, yes, he received important cables every day. Probably some sheriff off yonder wanted him to look for a fugitive supposed to be in Denver. He searched his desk for the file on the jewel robbery. That was what the hearing was about—he absently slipped the envelope out and tore it open.

It was from Major Bowen in Prescott, Arizona:

SAM T.—HAVE JOB FOR YOU IN ARIZONA—
STATEWIDE MARSHAL—CAN YOU COME
AT ONCE. GERALD BOWEN.

He blinked, went to the sunlight streaming in the window and reread the part about going to work in Arizona. He shook his head, beat the paper on his other hand. Thank God he didn't have to do this stuffy detective work any longer.

"Good news?" the nosy boy asked from the corner of his stall wall.

"Damn good news." And he smiled to himself.

"You inherit a fortune or something like that?"

"No, but I suspect I just inherited a new lease on life."

"Huh?" The boy made a face that he didn't understand.

"Never mind; get Shannon over here. He's got to be in court at two for me. I've got a good lead to follow."

"Yes, sir. But you sure don't make sense."

Didn't intend to explain it to you, you little smartass. He needed to get everything ready for Shannon to handle the case. One of the newly hired men could learn how to do it. They would have to do lots of things around here when he was gone—to Arizona. Whew, he could hardly wait to tell Shirley the good news. They could go to Prescott together; she didn't have any family ties here. He wet his lips and shook his head, still taken aback by the wire. Major Bowen, you are a prince of a guy, like always. It would be good to see him again. It had been years.

He left the court detail in Shannon's hands with brief instructions, went out the front door and two blocks away stopped off in front of Lou's Bathhouse. From the sidewalk, he took a quick look at the towering front wall of the Rockies. Still some snow up there on the high peaks. Then he pushed inside the spicy-smelling shop. He smiled at the friendly Chinaman who always bowed and talked pidgin English at forty miles an hour.

"I need a bath, and give these clothes a pressing."

"Yes. Yes. Have you white shirt all ready ironed for you, Mr. Mayes."

"Good."

In the backroom, Sam T. settled into the tin tub of steaming water. The bathhouse was so hot and humid it made him sleepy. Maybe he should go home and nap before he went to Shirley's. No, he wanted to tell her the great news. She would be excited. He'd have to wire the major and tell him he was coming. He found himself so relaxed, he closed his eyes for a second.

"You very tired, Mr. Mayes?" It was Lou's daughter Lee with a back scrubber brush in her hand who awoke him. The first time Lee came in to scrub his back while he was bathing, he about died from embarrassment. But the girl acted very proper and didn't seem to mind naked men half as bad as naked men were shocked to see her. He never heard a bad word said about her, and she sure did get his back scrubbed.

"I'm fine, Lee," he said. "Just enjoying the bathwater."

She proceeded to scrub his back with the brush. When she finished, she leaned over and smiled at him. "You plenty clean now."

"Thanks," he said and flexed his stiff back muscles. Sitting on those boards in the loft for hours hadn't helped his back a lot.

When she left the room, he stood and reached for a towel. His clothes should be ready by this time. He dried off and Lou stuck his head in and hung up his suit and pants.

"Make clothes much better."

"Thanks, my friend," he said to the bowing Chinaman.

He arrived at Shirley's front door in midafternoon. The sweet flowery aftershave surrounded him like a patch of flowers. Whew, he could get tired pretty quick of that odor.

"Why, Samuel? Whatever are you doing here at this time of day?" She stood back in the doorway looking a little aghast.

What was wrong with her? Did she have someone else in there?

"I had to come by to tell you some good news." He handed her the bottle of champagne. She read the label, then blinked her eyes as if in distress. He'd brought her bottles like this before. What was so wrong with this one?

"My, such fine champagne." She grinned at him as if to make up for her coldness. "Oh, my. Come inside. I am so sorry, but you took me unawares. I'm not dressed—"

"You look wonderful."

"Not quite. My hair . . ." She ran her fingers through the piles of curly locks that streamed down to her shoulders

"Trust me, you look great." He reached out and caught

her by the waist, closed the door behind them. She didn't have her corset on either; he knew that by touch. Good, he liked things raw so he could feel her ribs and flesh under the dress.

Their mouths met and then she pushed herself loose. "I guess I'm not ready for this. Excuse me. What is this good news?"

"Let's go in and open the champagne first." He herded her into the dining room.

She found the glasses in the sideboard and set them out. He popped the cork with a minimum of outburst and poured the pale bubbly.

"We are going to Arizona!" he said and raised the glass.

"Arizona?"

"Yes." He bent over and kissed her on the cheek. "I have a new job in Arizona. Aren't you excited?"

"Well, yes, for you. Doing what?" She looked bewildered at the notion.

"Marshal's job working for an ex-commander of mine, Gerald Bowen."

"Is it a good job? What will he pay you?"

"Hell, girl, I have no idea, but aren't you thrilled?"

"Quite frankly, no."

"You don't know the major. Well, he's a great guy and he's asking me to come out there."

"And do what? Be some hick town marshal? You have your future to think about, Samuel. *Our* future."

"I just figured our future would be in Arizona."

"Samuel, that is a territory. It still has wild Indians running all over it. If you think I am going to—wait!" She held up her hands to ward him off. "You finish your drink. Let me go and get decently dressed and then we will discuss it."

She guided him to the sofa. "You look tired."

"I've been up . . . oh, quite a while. All right, you go dress if it makes you feel better and then we can talk some more." He tossed down his drink, handed her the glass and slumped on the couch. Through his half-opened eyes he studied her shapely backside going down the hallway. Great girl—he'd convince her. She would see it his way—little woman needed some talking to, was all.

His head slumped, he shut his eyes and fell sound asleep.

CHAPTER 4

Lamas and Black stood by the corral in the darkness. The sound of a guitar being strummed floated on the warm night air. Some cowboy on the long porch played a tune.

"Clanton needs cattle very badly," Lamas said softly. His back against the poles, he looked toward the lit open door and windows of Clanton's rambling house. Overhead a spray of stars filled the inky sky. Lamas's thoughts were not on the Texan or their conversation, but rather on a lusty woman who lived nearby that he planned to lie with later. All this robbery business had separated him from female company for too long and the thought of her made desire rise in his groin.

"That means there ain't any around handy to steal," Black said with sarcasm in his tone.

"Yes, or he would have rustled them." Lamas grinned. He knew how much Black distrusted the old man.

"So what do we do?"

"Find out where they are at."

"The cattle?"

"Yes. It's late in the season for anyone to be driving them out of Texas, but there could be a herd coming. You go find out. I will meet you at the San Bernardino Spring with the others in two days."

"You calling all the men back?" Black frowned at him.

"No, they need the rest. Besides it would take too long to get them back here." Lamas shook his head at the notion. "Send word to that border cathouse for Sanchez, Sarge and Jimmy to meet me at San Bernardino Spring, the five of us can handle one herd of cattle."

"Two thousand cattle?"

"Whatever. You are the cow man, amigo. That is lots of money, my friend."

"He pays us ten, then he gets twenty-five or more from the army."

"Oh, he must rework the brands, amigo." Lamas clapped the big man on the arm to reassure him the deal was not all bad. Why worry what the old goat made off of them?

"That ain't no trick to change a brand." Black made a sour face in the starlight. "But I'll saddle up at daybreak, go tell them others where to meet you and go find them if they're some cattle coming."

"Good. Be careful. I count on you."

"There's word that Diego Fernandez got snakebit and died at a water hole," Black said.

"We will miss him. How did you learn that?"

"One of Clanton's cowboys bought that fancy holster off some bronco Apache come down through here, needed money. I saw it hanging in the bunkhouse and got to asking questions. It's sure enough the one I told Diego he could have from that rancher. The Injun told the cowhand the story about finding his body and a dead snake he must have killed after it bit him."

"He was good soldier. I feared he was dead or he would have been at the woodcutters' cabin."

"Me too. He was sure loyal to you. I better get some sleep. Me and ole Roanie's got lots of ground to cover come daylight."

"*Vaya con Dios*," Lamas said.

"Same to you." Black sauntered off in his high heel boots for the bunkhouse portion.

Lamas turned his ear to listen to the music again. No one looking or in sight on this side porch. He slipped in the corral, caught his bay horse and quickly saddled him. He needed to ride into the border town and speak to Juanita. He mounted and rode off softly in the night, so only the very sensitive would even realize his absence.

Close to her casa, Lamas rode along the creek where the starlight filtered through the cottonwood leaves that rustled on the gentle night breeze. The walls of her place in sight, he dismounted and tied the horse. He wanted the bay to be there in case he was forced to leave quickly. Then, being careful not to stumble over a bed of flat cactus and fill his fine kidskin boots with painful needles, he carefully picked his way along to the back entrance.

He smiled when his hand touched the strip of velvet cloth on the thick wooden gate. It was safe. Her man was gone. He shoved the bar across and entered the courtyard. Starlight danced on the tile and the water in the small fish pond. He could see the French doors to her bedroom standing open and smiled to himself over his good fortune.

He found her asleep, sprawled facedown on the white sheet. He removed his hat and coat while he studied her subtle form in the dim illumination of the room. Good that he could see well in the dark to appreciate such beauty. He removed his shirt and toed off his boots.

Undressed, he eased himself down on the edge of the bed and gathered her in his arms. Warmth radiated from her lush body; the rich musk filled his nose. His mouth sought her neck and when she emerged from sleep, her hands sought his face.

"Ah, Lamas, my lover, at last you return." Her hungry mouth found his and they were lost in lovemaking.

He awoke before daybreak and sat on the edge of the bed considering her. Lovely woman, but like so many others, even she did not satisfy him but for the instant. What did he search for? This one made love like it burned her up, consumed her. He could find no fault with her ripe body. What was wrong with him?

"Lamas, you mustn't leave me so soon." She reached for him.

"Have you heard of any more silver shipments coming up from Sonora?" he asked softly, leaning over her. Let her beg him; he wanted information in exchange.

"No, but did you hear that the Clantons killed all those men in the Peloncillos?"

"*Mucho* bad hombre, that Clanton." He kept his amusement to himself about the old man getting all the blame for his own robbery.

"Oh, he must be bad." She swept a sheet over them to wrap her nakedness.

"If I promise to learn more about the next silver train, will you stay in my bed until the rooster crows?" She pushed her pouty lips at him.

"I promise."

Lamas and the others waited for Black at the San Bernardino Spring. A great pool of water fed by an artesian spring under some gnarled cottonwoods marked a watering hole for the Chiricahuas, who for centuries rode from their mountains by this place on their way to the Sierra Madre. So fierce were the Apaches that despite several tries, the Perez family who owned the king's grant had abandoned cattle raising on the vast land that stretched for miles on both sides of the border.

Since the Apaches were moved north to San Carlos, Lamas decided, at last the family could use this large holding. Where was Black? He studied the waist-high yellow grass that waved in the wind. In the distance, the brown sugar loaves of the Peloncillo Mountains rose. Time for the Texan to appear. If he didn't arrive by nightfall, Lamas would send the men out looking for him.

"Maybe he got snakebit like you said happened to Diego." Sarge spat tobacco to the side of the fallen tree trunk he sat upon.

"It would kill the snake," Lamas said.

"That sumbitch may be tough, but by gawd, ain't many ever lived through a sidewinder bite. Had a big Polack private, name was Whizacowski, and he got bit one morning. Reached down for his saddle and the damn thing had crawled under it overnight and it struck him. Big man, he died before noon that day."

"If Black is dead, we will know in time." The ex-soldier was not Lamas's favorite person to talk with. Somehow Sarge's personality grated on Lamas and, while the man did his job, Lamas never felt comfortable in the noncom's company, especially at layovers like this. Something he could not put his finger on about the man and his ways.

"Yeah, but maybe the buzzards'll eat him first—'fore we find him."

"He's too damn tough for them to want a chunk of him." Lamas looked off to the south, not anxious to continue their discussion.

Sarge just nodded. "I never liked Texans. Fought them bastards in the war."

"I guess nobody has to like anyone," Lamas said. He grew weary of the man's words and tired of the boy's bad cooking. Maybe he should ride to Naco and find a woman to cook for them. She would have to be ugly, so his horny hands didn't keep her from cooking—though there wasn't one that bad-looking in all of Sonora or Arizona, and he could throw in New Mexico too, for that matter.

"He's coming," Sanchez said, matter-of-factly. "It is the roan horse. I know his pattern."

Lamas stood on his toes. He never doubted the things Sanchez could see or hear. Black was coming and he wondered if he'd found a herd for them to steal.

In a short while, Lamas heard the hard-breathing horse and Black appeared. The roan was lathered in sweat and dripping.

"Jimmy, walk that hot horse for him." Lamas made a side motion with his hand to hurry the boy to it. If the roan was not cooled, he might get stiff.

"Find any cattle?"

"Fifteen hundred."

"How many hands?"

"Half dozen."

"Do they look tough?"

Black shook his head, stepped over and poured himself a cup of coffee. In an instant, he spit the mouthful out with a bad face. "Who made this?"

He looked hard at Sarge, then Sanchez, but neither man offered a word.

"The kid," Lamas said sharply. "Are they toughs?"

"Naw, it's a family. Bunch of boys. Be like taking candy from a baby." He tossed out the contents of the pot and held it up, making a face while the black slag drained out. Then he swirled water in it and redrained it. The entire time, Black made impatient faces at the other two.

"I ought to kick both your asses for letting him do that. Where's the damn Arbuckle at anyway?"

"In the pannier." Sarge pointed his jackknife at it and went back to whittling.

"How far away is the herd?" Lamas asked, more interested in the herd than the state of the coffee.

"We can take them tomorrow might. Have the cattle at Clanton's in two days, if we've got enough horses to ride."

"I'll go get some horses," Lamas said, anxious for an excuse to leave the camp and find some food worth eating.

"Better have four apiece and a wrangler to keep up with them. It will take all of us to keep that large a herd moving."

"I'll do that." Lamas hurried to his horse and tightened the cinch. This cattle rustling would be like shooting ducks in a barrel, or was it fish? He shrugged. Never mind; Black was back with good news. To celebrate, Lamas would eat some real food in town, get some horses and help. He hoped the others did not kill one another while he was gone. He gave a shudder, thinking about the terrible coffee that boy had made for them. His bay could not go fast enough.

After a good meal in Naco, Lamas found a man he trusted to wrangle the horses. His name was Valdez. The two of them rode up to Turkey Creek and rented the horses from a rancher, who eyed them very suspiciously.

"You don't intend to steal my horses?" The man looked at him out of one eye, the other closed to the midday glare.

For ten cents he would cut this man's chicken neck off at his shoulders, but no, he only needed the horses for a few days. To arouse such a rancher would be foolish. These cattlemen could be the source of a fresh horse in desperate times. They didn't blab to the law, had their own code about loyalty and silence.

"Señor, this silver cross I wear"—Lamas held it up for

the man to see—"belonged to my mother. To show you I am only renting your bangtails, I will leave this treasure with you until I return the horses. Money could not buy it, señor." He removed his sombrero and handed the man his cross and chain.

"Since you're willing to do that, I reckon you are only renting them ponies. That blue roan will only buck when you saddle him. Gets over it. Them others just crow-hop a little on the start." The man held up the cross so the sun shone on it. "Guess you are proud of this thing. Ride easy, boys." And he waved the two of them out the gate.

If only the dumb gringo knew that. Lamas had taken that cross from a dead man, he might not even have put it over his head. Lamas and Valdez drove the horses ahead of them and rode hard for the San Bernardino Spring.

When they returned with the remuda, Black walked among them and Lamas could tell by his look he approved of the rented horses. They made plans to intercept the herd after sundown. Take the night herders out first. Then Black and the kid would ride guard on the cattle while the others took care of the crew in camp. At daylight, they would turn the herd south and cross into Mexico before the Mexican officials even suspected them. They would rest the herd overnight at a place called Fria, where there was water, and then drive them hard to the old man's the next day. Simple enough plan.

Valdez was to bring the fresh horses to them at first light. Lamas felt things were set. He didn't bother to eat any of the beans on the fire, though he knew that Black had cooked them. They took naps until sundown, then set out.

Past midnight, Lamas heard cattle bawling and shared a nod with Black. They came down a steep hillside and Lamas worried that their horses' shoes clacking on the rocks would be heard. The herd was bedded in a valley and he could make out the ribs of a wagon. He listened to some herder singing, so if his horse ran into a sleeping animal they would be awake enough not to spook him and stampede. These cattle came a long way from Texas, so there was not much danger of them jumping up—they would be trail-sore enough to hold. Still, shooting around them could cause him and his men troubles the rustlers did not need.

They reined up in an arroyo and waited. Lamas sent Sanchez. The Indian brought the first herder down with a thud in the night. Black took the man's hat and horse to ride in the herder's place so his outline would not spook the other rider. On foot to get the second rider, Lamas hurried behind the Yaqui. He almost walked into a cactus bed, but Sanchez saved him. Grateful, he nodded and they both squatted down. The second cowboy drew closer.

When he came past them, Sanchez grabbed him and jerked him from the horse. His knife found its mark before the rider could hardly protest. Where was the boy? Damn, time was precious. Sanchez led the horse back to where Sarge and Jimmy were sitting.

"Get out there and ride around them like Black," Lamas hissed at the boy.

"Yes, yes." He was mounted and gone.

Sanchez led Lamas and Sarge around the herd the other way. Soon the smell of smoldering mesquite reached Lamas's nose. The fire had about burned down; only the orange glow of a few logs remained. Bedrolls were spread about the campground. Sanchez slipped to the far one, raised his knife and plunged it repeatedly into the sleeping cowboy. Sarge took another, but his knife missed the mark and his victim began to shout and cry out. Nothing else to do: Lamas drew his pistol and shot the man beneath him squarely in the face. Sanchez stabbed another in the back trying to escape. His Colt still smoking, Lamas shot the last one in his bedroll before he could get to his pistol.

Sanchez cut his victim's throat. Wiping the knife blade on his pants, he searched around. Sarge had reached the wagon.

"Look what I found," the noncom shouted and drug a kicking, swearing young boy out. "They had a cub in there."

Sanchez made a sign with the side of his hand across his throat. Sarge nodded and did it. The boy's cursing stopped. Lamas looked anxiously into the night—good, thank God, the shots had not spooked the cattle.

The Yaqui, without instructions, began to loot the dead bodies. He put their few valuables in a pile and worked around until not only the bodies but the bedrolls had been searched. Sarge made a torch and checked out the wagon.

He climbed out and shook his head. "Food and gear is all I could find."

"Put their bodies in it," Lamas said, squatting by the fire. "We will burn it when we leave. It will look like Apaches did this." He was anxious to get back to his own hacienda, Los Palmos. Perhaps he could return home after these cattle were delivered to the old man

He had plenty of money and gold. What more could he want? Respect. Hard for a man whose mother was a *puta* to draw respectability. He owned a hacienda, had many fine horses, knew many rich people—perhaps if he married some rich man's daughter and sired children from her. He would think on this matter. Those repeating rifles he would soon deliver to Don Marques, perhaps

that transaction would raise his esteem among the
wealthy landowners in Sonora. The arms should be at the
storekeeper's warehouse in Nogales soon and he would
slip them into Mexico. Don Marques could not even buy
them. The government officials in Sonora would only
allow him to buy one rifle. One rifle, ha! He would show
them. Don Lamas was going to deliver a wagonload of
.44/.40s and ammunition to the man.

Don Marques would brag to his influential friends
about the feats of Don Lamas. Then perhaps a daughter
of such rich men would fill his bed this winter. He would
go to high society fandangos and fiestas with her. Oh, his
wedding to her would be so fancy they would never forget it. Yes, the boy they called Chupo, who was a pistolero at fifteen, would be Don Lamas, the rich rancher, to
everyone.

Which daughter would he choose? There was the Baca
girl . . . he was brought to awareness by Black.

"Which shift do you want? Now or two hours from
now?"

"Now is fine." He jerked down his waistcoat. Why was
he to ride herd like a stupid peon? No matter; he was the
one who sent the *soldados* home. He did that too soon;
they could have helped drive the cattle. Lamas went to
find his horse. In two days, this sea of *vacas* would be a
large pile of ten-dollar gold pieces. Maybe Black didn't
like Old Man Clanton, but he would like his share of the
money.

Lamas chuckled to himself, mounting up. This way
there would be more time for him to think about the
woman he would choose for his bride.

They drove the cattle on the run the last five miles to Old
Man Clanton's. Earlier, Sanchez thought he saw dust in
the north, which could mean Federales. His report put

Black into motion and he set the longhorns in a trot. Once moving, they became a boiling, bawling dust storm.

Lamas hated his fresh mount, but he whipped and spurred the lazy gelding to keep the cattle going. At times, visibility close to the herd shut down to a few feet. The cloth over his mouth became clogged with dirt. Alkali burned his eyes, but he kept moving in close to quirt the slow cattle and curse their ancestry.

"We are there!" Black shouted and rode in close to him. The Texan pulled down the filthy mask and his chin shone white against the dirt and grime around his eyes and forehead. Lamas laughed at the sight of him.

"Good," Lamas said and drew his horse back. He let the wind carry away the dust of the herd, and the steers spread out on the flat grassland when the other riders dropped aside. Maybe a bath would make him feel better, and there was Juanita to think about too. He would visit her one more time before going back to his hacienda. No telling, perhaps she had learned something more worthwhile in his absence, like a silver shipment being smuggled in to avoid the customs. It amused him that they blamed the old man for that robbery.

"No need in me going to Mexico with you," Black said.

"No, but wait until I return in the morning and see what information I can learn tonight."

"That'll be fine. You going to pay the horse wrangler to take them horses back?"

Lamas nodded. "He can handle it alone."

"Good. See you about breakfast." The big man reined the gray around. Lamas smiled after him. No way that horse bucked very far under Black. Black must be anxious to get back to the widow women in the Santa Ritas. He once worried about Black, who never acted interested in woman captives, *putas* and the like, so he had his tracker follow the Texan. When the Yaqui returned to the hacienda to tell his findings, Sanchez laughed freely over Lamas's concerns about the Texan.

"You have no worries, he is a stallion," Sanchez said.

"You saw him do it?"

"*Sí.* I felt sorry for that poor woman." He held out his forearm stiff like a giant phallus. "It was that big." They both laughed.

Lamas knew the big man must be anxious to return to her. Sanchez never spoke of the woman's beauty. All Lamas knew about her was she was a widow and had a small ranch. Black spent his off time at her place.

Lamas booted his horse for the house and corrals. First he would see Old Man Clanton and then take a bath. Ah, yes, Juanita's voluptuous body filled his thoughts.

Lamas dropped heavily from the saddle. Old Man Clanton stood on the porch scratching his privates and waiting for him. His gray beard was shaggy and he wore clothes as rumpled as if he slept in them. The head of the gang looked more like a derelict than the boss of a major ring of outlaws and ranching scion.

"Didn't take you long to find them," Clanton said and spat in the dust at the edge of the porch. Some brown juice ran off his thin lip and into the stained white beard.

"I beat you to them." Lamas smiled because he knew that was exactly what the old man thought. Probably made him mad that he hadn't learned of the herd first.

"Yeah, you did. Still lots of work to do to them before I get my money. I'll have to rebrand them and let that heal."

"And then sell them for a big profit to the agency at San Carlos."

"It damn sure ain't all profit." The man looked affronted that Lamas would accuse him of making a lot of money off the deal. "Come on inside." Clanton squinted hard at something in the distance, then spat again, turned and led the way.

"You have a wonderful ranch here," Lamas said, following the man, who stunk like a bear of sweat and fecal odors.

"Yeah, it makes a good place to change brands. They ask too many questions up there in Arizona. I come down here into Mexico and can do what the hell I like."

"And you can still sell beef to the Indian agency and the army?"

"Yeah. Horses and mules too." Clanton offered him a seat on the bench at the great dining table. He poured them both some whiskey in cups and Lamas thanked him. The old man took his place in the captain's chair at the head.

"Well, you can count the cattle and pay me tomorrow."

"Fine. What's your tally?"

"Fifteen hundred."

"Good." The old man wiped his mouth and beard with his palm. "You going back to your place?"

"When I get paid."

"I'll pay you."

"I never doubted that or I'd never went after those cattle."

"What in hell's name do you do with all your money?" Clanton leaned back, folded his hands over the wrinkled shirt and cocked one eye at him.

"I have a hacienda. Los Palmos. Like you say, it is expensive to have help and to fix up a run-down place."

"Amazing. It seems like only yesterday you were a cocky, sawed-off pistolero running around here. Today you have a hacienda and dress like some rich feller." Clanton shook his head in disbelief.

"Chupo, they called me back then."

"Yeah, I recall you from back then. You have good

men working for you. All business, but you ain't no fool, Lamas. Thing worries me is every day they keep getting more laws and more badges on both sides of the border. Makes for more pockets to fill to do business, less profits. What are we going to do when we can't buy them off?"

"By then, I hope to live on my hacienda and forget this business."

Clanton shook his head and scratched his thin white hair on top. "No, you'll never have enough money to live like that. It's in your blood. No way you could raise enough cattle or make enough money to do that alone and live the good life." He drank half his cup of whiskey and then belched.

"Maybe you are right." No need to tell the man that the cattle money was only a small portion of his fortune. He could live like a king on the proceeds of these last robberies alone.

Clanton nodded. "I know I'm right about that. Here, drink up. It's time for another snort." He reached over, ready to refill Lamas's cup.

Lamas waved off his offer of more. He didn't like the sharp whiskey that well, and besides, he didn't fully trust Clanton. The old man might get him drunk and try to swindle him out of his fifteen thousand dollars.

Bored with Clanton's conversation, with no excuse to leave, he whiled away the afternoon listening to the old man brag about his ventures, how he had bribed the agents and always got extra money for the beef he delivered. When the old man called to her, a buxom Mexican woman came in the room with more whiskey.

"This here is Felicia," the old man said and pulled her by the waist to him. "Good-looking, ain't she?"

Lamas agreed.

"She's that damn good in bed, too." The old man

laughed aloud and she slapped at him and made a face. He finally managed to stop laughing and fighting with her long enough to say, "Well, it's the gawdamn truth."

Lamas excused himself and went to take a bath. The ranch bathhouse was a small building with two tubs that a Mexican tended, heating the water for the users. After Lamas dried himself on the cheap towels, he began to dress into his clean change of clothing. Pulling on his pants, he wondered if the old man ever used this place. Bad as he smelled, he doubted the worker had to haul much water for his boss's usage.

The triangle's ringing called, the crew to supper. On his way to the house, Lamas found Black lingering behind and waiting for him.

"Feel better?" Black asked, looking fresh in his clean change.

"It helped. The old man is going to count them tomorrow and then pay me tomorrow night. Perhaps you should go along and keep him honest."

"Whatever you say, boss."

"I know you don't like him, but think about the money and he's *bueno* enough."

Black chuckled. "A man could put up with fresh shit clear to his chin if the price was right and he knew it wouldn't be like that every day."

"Right." Then they grew silent and merged in with the rest of the hands to enter the house. The long table flanked with benches quickly filled with cowboys. Old Man Clanton sat at the head and ate his buttermilk and cornbread. Platters of beef, steaming bowls of rice and beans, along with piles of tortillas and light bread were up and down the length of it.

The men, for the most part, were silent and passed the bowls and platters around. The woman Felicia and two teenage girls went around the room and filled their coffee cups. At Felicia's directions they replaced the empty bowls with new ones heaping with more food.

"By gawd, we eat good, don't we?" Clanton shouted at Lamas.

"*Sí*, you always eat good, Clanton."

A bunch of the cowboys grinned and agreed.

Later, under the starlight, Lamas rode to Juanita's house. Tired, he still looked forward to a night with her subtle body in his arms. The luxury of her great feather-bed, much like the one in his own bedroom at Los Palmos, intrigued him.

At the gate, the strip of velvet hung down as an invitation for him. He opened it and saw her standing in a lacy gown with the light of the room outlining her shapely figure. Her body looked yellowish red under the gauzy white material.

"Lamas, I didn't expect you back so soon," she said and ran to him.

"Why?" he asked, looking down into her lovely face. Was she to meet another lover this night?

"Oh, no. I mean I am so glad to see you are here." She stood on her toes and pursed her lips for him.

Good. He kissed her and swept her up in his arms. Her hands squeezed his face and her mouth became a hot volcano on his own. He put her gently on the bed and then laid down in the fluff of the mattress beside her. Their eyes locked on each other.

"Oh, Lamas," she moaned and hugged him tight.

Later, he sat in a chair and stared into the starlight reflected from the tile in the patio. Juanita slept, exhausted from their fling. He could hear her soft breathing above the crickets chirping.

A wife must be his next goal. One of nobility and high standing, who could read to him. Years ago, a *puta* taught him how to count money. She showed him how to write his name and how to read, but it was far from a finished education. Some daughter from a fine family could be his teacher and have his sons. He would be respected then. Don Lamas of Los Palmos Hacienda. He liked the sound of the title.

"You can't sleep?" Juanita asked, rising sleepily and rubbing his shoulders. "I am sorry. What can I do for you, my lover?"

"Nothing, I cannot sleep is all. Not your fault." He reached back and felt her warm flesh and patted it.

"The Lucky Shot Mine is sending their payroll by stagecoach this week." Standing behind him, she pushed her firm breasts to the back of his head and ran her palms over the sides of his face.

"From Benson?"

"No, from Nogales."

"When will they send it?" He raised an eyebrow at anyone sending a payroll in such an out-of-the-way route.

"Friday."

"Why from Nogales?" He frowned at such an impossible thing.

"No one would suspect it."

"You are certain?" He twisted around and moved her naked form onto his lap. She acted grateful for his attention and kissed his forehead.

"Yes." She used her fingers to comb though his hair. Their mouths met and they spoke no more.

CHAPTER 5

Alone, Sam T. waited on the platform of the station. His steamer trunk was loaded on the handcart and ready to go in the baggage car. This was it. Himself and all of his worldly possessions were ready to embark on a new adventure. He cast a glance towards the snowcapped front range of the Rockies. Shirley McKenzie had even declined his offer for her to see him off. Her absence left him upset and he tried to reason out why she refused even that request. While there would be other women in his life, somehow he had thought Shirley McKenzie was the right one. However, she had no interest whatsoever in Arizona Territory or taking up a new life there with him. She even had the gall to accuse him of being a sugarfoot for taking the job. He chuckled to himself at the notion of her outrage.

No, he was better off without her, in that case. This job Major Bowen offered him couldn't be any more boring than doing detective work for the Great Western Agency in Colorado. He'd had his fill of it. The locomotive's steel wheels screeched to a halt beside him and great clouds of steam engulfed him for a minute, then swept away.

The conductor placed a stool for the passengers to use. Sam T. stood back and waited for the others to climb on. A couple at the end of the line moved up the stairs, then he went on board the train. The car looked sparsely filled. He chose a seat on the right so he could look at the mountains going south to Raton, where he would transfer to the Atlantic and Pacific Railroad for Ash Fork, Arizona. Then his itinerary called for him to take a stage to the fledgling capital of Prescott. Resigned to making the trip by himself, he looked forward to seeing Major Bowen again. New job, new land and somewhere down there perhaps even a new woman. He drew a sharp inhale of the piercing smell of coal smoke from the locomotive's stacks.

From the corner of his eye through the smudged pane, he observed a familiar figure hurrying down the platform. It was Shirley. For a long moment, he considered rushing to the end of the car. Then the conductor's "All aboard" sounded.

He fought with the window, clasping the squeeze levers. At last the stiff lower section slid.

"Shirley," he shouted. She stood flush-faced, out of breath. The train had began to chug. The force of the start about jerked him down.

"Write me," he said, feeling helpless.

"I will, Sam. I'm sorry. I'll miss you—" The sadness and sincere look on her face hurt him. Why hadn't she said something sooner?

He slumped down in the seat. The bitter-tasting smoke from the stack blew in the open window. Nothing mattered as he sat in a daze. Their relationship had all been over; now it was back. At the last minute, she must have regretted her indifference and come to the station. Stubborn woman, she could have been sitting with him, beside him. They could have been going there together.

What made her change her mind?

"Excuse my bold curiosity. Was that your wife?" a young woman asked from across the aisle.

"No, just a good friend," he said, barely aware of her. She looked to be in her early twenties, with brown ringlets of curls framing a pert face.

"I thought for a moment you were considering disembarking," she said.

"No," he said softly. "Maybe I should have, but we said our good-byes earlier."

"Sounds very final."

"It is. I mean it was. Excuse me, ma'am, my name's Sam T. Mayes." He removed his hat for her.

"Mrs. Julia Riley."

"I take it your husband is not here."

"Oh, no, Mr. Mayes. He's a lieutenant in the army, stationed in Arizona."

"Isn't that interesting. I'm going to Arizona."

"Oh, yes, Mr. Mayes?"

"Sam T. is better."

"You may call me Julia." Her warm smile would have melted icebergs in the Arctic.

"Your husband—he's stationed there?"

"Yes, but I am going to the capital, Prescott. He's at an army outpost right now."

"May I?" He rose and stepped across the aisle when she nodded. Talking with beautiful women came before gazing at mountains. He swung the seat back so he could sit and face her.

The car was loosely populated with plenty of empty spaces and the morning sun streaming in on them. He removed his Stetson and sat down. He found a striking resemblance in this lovely woman to another in his past. The memory of her ate at him like burning gunpowder.

"Oh, be comfortable and wear it," she said to dismiss his chivalry. "You look rather striking under that wide-brim hat."

"Thank you." He gazed out across the yellow grass plains that stretched forever to the east, so that it did not look overly apparent he was struck with her good looks. Mrs. Riley's beauty was gut-wrenching and Sam T. considered it a crime she was without an escort on such an adventure.

"May I ask your business?"

"Law enforcement. I am going to take a job in Arizona."

"Like a U.S. marshal?"

"Sort of like that."

"I'm sorry I am so nosy." As if taken back by her own boldness, she ran her full lower lip across her even teeth.

"Julia, you can ask me anything your heart desires." He shook his head to dismiss her concern.

"I really am quite concerned about my husband, Aaron. He's in the field all the time with, well, buffalo soldiers. You know, Negroes, and I am not certain how trustworthy they are."

"Rest easy, little lady," he said with a grin. "He's better off with them than white ones. All the army can attract these days on their low pay are criminals looking to escape jail time and foreigners who don't speak or understand English."

"Oh, I never knew that."

Sam T. leaned back in the seat. He'd take buffalo soldiers anytime to foreigners who didn't know a word of English. Whew, the state of the U.S. military was a mess and no one worried about it. The North would never have won the war under the current conditions. He felt more at ease with her by the minute and savored his good fortune. The clickety-clack of the car's wheels on the expansion gaps sang a song, "*Going to Arizona, going to Arizona.*"

The train made frequent stops before it reached Colorado Springs. At one point four men that Sam T. considered hardcases came on board. They wore a certain lean, harsh look. For him, these men in cowboy garb fit the role of trouble. A whiff of whiskey perfumed their passage, as shouldering saddles and war bags, they moved purposefully down the aisle. When the conductor reached Sam T. and the lady, he took a strong look down the car in the direction of their loud voices.

"Sir." He bent over as if checking Sam T.'s ticket. "Should those Rebs decide to restart the war, please inform me."

"There won't be any informing necessary," Sam T. said.

"Very well." The train man straightened, checked his gold watch. "We should be in the Springs on time today." He snapped the timepiece shut and moved down the aisle to punch the other tickets.

"Do you have family?" she asked, bringing Sam T. back from his thoughts.

"No, ma'am. I never stayed in one place that long."

"Oh."

"Law enforcement is not the kind of job where you go to work and then come home at night"

"I see—"

"Several years ago, a very lovely woman came into my life. She was murdered. You remind me very much of her."

"Oh, I'm sorry I didn't—"

"You didn't, Julia. I was only explaining. I guess after that I have been afraid to, well, seriously involve myself with another woman." Except perhaps Shirley, who failed him when the chips were down. Out the window, he studied a sod shack and the clothes on the line waving in the strong wind. Would his life be different if Sharon had lived? Would he have been a dirt farmer with a big family of kids? In fifteen years, they could have had a passel. Fate instead dealt him another hand.

He could hear the raucous talk of the cowboys up the aisle. With his back to them, he could not see what they were up to. Obviously, they were passing the bottle around.

"Are they having a high old time?" he asked.

"Yes," she said, looking about ready to snicker.

Sam T. twisted around and saw the wave of the jug, then the car door opened and the whiskey was quickly secreted again. The conductor strode through the aisle and their voices became subdued. If there had been no woman on board, their actions would not be so bad, but besides Julia, by Sam T.'s appraisal, there were a half dozen respectable ladies in the car.

The conductor passed on to the next coach and the party began again. It was when "sons of bitches" and other words grew louder, that Sam T. rose to his full six feet. He gave Julia a reassuring nod and strode down the car, using the various seat rails for balance against the rock of the train. The cowboys grew louder and he considered their talk fit only for barnyard consumption.

He stood over them before they looked up and noticed him.

"Want a snort, dude?" the red-faced one asked. Sam T. judged them to be in their early twenties. They were drunk enough to have a cocky edge to their ways.

"Gents, the fun's over. There are ladies aboard this coach."

"Where?" the short one asked and used his hand as a visor to look back the way Sam T. had come.

"So?" said the hardest-looking of the three.

"Time to button your lips, boys," Sam T. said.

"And who's going to make us do that?"

Sam T.'s hand produced the short-barreled sheriff's model Colt from his shoulder holster so fast the small one gasped.

"Now on your feet," he said, waving it toward the end of the car.

"Who the hell are you?" the tough one demanded. "I'll kill your ass—"

Sam T.'s slash with the revolver butt caved in his high-crown hat and sent him sprawling over the other one's lap. The whiskey bottle shattered on the floor. In an instant, he forced the muzzle in the redheaded one's face.

"Get your hand clear of that iron or die."

A woman in the car made a stifled scream. Sam T. never looked away from them. Every nerve in his body stood on end. Three to one and any move they made could make him a dead man.

"Get up real easy. You're getting off here." He took a half step back to make room for them to get out.

"We—"

"I'll take over here, sir," the conductor said, coming down the car.

"Listen, we never—"

Sam T. turned to the man. "They got awfully foul-mouthed."

"No problem, we'll be stopping here in a minute. Get your gear and get ready to get off," the conductor said, pulling their guns from their holsters.

"But we paid—"

"Who the hell are you, mister?" the hard one asked, holding his hand out to silence the others.

"Sam T. Mayes. What's your handle?"

"That's for you to find out, but if we ever meet again—"

"You better come armed, mister. Better come damned well armed." Sam T. watched them file forward. Satisfied they posed no threat, he moved the cylinder back so the empty one was under the hammer, then holstered the Colt.

The conductor thanked him and herded them out. Sam T. watched the short cowboy move out of the car behind the other two, packing his war bag and saddle. The train braked for the next whistle stop. Several passengers nodded their approval when Sam T. came back up the aisle.

"Weren't you afraid?" Julia whispered when he took his seat.

"No, it wasn't my time."

"You mean to die . . ." She blanched under her creamy complexion.

"Yes, ma'am, sorry I am so blunt."

"No, I just never knew a man before who considered that." Then her face reddened. "I am being far too personal."

"Don't worry about it," he said to reassure her.

He sat back and through the window studied the shriveled corn plants needing rain. Laid out in wide check rows, the field looked large, and in the distance someone cultivated with a team of grays, hoping to churn up moisture from the ground. No, God never meant for him to be a farmer.

The quarter moon came up over Mount Lemmon. Jesus Morales stood in the white light and teetered in his sandals. He put his hand against the stucco wall for support. He felt woozy from too much drink. It must be two more blocks to his place. If he could only make it there. He set out again. His movement unsteady, he weaved his way down the street. Then his feet became tangled and he stumbled over something that grunted and soon a pungent odor rose in his nose. Pig shit. He had fallen in a hole dug out by some neighborhood sow.

A force rose behind his tongue and soon he began gagging up violent vomit. His stomach turned inside out. He had to escape the pig wallow or he'd puke up his guts. In desperation, he managed to crawl twenty feet between vomiting and gagging, to fall face down and pass out.

He awoke to someone kicking him lightly in the ribs. Blind, he swatted at it. Still his tormentor persisted. He tried to open his dry eyes. Then he could smell the musk. It wasn't someone, it was some thing. A large black sow was trying to root him over. He kicked at her to get away. What time was it?

"Get away, you stupid sow!" At his words, she backed up a little and glared at him out of small beady eyes.

At last, he raised up. His shirt filthy and sour smelling, he kicked with impatience at the snuffling pig. "Go on!"

Where were his sandals? He searched about in the shadowy darkness. It must be close to sunup, time for him to go to work at the adobe brickyard. His mind clouded and, dizzy, he fought to his feet. Where were his sandals? Lightheaded, he started back in the direction he had come from. He searched around the slop hole in the alley where women threw their wastewater and the pigs had rooted a place to mud-bathe. Too dark to see. Maybe they were in that slop hole.

The thick odor of hog was strong on his clothes. He was filthy and coated with dried mud and shit. At last he gave up his search and went stumbling off to Raphael

Ortega's adobe pit. He couldn't afford to miss any work; he was penniless. Gawdamnit, he smelled bad, like he had shit his own pants. He reached Green Street, crossed it and went up the alley to where the excavation some twelve feet deep had eaten up two city lots.

"Whew, you smell bad," Conteras said and backed away. "Did you make love to a pig last night?" The little man laughed at Jesus' expense.

Jesus mumbled something unintelligible and picked up the handles of a wheelbarrow. He pushed it down the ramp. The small steel wheel made a ringing sound that pierced his head. His day had begun. He lifted the pick-axe and made the first of ten thousand swings into the hard-packed brown clay. It crumbled slowly and he used the spade to load the wheelbarrow with it. When the small box was full, he glanced with dread at the ramp and began to shove it up the steep way. His shoulders hurt, his stomach growled and churned empty. At last he dumped the contents, went by the water barrel and took a gourd of the tepid liquid. He let the refreshing water slide down his throat and then he hurried back to his digging. He needed this job.

On Jesus' third trip up the ramp, Conteras came out and told him it was time to mix the clay and straw. He hated that worse than mining the dirt. The sun stood high in the morning sky. He shoveled the four-by-four mixing bin half full of clay, added water and began to fork straw on top. Then, by treading it with his bare feet, he mixed it. The hotter the day grew, the worse the smell came from his clothing. It was a deadly mixture of sour puke, pig manure and his own foul body odor. He finally had to quit stomping the mixture and went to relieve himself in the small outhouse.

The stifling-hot privy buzzed with flies, and the smell wafting up from the pit underneath only made matters worse. He finally finished and tumbled outside to gasp for fresh air.

"Why do you use it?" Conteras came over and asked. "You smell like you already shit on yourself."

He ignored the man and went back to tramping the adobe. If he let Conteras get to him, he would probably kill the man. Then what would he do for work? Even prison might not be as bad. They had a new prison at Yuma. It couldn't be much hotter than this hole. He daydreamed of the cool Sierra Madre, the White Mountains, under the Mogollon Rim in the north, when he was an army scout, not an adobe mud mixer.

"Work that straw in better. Some of that batch you made last week broke on the builder. He wanted his money back," Conteras said.

Jesus looked over at the little man. He resembled a small feisty dog, only inches shorter than Jesus. Still the man lorded himself over Jesus. He hated his thin mustache, he hated Conteras' fat wife, Corita, who brought bean-filled tortillas every day. No meat in them. It was Jesus' only meal of the day because the fifty cents Conteras paid him each day went for something to drink. More than anything else, he hoped the cheap liquor he could afford would get him through the night and part of the next day as well. So he would dig some more clay and mix some more with straw and then pack it in the forms to set up. In two days, he pulled those forms and stacked the still-damp bricks, each one tipped on the next one in long rows to dry for a month. Ortega owned two more lots beside the pit where they dried the bricks.

Jesus tamped the forms full and the sun grew higher. Soon his boss's wife came. She had a ponderous belly under a thin dress and he could see the rosette of her nipples, big as silver dollars beneath the material. Corita reminded him of that alley sow; he hated her.

"Time to eat," she announced and he stopped his work.

"You smell bad," she whined. "Stay downwind." With her pudgy fingers she directed for him to go around her.

Maybe he would kill her with his bare hands. Instead he took the wood slab with the two burritos on it and stepped aside. Conteras was in the next yard arguing with a builder.

"You must have rubbed on a pig," she said, busy feeding her face. Then she grimaced at him. "Don't come around me stinking like that. Whew, you smell awful."

"Go to hell," he mumbled.

"You talk to me like that, you won't get any more lunch."

Who cared? It was slop that she brought him anyway. Besides, Conteras made her bring him something to eat. It wasn't out of her generosity that she fed him. In fact, all she did was insult him. If she thought he cared about her fat butt, she was stupid. He would make love to a cow first. Oh, many times he had seen her fat thighs when she sat with her legs spread apart and acted like she was hot. They appealed to him like that pig did rooting him in the Green Street alley. He hated her.

The food only upset his stomach. He sipped some water and began to swallow his own spit. Something an Apache woman taught him: A man's own saliva was better than any medicine to settle his stomach. Soon he was back to work shoveling the wet mixture in the wooden forms to make more bricks. The work was hot and he was slow.

Conteras came back and grumbled he wasn't working hard enough. Jesus told him what he could do and went on tamping the forms full.

"First thing in the morning, we will pull the forms on those you did yesterday. There better not be any broken ones," Conteras warned him, then he went and laughed with his fat wife about something. Maybe about Jesus.

Jesus recalled how it was when he was an army scout. Never, even on the worst days when he scouted, did an entire bad day compare to ten minutes on this job. The sad part was they didn't need scouts anymore. The Apaches were on reservations. No more bronco Apaches, no more raids to Mexico. The midday sun grew hotter as he tamped the filled forms. Someone came to see about adobe bricks, and as Conteras walked by he made a comment about Jesus' work. Jesus considered clubbing him to death with the shovel. Tonight he would really get drunk, so he could face the two of them the next day.

"Cool in the Madres," he mumbled in singsong fashion, to take his mind off of the heat, filling the forms with the mixture.

"Why don't you go there, then?" Conteras asked, passing by him.

He silently snarled at the man's back. He would if he could. But he had no money. There was no way to get any and nothing to ride. Besides, what would he do there? Live like some bronco Apache? Tonight, he would drink himself silly and forget it all. That he wanted to do more than anything else—forget it all.

Major Gerald Bowen returned from his latest meeting with Governor Sterling and kissed his wife Mary on the cheek. "I'm going to Tucson tomorrow. I should be back in five days. If Sam T. Mayes arrives here while I'm gone, have him take a room and tell him I'll return shortly. I want to arrange it so he has some help waiting in Tucson and can get right after those outlaws."

"So Governor Sterling is going to allow your marshals?" she asked.

"He is. I don't think he's all that much in favor of them,

but he's going to let me hire a few men. He wants this Border Gang stopped worse than anything else. They are marauding all over southern Arizona."

"Gerald, you aren't going down there after them by yourself?"

He shook his head. "No, my dear, my experience is not in pursuing criminals. I suspect I have delegated authority too long to get back on the trail. And I know Sam T. will need a good sharp man to help him. If I can hire him, Jesus Morales is the man for the job. But he may have a much better job than I can afford to outbid. That's why I'm going down there."

"He was one of your scouts at Fort Grant, wasn't he?"

"Yes, and he's loyal and hardworking. I hope I can locate him. I have no idea what he's doing these days."

"Where will you look?"

"Tucson." He shrugged, uncertain where he would find the ex-scout. His concern was if he could hire him when he located the man.

"Don't drink any bad water," she reminded him and busied herself gathering his extra clothing for him to take along. "When do you leave?"

"First thing in the morning on the stage."

"For how many days?"

"Five or six," he said, taking his well-oiled Colt from the wooden case in his desk drawer. He decided he'd better start packing it on his person.

Up the street in the Harrington House, Ella Devereaux wondered why Major Bowen purchased a round-trip ticket to Tucson on the stage line. A few moments before, Sassy had brought her the note from the young man who worked in the stage line office. She reread it: *Major Bowen bought a two-way ticket to Tucson today.*

"Missy," Sassy interrupted from the doorway. "Mr. Killian is here to see you."

For moment she considered where in the house she should meet with the city councilman. Would an intimate meeting in her apartment be necessary? It might not be a bad idea, if Governor Sterling's actions were close to shutting her down.

"Show him up here," she said, then fluffed the front of her dress, made a close examination of her breasts and cleavage. Satisfied that she looked presentable, she rose when Sassy brought the tall thin man into the room.

"Why, Horace, so good to see you. What brings you here? Oh, Sassy, go get some brandy for the councilman. You do like brandy, don't you, Horace?"

"Be fine, Miss Ella."

"Here, take a seat." She showed him to the overstuffed chair behind the wind-fluttering lace curtains, then sat down opposite him.

"What can I do for you?"

"It's come to our attention . . ." He trailed off when Sassy returned to the room with a tray, decanter and glasses.

"Set it here and I can handle it." She dismissed the girl after Sassy placed the tray on the small table between them.

Ella poured them both a drink. "Continue, sir. Sorry you were so rudely interrupted."

"Aw, that ain't nothing. The city council needs to hire a new marshal and he's going to cost forty dollars a month—"

"Your council wants Harrington House to underwrite his salary?" She posed a warm smile for the man as if his request pleased her.

"Yeah, that's right," he said in relief.

She raised the glass and tried to hide her relief. "A done deal, sir. Tell Chief Wallace it will be in my regular envelope next month."

The man looked as if a ton of weight had been taken from his shoulders. He smiled and sat back in the chair. "I told them boys at the meeting last night that you would understand the need for more enforcement. Why, those rowdy cowboys and miners become more than a handful anymore."

"Anything to make Prescott more respectable," she said and toasted him with her glass.

"You sure have a fine place here, Miss Ella."

"We try to please. Do you have any need? I mean, a personal one?" she asked in low voice.

"Well . . ."

"Don't be bashful, now. What could I arrange for you?"

"Middle of the day and all . . ." He shrugged.

"How about I find, say, a fiery redhead?"

"Oh, yes, but I have to be back—"

"Come, my dear." She rose and offered him her arm. Then they strode from her room down the hall.

She knocked on the closed door. "Strawberry, my dear. I have special company."

"Just a minute, Missy."

Ella turned and smiled at the man. "I am certain that she won't detain you too long."

Strawberry appeared in the doorway in a white shift. "Oh, good day, councilman. Come in." Then, with quick look of *I'll handle this* behind the man's back, Strawberry closed the door after him. Ella went back down the hallway, satisfied Horace would be well taken care of in there.

If the council expected her to pay for the new town

law, then they weren't planning on shutting her down in the near future. Her other concern, though, was about Bowen going to Tucson. Why? Perhaps she should wire Senator Green and warn him. Back in her room, she sipped her brandy and considered the governor's mansion half a block away. Things were happening fast in this new territory and she needed to keep abreast of them.

CHAPTER 6

Bowen hopped aboard the stage in the predawn light and arrived in Tucson twenty-four hours later. Groggy and sore from the stiff ride, he took a room at the Congress Hotel. In the hotel bar, he asked if anyone knew of Jesus Morales' whereabouts. The Mexican waiter promised to find out and let him know if anyone knew of Morales. In return, Bowen promised him a dollar reward for the information.

Bowen ate a breakfast of ground pork, eggs and peppers with tortillas, then went upstairs and tried to sleep a few hours in the hot room. Despite the open windows, the air in the room proved stifling. After a short while the heat grew worse, so he rose, took a sponge bath and went downstairs.

"Señor, señor. They say that Jesus Morales works at an adobe pit off Green Street," the waiter said aloud when he spotted him.

"What does he do there?" Bowen asked suspiciously. Adobe brickmaking hardly sounded like something the suave Morales would be involved in. "Does he own it?"

"No, Raphael Ortega owns it. He is a worker there.

The pit, it is across town." He made a vague wave of his arm.

Bowen paid him. Uncertain this could be the right man, he bought himself a whiskey at the bar, then ordered some lunch and took a seat at a table. What would Morales be doing there? Probably a blind alley, but he would go see this Morales after his meal.

When he went outside the hotel, he found the driver of the cab knew the location of Ortega's adobe pit. Bowen climbed in, reset the Colt at his waist under his coat and squinted against the too brilliant sun. The man drove slowly through the residential district's narrow streets and cur dogs yapped at his lanky horse's heels.

He drew up in an alley. Beside them, rows of light-colored adobe bricks ran side by side like snakes to the back fence. A short man with a mustache came from under a palm ramada and smiled.

"Ah, you need some bricks, señor? We have some good ones."

"I am looking for Jesus Morales. Does he work here?"

"*Sí.*" The man acted as if he knew little about the matter. A simple yes and that was all.

"I need to talk, to him. Where is he?"

"In the hole." With that said, the man turned on his heel and went back to the ramada.

Bowen frowned and then headed for the obvious pit, for he could not see into it from where he stood. He looked over the edge and discovered one man swinging a pick in what he figured must be an oven from hell.

"Jesus?"

The rumpled-looking man in filthy clothing let go of the pick and turned to look up from under a worn-out straw hat. He blinked his eyes in disbelief.

"Major Bowen?" he managed in a cracked voice.

"Yes."

"What are you doing here?" Jesus asked.

"What in hell are you doing down there?"

"Working. Why?"

" 'Cause I've got a helluva lot better job for you than this."

Bowen blinked in shock when Jesus dropped to his knees, made the sign of the cross and began to pray out loud to the Virgin Mary.

"You are hiring my help away?" the little man demanded, coming from the ramada as if Bowen had no authority to do such a thing

"Yes, I am. Jesus, get up here. We've got things to do." Bowen had no time for this little banty rooster of a pest.

When Jesus neared the top of the ramp, Bowen could see his eyes were filled with tears. This ex-scout who had fought Apaches like a tiger was crying over this new-found offer. Bowen could hardly believe it. Jesus bawled like a baby.

"Jesus, what's the matter with you?" he asked

"Oh, Major, what do you need from me?" He wiped his wet eyes on the side of his hands.

Bowen could hardly believe it was him. It appeared the man hadn't bathed or shaved in weeks. Was this really Jesus Morales? What had caused such a dramatic fall?

"We can't talk here. Where is there a bathhouse?"

"We can go to the Santa Cruz River." Jesus motioned toward it.

"No, I mean a bathhouse." Bowen shook his head to dismiss that as the wrong answer.

"If you are quitting in the middle of the day, I am charging you for lunch," Conteras said.

"Go to hell!" Jesus said.

"You owe me—"

Jesus reached out and caught the man's shirt in his fist.

He drew him close to his face to make him squirm. "Go to hell, Conteras!"

"You can't quit—"

"Come on, Jesus," Bowen said. "He ain't worth killing."

He released the man and turned to Bowen. "Where are we going, Major?"

"Get in the cab. We're going to find you a bath and a clean suit of clothing." Bowen considered the nasty, battered straw hat on the man's head. He removed it and sent it sailing off into the pit. "And a new hat too."

Jesus grinned at him. "Good. I hated that one since the day I found it."

"Where can we go?"

"To Tia's."

In Spanish, Jesus rattled off directions and the driver nodded. They both climbed in the cab and the man made a U-turn.

Jesus opened his mouth, but was too overwhelmed with emotion to speak. Bowen read the question in his eyes.

"I'm the head of a new law enforcement agency, but it's a secret. You heard of the Border Gang?"

"Who has not heard of those killers?" Jesus asked as he recovered his composure.

Bowen searched around to be certain they were alone. "Do you know who they are?"

"Mexican bandits."

"You know their leader?"

"I could find out."

Pleased with the answer, Bowen nodded his head. He felt excited for the first time since he had found his ex-scout. Maybe his decision to hire the man wasn't so foolish after all. Morales's condition had worried him, but he sounded like the same man who scouted for him—ready for duty. He hoped so, anyway.

"Good. Sam T. Mayes will be here in a week. He will be the marshal in charge. I'll pick out some good horses for the two of you to ride, and pack animals. Sam T. can get the supplies you will need when he comes."

"For this man Sam T. Mayes?" Jesus acted like a man in shock.

"Yes. He will be the marshal. You'll be his deputy. It pays two dollars a day."

"What else do I need to do?" Jesus uttered another prayer.

"Can you find Too-Gut?"

"I think so, for two dollars a day." Jesus shook his head in disbelief.

"All right. Tell him he gets the same pay. You and Too-Gut will help Sam T. round up this gang."

"This Border Gang is tough, I hear." Jesus frowned at him.

"There isn't anything you, Too-Gut and Sam T. can't whip."

"You know what I am thinking?"

"What's that, Jesus?"

"That three men can make an army."

"Three good men."

Jesus slumped in the leather seat. He shook his head warily and looked disappointed.

"You afraid?" Bowen asked.

"No, Major, but I think it will be as much work as the adobe pit."

Then both men laughed.

Tia's place was a small house in the center of a few irrigated acres. An attractive woman in her thirties came to the door, made a face at the sight of Jesus and then smiled at the major.

"Tia, this is my new boss. He wants a bath," Jesus said.

"For him," Bowen said, when she looked at him with a questioning look.

"Come, the water will be cold. I have no time to heat it." She sounded concerned and ushered them inside the front doorway.

Bowen spotted the high-backed tin tub in the center of the room. The short, shapely woman made several displeased faces at Jesus' condition. At last she spoke. "Take those stinking rags off."

"I have no clothes to change into—"

"Take them off before you smell my house up any more. I have seen you. He don't care." She gave a head toss in the direction of Bowen.

"Excuse me?" Bowen said. "I am going to the store and find him some new clothes."

"Good. He needs them," she said and showed him to the door.

Bowen watched her run next door and then across the street. Quickly, she recruited several women to go with large ollas for the bathwater. He climbed in the taxi and told the man he wanted to go to a large store.

The mercantile was expansive. Bowen purchased a white cotton shirt without a collar, a pair of canvas pants, suspenders, a wide-brimmed straw hat with a Chihuahua crush in the top and two pair of underwear. Since he didn't have Jesus' size, he decided he would wait on boots. Then he saw a bandolier that held .44/.40 cartridges. What would Jesus Morales be without a bandolier? He ordered it from the clerk and the shells to fill it. Then he chose a used .44 pistol from the gun case, a large-bladed hunting knife in a sheath, along with a holster set. Next he went through

the silk scarfs until he found a powder-blue one. Satisfied with his purchases, he paid the man, took his pack-
ages and went out to the cab driver.

"Back to Tia's place," he said and sat back in the seat.

She was finished shaving Jesus when Bowen arrived.
Jesus's thick black hair had been given a long-overdue
trim. He stood up in the sheet gown she had him wrapped
in. Jesus blinked his bloodshot eyes in disbelief at the
armload of things Bowen brought in.

"I didn't know your boot size," Bowen apologized.

"Oh, that is all right," he gushed. "Go and I will dress,"
he said to her.

"No. I get to help you," she said, acting excited about
examining the purchases. She held the new canvas pants
out at arm's length and nodded her approval.

"All right," he said and started to take off the sheet.

"Wait. Put these on," she said and shoved the new set
of one-piece underwear at him.

He shrugged, took them, then threw the sheet over his
head. Both she and Bowen laughed at his antics under
the covers.

"He never had any of that to wear before," she said
privately to Bowen. "He may not know how to put it on."
Then she raised her voice. "Be sure those buttons go in
front." They both laughed hard until the thin frame of
Jesus emerged dressed in his one-piece underwear.

"What are you telling him?" Jesus asked with a frown.

"You look pretty good," she said, smugly going around
him in a circle with her hands on her hips to inspect him.

"Let's get dressed. That cab driver is getting restless,"
Bowen said to hurry them.

"Who is going to fill this?" she asked, holding up the
cartridge belts.

"He'll have time to do that before Sam T. comes."

"Oh," she said. "Will this Sam T. need a bath too?"

"Not that bad, I hope," Bowen said, amused at her humor.

His pants on and tucking in his new shirt, Jesus leaned over and kissed her on the cheek. "But you can fill those belts for me while I am gone." He indicated the bandoliers.

Bowen considered her for a minute. "We will need to have supper when we return. Maybe some wine and goat?" He handed her some money.

"Too much—"

"A fat goat," he said and they exchanged a smile.

"For this much we will have a fiesta."

"Good," Bowen said. "A fiesta is what we want."

The bootmaker was a tiny Mexican man in a small shop on a side street. When they came inside the room, it reeked of rich leather smells. The owner sat on the floor, cross-legged and taking a hammer to the sole of a new boot.

"Sancho?" Jesus asked softly. "Any used boots to fit me?"

The man peered over at Jesus' bare feet as if calculating their size. Then he acted as if in deep concentration for a long moment before he spoke. "On the second shelf," he said in Spanish.

Jesus moved by. Sancho looked at the major's feet and then nodded, saying, "*Cuatro*."

Bowen went by the man to look at the fourth shelf.

"Sancho?" Jesus called out, pulling on a pair of high top black boots. "Do you know about the Border Gang?"

The old man shook his head warily. "They say if you speak of them, they will cut out your tongue."

His boots on, Jesus stalked to the front and squatted down near the bootmaker. "Who are they?"

"They say they are the wind."

"I say they are killers."

"Worse than that," was all the old man would say.

"How much?" Bowen asked, indicating Jesus' boots.

"Used. Two dollars."

"How much for the names of the gang members?" Bowen asked.

"I am an old man. They have many spies here." He shook his small wrinkled face as if unable to answer him.

Bowen paid him the two dollars and they climbed in the cab.

"It won't be easy to learn their names, will it?" he asked Jesus.

"I will find them," Jesus promised and stretched his new footgear out to inspect them.

"I believe you will, Jesus. I believe you will." Bowen felt certain he had made the right decision. All he needed was Too-Gut and Sam T. there and they could get started.

Tia's fiesta proved a success. Musicians played in her backyard. They feasted on roasted goat, peppers, beans and rice. The wine flowed and a small boy ran to the nearby cantina to refill the buckets of beer.

Bowen enjoyed the songs, and his Spanish, while not polished, was good enough for him to understand a portion of what they spoke about. He sat at a small table in the shadows and Tia made certain he had plenty of food and drink. She introduced various people to him, her neighbors, relatives and friends, giving him credit for the fiesta.

Jesus came by in a while and squatted on his heels. "They say these bandits are from Mexico. The one who leads them is an hombre called Lamas."

"Lamas who?" Bowen asked under his breath.

"That is his name."

"How does he do all this and no one sees his gang until they do some crime?"

"They are like the wind, Major. Like the wind."

"Too-Gut could find their tracks. They must leave tracks."

"*Sí*, I will find him."

"They know nothing more than his name?" Bowen asked, impressed at last that they had a handle for the gang leader.

"No, Major. He is perhaps a ghost."

Bowen nodded and considered the matter for a long moment. He understood how superstitious these Mexican people were, but there was nothing supernatural about the man they dealt with—he was alive. He gazed at the Chinese lanterns stretched over the dancing couples; Bowen felt convinced his plan would work. Sam T., Jesus and the Apache tracker were the force to bring this Lamas and his killing spree to an end.

Sam T. showed Mrs. Julia Riley to the train at Raton. He eyed the people gathered on the platform out of habit, saw no one that appeared to be a threat, then followed Julia onto the coach. They chose a seat a third of the way down the car and he flipped the seat back over to take the one facing her.

"I have noticed something," she said, settled in her place. "You never miss examining every man that comes along. How many enemies do you have?"

"Maybe a few, maybe hundreds."

"I see."

The locomotive began to jerk the cars. The train soon sped toward Santa Fe. From beneath them, the clack of the rails became a song and the sway of the car, their dance. Waltzing to Arizona, he mused, with a lovely partner. He turned and studied the drab-looking junipers through the grimy glass.

A sweltering sun blazed across the azure sky. A lone gliding buzzard circled the five riders lined up along the crest of the desert rise. Lamas gazed intently on the distant stage stop below. Shimmering heat waves distorted his vision of the adobe buildings and surrounding horse pens. Nothing looked out of place.

He pushed back his sombrero; the leather thong stretched across his throat. Then he raised up in the stirrups and with devilment in his heart turned to grin at the Texan beside him.

"Well, Ezra, my compadre, we have at least two hours before the stage arrives."

A scowl flicked across Ezra Black's face. Only Lamas had the nerve to call him by his first name. The Texan's brittle reaction amused Lamas each time.

"Yeah, Lamas," he drawled, "and maybe the stage that comes will have that payroll on it."

"It will be on it, my friend." Lamas laughed aloud, still amused at the frown on the Texan's face. Ah, lovely Juanita, the big man did not know about his source of information for this robbery. He glanced down at the squat adobe buildings and his blood pumped faster in anticipation of seeing lots of money in the strongbox. Turning in his saddle, he surveyed the others. Sarge, wearing his blue faded army uniform, grinned and rubbed his palms together in a greedy gesture. The sleepy-eyed kid Jimmy wore a look of boredom on his pimpled face. Lamas's Yaqui, Sanchez, the dependable one, weighed down by cross-belts of ammunition, had dismounted to check on his cinch.

Jimmy roused himself and pushed back his dusty Stetson. "Are we going down there?" he asked lazily.

Black frowned at Lamas. "Where the hell has he been?"

"Maybe we should send him down there alone," Lamas said.

The kid's eyes flew open. "Huh?"

A soft ripple of laughter from the others drew a flush to his face.

Lamas leaned back in his saddle and sighed with satisfaction. He and his army were ready. When the Halsey coach from Nogales arrived, they would be in place. Good planning. Always his good planning made such things work so well, he silently gloated.

Nudging his horse with a rowel, he signaled for his men to follow him down the slope toward the stage stop.

The stagecoach continually jolted until every muscle in Justine Stauffer's body cried out in protest. She felt disgusted with the constant billowing of fine powder that blew through the open side windows and crept through the cracks. Her brown dress turned a dull gray, and she could feel the dust crusting her fair skin. Her husband, Tom, was engrossed as usual in a sheaf of impressive-looking papers covered with facts and figures. Though his hip pressed against hers, she felt isolated from him.

The coach lurched roughly, sending Justine sprawling over Tom's lap, crushing his precious documents.

"For God's sake, Justine! Can't you sit still?"

She looked at her husband reproachfully, too wary of him to spout the words that sprang to her mind. It wasn't her fault that the stage jerked her around like a rag doll.

Allowing herself a meek "Excuse me," she turned away from Tom and crouched in the corner, wondering if the torturous journey would ever end. Maybe she would find the courage, when they returned to Tucson, to leave Tom.

Why she had accompanied him to Tombstone on this business trip, she simply didn't know. He obviously did not desire her company. Dan Narrimore, the wealthy mine owner, had much more to offer her. His handsome good looks, sophisticated manner and splendid home were growing hard to resist. A vision of Dan brought a small amount of comfort to her weary spirit. Even though she found his company more desirable than her husband's, when it came to making a break from Tom, she was a coward.

A lump formed in her throat. Saliva refused to surface in her mouth and even swallowing did not erase the lump. Her blue eyes opened and she glanced at the timid little man on the facing bench. Bailey, her husband's assistant, stared straight ahead, his thin white hand gripping the window frame. Justine admitted that he was probably worse off than she was. Poor Bailey. He had few interests in life other than his work. There were times when she suspected he knew more about mining than her engineer-degreed husband. Bailey painstakingly wrote the reports that were filled with tedious details while Tom played the social role.

But, Justine wondered, what did men like Bailey think about? Had he no desire to make love to a woman? To her knowledge, he had never shown an interest in any. He seldom drank. Perhaps Bailey's passion was satisfied by his work. Maybe his pulse quickened at the words he produced with a pen.

Justine smiled. Bailey would be shocked if he knew her thoughts; his prominent ears would burn scarlet with embarrassment. She recalled that Tom had, at times, deliberately taunted him by saying, "Bailey, why don't you go find some lady tonight and relax?" Her husband enjoyed disconcerting the man. It was apparently a part of Tom's lord-and-master role, which he played so naturally. Yes, Bailey was in a worse position than she was. Yet he never showed any desire to escape.

From outside, the "Hee-yah" of the driver, the drum of hooves and creak of the coach caused Justine's head to pound. The headache did provide her with a small consolation—it momentarily made her forget about the dull ache below her stomach caused by an expanding bladder. The last stop had been miles earlier, and if she didn't get a chance to relieve herself soon, she feared embarrassing consequences.

When Tom withdrew a fat cigar from his breast pocket, it posed the final insult. Earlier she had heard him offer one to Bailey. The little man had clamped his lips and shaken his head vehemently.

Tom's first attempt to ignite the cigar failed. The sway of the coach and the elusive tip prevented him from lighting it. The match burned his fingers, causing him to swear harshly.

Justine avoided his eyes, expecting him to blame her, as he seemed to do for everything that went wrong. There was little evidence of the man she married three years earlier in the curt individual that Tom had become. Even his lovemaking was selfishly inflicted. Other than her legal obligation, she found little reason to remain with him. Despite that knowledge, when the opportunity to leave Tom had presented itself, her courage had evaporated like smoke. All her resolve wafted away at the word *divorce*. She would be a marked woman, shunned by her own family. Her mother's stern warning, *Marriage is forever!* branded Justine's thoughts. There was no place in Tucson society for a divorced woman. A discreet affair was one thing, but divorce was dirty laundry hung out for all to see. It was a difficult choice to make. She could either continue to live an unhappy life with a husband who no longer cared about her, or she could divorce him and be ostracized by society.

Another bump crushed her against the side of the coach, causing her bladder to protest. She sucked in her stomach. The pungent odor of the newly lit Havana cigar filled her nostrils. She held her breath, fighting the sneeze that tickled her nose, but failed to control the involuntary action.

The small sneeze drew a cold stare from her husband. His impatience was not tempered any when Bailey blessed her. Tom turned an icy glare on the pitiful assistant.

Justine felt sickened as she watched Bailey cower before her tyrannical husband. Oh, Lord, she prayed silently, let the next stop be soon.

Lamas hoisted his feet up and planted his polished boots on a chair. Grundy, the wide-eyed, whiskered relay station operator, sat across from him and acted ready to agree to any condition.

Thoughtfully, Lamas studied the station agent. Why was death such a threat to the man? he wondered idly. Surely dying would be no worse than living in this miserable place. The man's woman was such a slovenly fat squaw that it probably required a gallon of whiskey to get drunk enough to climb on her round belly.

Lamas never allowed himself to get that drunk anymore. Not since his days as Chupo, the pistolero, when he knew no better. Well, the ugly woman would not go to waste, he mused. Perhaps the rat-faced Sanchez would use her; he was not fussy.

A glance at the door reassured Lamas. Ezra Black stood in the frame, his rifle at the ready in his arms. Satisfied, Lamas turned back to Grundy.

"You give a sign, a hint, a warning of any kind to the driver or anyone, and you're dead, amigo."

"Not me, Señor . . . ?"

"Never mind my name. Just remember, one wrong move . . ." Lamas made an expressive movement of drawing his finger across his throat.

Grundy swallowed visibly. "Yes, sir."

The gang leader smiled and stroked the beard stubble on his face. It would be good to be back home and shaved every day. He glanced around the room, which served as a rest stop for the passengers while the horses were being changed.

"Sarge is on the roof," Black reported. "Jimmy's watching those two boys who switch the horses."

"Sanchez!" Lamas shouted. Immediately the Yaqui appeared at the door. "You go watch those boys. Send Jimmy here to me." The horse handlers were Mexican and there was a chance that they would not understand the kid's orders. Lamas did not want any mistakes before he had the stage occupants inside the room. Besides, he did not trust the unpredictable Jimmy. The kid was wanted in Texas for murdering his stepfather. He was only eighteen, a tough enough hombre, but much too stupid and lazy at times.

Dust filtered down from overhead. Sarge's footsteps on the stick-and-mud roof made a soft cracking sound. The army deserter was as deadly as a sun-warmed sidewinder. Lamas relaxed at the knowledge. His men were set for the arrival of the stage from Nogales. Today it would produce a payroll and perhaps a rich passenger worth thousands to ransom.

"Ain't no strongbox on this one," Grundy warned.

Lamas turned to glare at him. Perhaps Grundy thought they would leave if there was nothing worth taking. That was an amusing idea, but Lamas felt certain Juanita knew more than this scruffy stage-stop keeper. As for the old man, his miserable time on earth would soon be over anyway. A simple snap of Lamas's fingers and the man's life would end.

Lamas sighed. His eyes locked onto Black's, who had moved to the table and was sipping from a cup of coffee.

"He know anything?" Black asked with a toss of his head.

"Who cares? For a dead man, he knows very little."

"Hell, mister, I . . ." Grundy moaned. He looked at Black then back to Lamas, his eyes pleading. "I don't know what's on that stage."

"I have no time for your weak answers!" Lamas warned him. "Talk or I will soon grow tired of your face."

The sound of a struggle outside drew Lamas's attention. Black rose and thumbed back the hammer of his rifle.

"Gawdamn you!" Jimmy swore. He appeared in the threshold, struggling to contain an Indian girl. She was dressed in only a shift, her bare brown legs flashing as she struggled.

"Hey, look what I found," the kid bragged. He glanced at Lamas and Black, as if expecting praise for his find. The girl began fighting him again. Lamas stepped over and slapped her with the back of his hand.

The girl's brown eyes blazed at him, but she froze. Lamas, reading the hatred in her gaze, merely smiled. "Settle down or I will cut your throat!" He repeated his threat in Spanish. The words subdued her struggles, but not until she had pried Jimmy's hand from her breast.

"Tie her up," he ordered. "After the stage comes, you can do what you like with her."

"She's mine!" Jimmy declared.

"Do what Lamas said, Jimmy," Black said. "All of us can try her after we've finished our business here." His words disputed the kid's claim.

With a half smile of amusement at the Texan's words, Lamas watched Jimmy drag her into the back room. She was probably in her teens, the offspring of the fat squaw, who cowered in a corner. She was not of Grundy's seed, for she had more Mexican mixed with her Indian features. After his men finished with her, they'd tie her on a horse and haul her back to some bordello, where he would sell her. The girl would probably be worth a hundred pesos in Sonora.

"Lamas!" Sarge shouted from the roof. "The stage is coming."

Lamas hooked his thumbs in his belt and rocked on his heels. At last, it was coming. Soon he and his men would be finished here and on their way home to Mexico with the mine's payroll. Maybe even have a hostage or two worth thousands of dollars in ransom. He smiled. More good planning.

"Stage stop ahead," Justine heard Tom say to Bailey. She opened her eyes to see Bailey nodding in approval, his facial features rigid as though carved in stone. No doubt he was as relieved as she was at the prospect of having a brief respite from the pounding coach.

Tom turned to her. "When I finish my business in Tombstone, I plan to go on to Prescott. You can stay at the house in Tucson or accompany me," he said with humiliating indifference.

She nodded meekly, inwardly despising her cowardice. Perhaps she would stay in Tucson. That would certainly give Tom the opportunity to chase some doxy, though the thought of her husband in some painted woman's arms did not bother her. As long as he was discreet, she didn't care. If he was satisfied by another, he would be less likely to force his unwanted attentions on her when he returned. If she was still waiting for him.

"Whoa! Whoa!" the gravelly-voiced driver shouted from the top as he pulled the stage to a swinging halt.

"Finally." Tom sighed.

The driver climbed over the side and opened the passenger door. "Get down and stretch your legs," he said.

Then, turning, he shouted toward the adobe building, "Grundy! You got coffee and grub ready?"

Justine glanced out the window toward the porch. A bushy-faced old man nodded from the doorway of the shabby building. For a moment she wondered about his rigid stance. Wasn't he glad for the company? Didn't he feel lonely out here in this isolated place? He did not seem particularly pleased to see them. She shrugged, deciding he was simply a dim-witted old desert rat.

Tom had stepped down and was walking toward the building, without bothering to help her descend the one iron step.

"Go ahead, Mr. Bailey," Justine said.

After Bailey was on the ground, he reached a hand upward. "Here, allow me to help you down."

"Thank you." She placed her hand in the man's thin one and felt her legs begin to buckle as she stepped down on the firm ground. It took a moment to regain her balance, then she released Balley's hand and straightened her hat. When she glanced around, she noted a very tall cowboy standing to the left of the building. He seemed disinterested in their appearance as he whittled idly on a stick.

"Ma'am, I'm sorry about the rough ride," the driver apologized.

Justine turned to him and shrugged. "I suspect there's little you can do about it. I'll survive."

"Er—Ma'am." He cleared his throat and avoided looking at her face as he said, "If you go around back, you'll find the, er, facilities." He pointed a crooked finger, obviously embarrassed. Since Tom had deserted her, perhaps the man felt it his duty to assist her. Justine mentally checked another black mark against her thoughtless husband.

The whittling cowboy leaned against the porch post,

completely ignored her as she passed by him. Justine had
expected a smile, a nod, some kind of acknowledgment.
She knew that despite her dusty and disheveled appearance, she was still attractive. Her confidence plummeted
at the implied insult. Squaring her shoulders, she gathered her skirt and stepped daintily around the building.

A few moments later, her mission completed, Justine
returned to the front porch. The tall cowboy was nowhere in sight. She stepped across the threshold and into
the cool, shadowed interior of the stage stop.

A handsome, swarthy man grinned at her openly,
exposing very white teeth. Justine frowned at him, re-
garding his look almost as a leer. He pushed his sombrero back on his head, appraising her with an insolent
stare.

"Welcome, señora. We have been waiting for you."

"W-what?" She darted a quick glance at her husband. He sat ashen-faced at the rough table. Bailey was
beside him, his eyes wide in a look of horror. When she
moved her gaze around the room, she noted the tall
cowboy. He was smiling now and tapping a pistol barrel
against his palm.

"Well, Lamas," the cowboy drawled, "I believe we've
struck pay dirt."

"Gawdamighty!" a pockmarked young man swore.
"I'll trade my Injun squaw for her right now."

"Shut up, Jimmy!" Lamas ordered. His coal-black
eyes never left Justine. "This one must not be marked,
for I think you are right, Black. We have a fortune here."

Justine felt his gaze strip away her clothing. A scorching wave of embarrassment swept over her, followed by
a shiver of fear.

The tall cowboy Black appraised her with equal in-
tensity. "Yes, sir. We have us a real prize."

"Jimmy," Lamas spoke sharply, "go tell Sanchez to

take care of those boys in the shed, and you two get some more horses ready.

"How many?"

"If you want to take the Indian girl, get two extras," Lamas offered absently.

"Hell, I'd rather have her." Jimmy laughed and pointed at Justine.

"Now, hold on!" Tom rose in protest.

"You sit down, señor!" Lamas ordered. At the outlaw's words, Tom wilted and slumped back in the chair. "Now, do I have all your money?" Lamas asked, searching each man's face for the truth.

"You!" he pointed at Bailey. "Do I have all your money?"

Bailey blinked rapidly and nodded his head. Lamas smiled in amusement. Obviously he had all the nervous one's money, but he enjoyed frightening the little man. "Are you lying to me?"

"N-no," Bailey stammered.

"Because if you are, señor, I will cut your throat very slowly from ear to ear. *Comprende?*"

Bailey gulped audibly. "No. I mean yes."

Lamas tired of his game, turned again to study the white woman. Her beauty took his breath away. Why was she there anyway?

"Take off your clothes," he said quietly. "I want to see all of my unexpected prize."

Justine looked at the man in horror. Surely he was joking. "I—I . . ."

"I am waiting, señora."

"I couldn't." Her legs threatened to fold beneath her. She closed her eyes, praying that she was simply having a nightmare. At any moment she would wake up and once more be in the swaying coach. It was a dream. Determinedly she kept her eyelids tightly closed and shut her ears to the heavy breathing of the men in the room.

"You take them off or my men will do it for you."

Oh, God, it was no dream. Reluctantly, she opened her eyes and stared at the cold, ruthless face of the swarthy outlaw. Tears welled her eyes and she put out her hands to hold this impossible thing away.

Lamas merely smiled with contempt. He folded his arms and signaled the boy and the one in army clothes forward. The men grabbed her while Lamas looked on with approval.

Justine groaned at the foul stench that emitted from the man with the army coat. His thick grubby fingers fumbled with the buttons on the front of her dress. The boy held her around the waist and laughed low in his throat. She struggled and tried to raise her hands to claw at their faces, but her strength was a pitiful defense against such strong-armed tactics. The scream that rose to her throat threatened to choke her.

"No!" Bailey shouted. "Let her be!" He lunged forward, but the roar of Lamas's pistol slammed into him and sent him sprawling backward across the table. Justine watched his demise through tear-blurred eyes. She did not dare look at her sniveling husband. Totally gripped with blinding fear, she closed her eyes and went limp in the men's grasp.

More guns erupted; the acrid smoke of gunpowder boiled up her nose. She opened her eyes to see the bloody bodies of her husband, the driver and the stage stop man, Grundy. A deep groan tore through her body. Then, with a sigh of relief, she felt herself slip into a world of blackness.

CHAPTER 7

Major Bowen walked two blocks toward the stage depot. He felt secure in the knowledge that Jesus would be searching for the Apache Too-Gut. The ex-scout also promised to have everything ready for the arrival of Sam T. The cool morning desert air provided a refreshing break from the daytime heat. Before the stage reached Maricopa Wells, he knew the temperature would be well above a hundred degrees. Prescott's mile-high climate would be a welcome reprieve from the sultry desert temperatures of Tucson.

He stopped and glanced back. A nagging feeling of being followed bothered him. Nothing he could see when he glanced back over his shoulder but some early vendors in the street, their burros laden down with water barrels and others bearing firewood which resembled bundles of dried sticks. A long-dead dog laid a few feet off the curb, drawing swarms of flies. Street maintenance in this city left much to be desired. He recalled the cab man avoiding a bloated cow carcass on one stretch of street they covered the day before.

A woman led a small band of bleating goats, loudly

advertising, "Fresh milk," in Spanish. Bowen eased into the alleyway, set his satchel down and waited. He didn't have long to stand there. The sound of running feet approached, then a wide-eyed youngster burst around the corner with a look of shock on his face when they collided. Bowen's fist shot out and grasped the boy by the front of his shirt.

"Why are you following me?" He drew him close to his face

"I—I—"

"Who hired you?" He reinforced his grip on the shirt and raised the youth on his toes.

"Señor Green."

"What did he want?" Bowen looked around to be sure the boy didn't have anyone with him.

"I don't know—he is a politico."

"Senator Green?" Yes, he knew that name from the past legislative session.

"*Sí, señor.*"

Damn. How did that legislator already know about his business? They must suspect something, or someone had warned them. He and the governor had a new problem. There was a spy in their midst. Someone he needed to ferret out.

"You tell Green I was, ah, buying sheep. Ask him how many he has to sell."

The boy shrugged when he released him. "He has no sheep, señor."

"Maybe he needs some. Tell him the market is going sky-high on sheep."

The youth looked frightened and confused. He backed slowly away. "I will tell him. I will tell him." Then he ran.

Bowen watched him until he disappeared down the alley. Oh, John will love this news, he thought. Senator

Green hired a boy to track him around Tucson. This one obviously had not followed him around the day before when he found Jesus, which was excellent. That matter should still be private. But who was the spy in the capital? He would need to start watching things much closer at Prescott. His own link to the marshals might even be in jeopardy. But by damn, he had a name for the Border Gang leader to share with John. *Lamas.*

He entered the stage depot and handed his valise to the agent.

"I'll take that. You're going to Prescott, sir? Well, stage departure is running a little behind this morning. Having to reshoe a horse."

"No hurry, as long as I get there in one piece."

"We should be leaving in thirty minutes."

"Good. I'll go out and sit on the porch where it is still cool."

"Sorry about the delay, sir."

"No problem," Bowen said and went outdoors to take a seat on the bench that lined the front of the office. He lit a cigar and sat back to consider the situation. At the corner of the building, a drummer who apparently must be another waiting passenger stole a snootful of whiskey from a small flask. Then, acting secretive, he pocketed it.

A stout woman in a too-tight corset came huffing and puffing up the sidewalk to the office door. Bowen guessed her to be in her thirties.

"Has it gone?" she asked, out of breath.

"The stage?" Bowen asked.

"Yes—"

"No, it is going to be late."

"Well, praise the Lord. I just knew I had missed it. Whew, you mean the one going to Prescott?" She wiped her sweaty brow with her palm and shook her head as if to get her bearings. Then, using the reflection in the window, she reset the wide-brimmed hat, decorated with lace and ribbons, on her head. She fussed with some resistant stubborn strands of her brown hair, using the window image for a guide.

"You going to Prescott?" she asked, not looking at him, still having trouble with her breathing.

"Yes."

"I'm Mamie VanKirk. I live up there."

"Oh . . . Major—I mean Gerald—Bowen."

"Military man, huh?" There was a peevish set to her lips.

"Retired military man," he corrected her.

"You live in Prescott?"

"Yes." He asked the woman what she did.

"I own the Bar TF Ranch. You heard of it?"

"No. My wife, Mary, and I are new to the area. We moved there about six months ago." Quite unusual for a woman to own a ranch, but she looked capable of handling things.

"You'll have to bring her to the dances we have out at the schoolhouse. Folks come from miles and miles on Saturday night. A little dancing never hurt a soul, did it?"

"I don't think it did."

"Sure never killed me. Well, Major, since we're going to be passengers together all day and night, tell me about your military career." She hiked up her dress like it was nuisance and took a place on the bench beside him. "There ought to be enough time to get in the whole thing."

Bowen wondered about Miss VanKirk. She had the brassy ways of some madam, yet despite her fashionable dress and hat, she looked like a woman trapped in a costume she didn't feel comfortable or accustomed to. It would be an interesting trip home.

He explained his career in brief and she nodded with interest at his telling about officers' school and the early war. Polite as she acted, he decided she could recite his whole story back to him without a stumble. He felt better when the stage pulled up and relieved him of any further talk.

Once on board and moving down the streets of Tucson, Mamie, Miss or Mrs., was not to be without knowing and continued to pry things from him. She also shifted and tugged at the oppressive corset, which he decided must be binding her. To be polite, he hid his amusement at the woman's obvious difficulty and discomfort.

"When we get to Maricopa Wells"—she leaned over closer to him and lowered her voice—"I will need your expert assistance."

"Mine?" he asked. What did she want?

"You are a married man?"

"Yes. Happily, thank you."

She looked perturbed at the drummer, who was drunk enough to hum hymns to himself in the opposite seat. Then she made a face. "I can't wait that long. Undo this damn corset for me." She scooted around and turned her back to him.

"Well, go ahead, I'm certain you've seen a woman's undergarment before," she said after a moment.

He looked at the coach ceiling for help, then began to undo the small buttons down the back of the dress. Mamie sat up straight and bounced on the bumps in the road. With stiff fingers, he undid some more.

"Go ahead; you have to unbutton the whole damn thing."

"The whole thing?" the drunk drummer asked in his stupor.

"You shut up and look the other way or I swear I'll

throw you out the door." She pointed an accusing finger at the man like a pistol.

"Yes, ma'am." The drummer swallowed hard and covered his eyes with his sleeves.

"Oh, for Christ's sake, Major, will you please hurry? I'm about to die."

He wouldn't bother to tell Mary about this episode. Then he became tickled. Actually she might even laugh about it too. At last the pinkish-colored corset became exposed. He panicked at the sight of the closure. Why, it was shoelaced from the middle of her back clear down to her hips.

"Unlace it. Will you please hurry?"

"I am. I am," he said and began to pull the lacing out of the eyelets.

When he was halfway down her back, the corset opened like an eggshell and she let out a great gasp. "Thank God."

"You want me to stop?"

"Heavens, no! I want out of this bear trap."

His hands full of the string, he managed to separate the last vestige and then leaned back from her to politely look away.

"Close your eyes; I'm getting rid of this damn thing."

He gazed out the window. Soon he began to feel her wiggling on the seat as she wrestled with the undergarment. At last she flung it on his lap with a loud, "There. Button me up, please," she added, holding the dress to her sides with her elbows.

"Yes, ma'am," he said, ignoring the white skin with the red marks like whip lashes across her back. The dress buttons proved hard to catch and he fumbled in his haste. The task at last completed, he settled back. "That's it."

She twisted back around. "Thank you. You're a true gentleman."

They both dropped their gaze to the pink corset upon his lap. She grabbed it and raised it up. Then she flung it out the open window among the passing saguaros and cat-claw.

"The damn dumb salesperson who sold me that ought to be shot, don't you agree?"

"Yes, I do, Mamie."

"Hell, I guess the truth is I'll never be a fashion figure, will I?"

Bowen felt trapped. Had it not been for the drunk drummer asking if he could look now, he might never have escaped her insistence for an answer.

They both laughed at the drummer instead.

Sam T. stepped down from the stage and looked around at the territorial capital. He assisted Julia and smiled at her exclamation. "It's a pretty place. I thought it would have cactus all over."

"I don't even see any here," he said, admiring the tall ponderosa pines scattered around on the hillsides. New houses and businesses were being built around existing ones and the sounds of hammers and saws rang in the crisp mountain air. In a westerly direction, he could see an unusual thumb-shaped butte sticking up.

"Mrs. Riley?" A corporal stepped forward and stood at attention.

"Yes, Corporal?" she said.

"Good. I'm here to get your things and get you, ma'am." Then he turned red from embarrassment over his choice of words.

"Well, corporal, my trunks are coming from Ash Flat by freighter, but I do have a small bag."

"You will be in safe hands," Sam T. said, seeing the young soldier's sincerity. "That freighter should be here in the next day or so with our trunks."

"The stage lines don't haul such things," she explained offhandedly to the young man.

"Yes, ma'am. I will wait at the coach for you." He snapped to attention, then turned and went to the waiting carriage across the street.

"I am saddened to part with you, Sam. You've been a fine companion to me the entire trip. Thank you."

He nodded. "You take care, Julia. If I can ever help, you be sure to call on me. Major Bowen will know how to get in touch with me."

"Perhaps you will attend a military function at Fort Whipple and we can meet again."

"Perhaps." He smiled at her. Damn, this proved harder than parting with Shirley.

"Maybe she will write you," she said as if she knew his thoughts.

"Maybe. Good luck, Julia." With an emptiness inside him, he watched her go to the conveyance as the corporal assisted her into the seat. He waved, then took his valise and headed for the saloon on the corner. A good stout drink might clear his head.

Mahoney's Saloon. Common Irish name as any. He pushed through the doors and looked over the crowd at the bar. Then he walked to about midway, dropped his suitcase on the floor and nodded to the bartender.

"Gawd almighty, Captain Mayes. Sure'n as the devil, it's you!"

"Mahoney?" He shook hands with the ex-noncom and blinked in disbelief at the man.

"You look wonderful, Captain. Wonderful."

"You look damn good yourself. Did every old cracker in the Tenth retire up here?"

"Major's here."

"I know. I came to see him."

"Damn, what'll you have? Rye?"

"Yes, and make it a double."

"I will. Hey, boys," Mahoney shouted, brandishing the bottle of bond. "Here's me old captain from the days in the war. A finer officer they never commissioned, and we rode the toughest damn detail in the world. Keeping the bloody telegraph wires up from Missouri to Fort Smith."

"Hey, here's to soldiers, blue or gray," someone shouted and glasses flew in the air for a toast.

"May those days be forever silent," Sam T. said.

"Amen." Then everyone drank.

"Where does the major have his office?"

"He's retired." Mahoney frowned and acted taken aback by the question. "He's got a house up on the hill. Go three blocks up the hill, and then halfway on the right you will see a nice white picket fence with a goat inside."

"He has a goat?" Sam T. batted his eyes.

"No, but the goat thinks so." Mahoney laughed and poured him a second double.

"That's all I need. Even for old time's sake." He had to report to Bowen halfway sober anyway.

"You get some time, you come back. We can talk about the old days."

"I'll sure do that. I need a few cigars."

Mahoney shoved the humidor glass at him; then, when Sam selected two, he refused to let him pay. "I owe you more than few cigars, Captain."

On his empty stomach, Sam T. felt the liquor, but he decided the walk would help burn some of the alcohol from his system. Suitcase in hand, he started up the steep street. A mockingbird scolded him. Some sassy blue jays fluttered overhead. He noticed a large, fine house to the left. Either a banker or mine superintendent owned the place. They had a black yardman cleaning up things. Must be a very rich person's house, so palatial.

He felt someone watching him as he made the climb.

Whoever it was, the person was at a second-story window and all he could see was a shadow on the curtains. Oh, well, some old maid or grandmother snooping on him. Unfazed, he continued up the hill to the third street and turned south.

The white-fenced yard was festooned in sweetpea vines. He decided this bungalow must be the major's house. Then he looked up and noticed a white goat tethered on a rope bleating at him from the hillside across the street. Mary's goat, no doubt, and he smiled.

"Captain Mayes!" she shouted and ran to the front door when he knocked. "It has been a long while."

He hugged the gray-haired woman and removed his hat. "Great to see you, ma'am."

"Have you eaten anything lately?" she asked, looking him over.

"No. Is the major home?"

"He's gone to Tucson to arrange some things, but he will be back tomorrow or the next day. Said for you to take a room and he would hurry back. Come inside and let's find you some food. You look wonderful."

"Feel great. Excited about this job he has for me."

"Well, I'll let him tell you about it."

"Sure, I understand."

"Good, because I don't." Then she laughed. "Oh, the things you men get into."

"Yes, ma'am."

She served him tasty leftovers and then offered him two kinds of pie, peach and apple. He took a slice of each and made her laugh.

Between bites, he listened as she told him about Governor Sterling and his log mansion. She went on about the library society that the local wives had recently founded and the women's group in the Methodist church.

"Who owns that big mansion I saw coming up the hill?" he asked, starting on the peach pie first.

"That is the Harrington House." She sounded taken aback.

"Oh," he said absently. "Harrington must have lots of money."

"It is a parlor house," she said in a lowered voice.

He almost choked on the pie and spluttered out an apology.

"It is all right. A Mrs. Devereaux lives there."

"Well . . ." He wiped his mouth on her cloth napkin. "She must have a good business."

"I suspect she does more when the legislature is in town. Then there isn't room behind that high fence to hide all the rigs."

"I would think so," he said and started on the apple pie. "I see your famous goat is grazing across the road."

"Couldn't find its owner and couldn't keep it out of my flowers." She made a rather peevish face.

Sam smiled as he sipped on his second cup of fresh ground coffee she fixed for him.

"You never married?"

"No, ma'am."

"Shame," she said and smiled. "Oh, please don't mention the marshals or Gerald's part in it around Prescott. He can explain. But it is very secretive."

"I'm sure he will, and I won't tell a soul." He came very close to telling Mahoney about his job. Good thing he hadn't and called it only a visit.

After eating, he headed off for a boardinghouse she recommended: a two-story establishment west of the creek and up the hill behind the governor's mansion. He promised Mary to return the next day, to see if the major had returned and to move the goat for her.

The walk back downhill was pleasant. A fresh breath

of the turpentine-smelling pines hung in the air. He skirted a few loose milk cows grazing along the street and went past the Harrington House. This was some fancy whorehouse, similar to the ones they had in Denver, Kansas City or Chicago. Sure enough, very ritzy for a frontier outpost like Prescott.

A matronly lady came to the door of the boardinghouse on his first knock.

"Mrs. Tremble is my name. Don't put up with drunks and loud snorers. Pay a week in advance and it costs four bucks a week for bed and two meals a day, breakfast and supper. Get your own lunch pail, I don't fix them."

Sam T. studied the woman. Tidy-looking and in her fifties, but he figured she could handle a rowdy one or whatever came her way.

"That's a room of my own?"

"No, that costs two bucks more."

"And if I don't take meals?"

"Well, you have to eat someplace." Hands on her ample hips, she glared back at him. "My cooking ain't that bad."

"Didn't mean to offend you, but I have to travel a lot."

"I understand. You won't be here to eat that much, then?"

"Exactly."

"Five a week and you can have a private room," she surrendered. "Where's your things?"

"A freighter is bringing my trunk down from Ash Fork. Stage line wouldn't haul it."

"They get too damn independent and the railroads will replace them." She gave a bewildered shake of her head. "They will."

"Yes, ma'am."

He paid her five for the first week. She stuffed it in her dress front and with effort led him up on the second floor.

The room smelled stale from being closed; with some effort she opened the window sash to let in some fresh air.

The room contained a bed, two chairs and a small table, a dresser and small rack to hang his clothes.

"Supper will be served in two hours," she said. "Come down and eat. Need to meet everyone. You're going to be here steady, I'll throw in a few meals. Don't wag your tongue about it."

"Yes, ma'am." He looked around when she left the room, then sat on the bed. Settled in Prescott at long last. He wondered about the secret part of the job. Must be some sort of undercover law work the major needed done. No matter. So far he liked what he saw of Arizona. It wasn't that different from Denver in climate and, despite Shirley's prickly-cactus comments, he had yet to see much more cactus here than they had in Colorado.

Ella Devereaux turned from the curtain after observing him again. Stranger in town, a big man dressed in a suit and wearing a Boss of the Plains hat. He carried a valise, so he was new. She could hardly make out his face. He went up and came back in an hour. Time enough to visit someone or inspect something. She drummed her fingernails on the polished top of the small table. She had business to take care of.

She went down the hallway and into Lily's room. The small brunette sat on the edge of her bed dressed in a cotton shift and looked up with a soft, "Hello."

Ella went to the window and studied the alley behind the barn. Her plan needed to work. It was the best one she had yet.

"That young man who works in the telegraph office . . ." She let her voice trail off on purpose. The girl knew his name well enough; Ella saw how her eyes shone whenever he dropped in. They never fooled her.

"You mean Brad Townsend?"

"Yes, he's kind of sweet on you, isn't he?"

"I guess so, Missy." She wrinkled her pug nose at the notion. "But he don't make enough money to come here very often."

"What if he came every week? On a weeknight, of course."

"He couldn't afford it." She dropped her hairbrush on the bed and sighed out loud. "I'd sure like it, though."

"He would too, wouldn't he?"

"I think he would," she said coyly.

"Send him word to come up here tonight and see me."

"How—"

"Lily, you aren't dumb. You've sent him notes before. I've seen you do it. Go down and get some paper and pen and write him a note. I need to talk to him."

"You ain't mad about that, are you?" Lily stood up, looked at her warily and started for the door.

"Of course I ain't mad. I need him to do some extra work for me, so you can have him one night a week." She reached out and swatted her on the butt with the flat of her hand to impress her to move faster. "Now get that note sent."

"Oh, that hurt me," Lily cried out, then headed for the doorway and reached back to gingerly rub the right side of her derriere.

"Don't fiddle-faddle around either."

"I won't. I won't." And she disappeared.

Ella drew in a deep breath. Brad could be the answer to the information she needed. A hard tug with both hands grasping it, she raised the corset and front of her dress up. Then, checking her cleavage and satisfied, she headed for the stairs. The kitchen help—oh, those slow-moving girls. They were even lazier than her doves who napped all day.

CHAPTER 8

Jesus Morales needed a drink bad. He rose to a sitting position on the bed and began to shake. He clutched his arms and his molars chattered uncontrollably. His actions awoke Tia. She sat up and hugged him tight to still his shaking.

"Oh, my God, my lover, you are like a man freezing," she cried.

"I am," he managed. "Got to—have a drink. I—had this—before."

"What do you need?" she asked, in the shadowy darkness of the pre-dawn.

"Anything—"

"Maria next door has something in a jug." She quickly pulled on her skirt and then her blouse. She looked at him with a pained expression, then she went to a trunk, found a blanket and wrapped it around him.

"I'll be right back," she said, then quickly dressed and rushed out the door.

He shook and with shuddering breaths tried to still his quaking. Somehow he must rid himself of these shakes before this man Sam T. arrived. He couldn't afford to disappoint him or the major.

Tia returned with a crock jug and he tilted it up with her to steady it until the liquor ran in his mouth. Then his throat constricted and threatened to choke him. He pushed the jug aside and began to cough. At last, with tears streaming down his face, he managed two more swallows of the fiery liquor. Some kind of mescal. Bad stuff, but he'd drunk worse before to get drunk on.

Weak and in a cold sweat, he began to settle down. She swept the damp hair from his face and kissed him on the mouth.

"You have been gone for so long. I was so pleased you came back to me. I don't want to lose you again." Her brown eyes were pleading her concern.

He nodded. He had missed making love to her for a long time, but he'd had no money, no good job to support her. No, before he could ever have asked to stay with her, he had to have a good job like the new one he held with the major.

"How will you ever ride out and find this Apache like you are?" she asked in a concerned whisper.

"I will take a little whiskey along. This will go away in time."

"No! You will only drink it and want some more. I know you will, and then that major will fire you and you will go back and dig adobe again like some animal." She folded her arms and sat pouting on the bed.

"No, Tia." He held up his hands in defense. "I won't do that again."

"Yes, you will, and then I can cry at night for you." She shook her head in disapproval. "No more whiskey, no mescal, no tequila, no wine, no more *cerveza*.

He shrugged. "You probably are right. Sometimes I can't control myself."

"I will go in the desert with you to find this one."

"Too dangerous." He shook his head.

"Jesus, I don't want you to have to work in that adobe pit ever again."

Her concerned look at him in the dim light made him want to hide. "Ah, *sí*, it's a bad place."

"I will ride Sam T.'s horse and we will go find Too-Gut," she said.

"It will be dangerous to look for him. Those Apaches steal Mexican women." No way she could go up there. She must stay there. What of her work? He knew she did domestic chores for some women in town.

"I will be with you. You will be sober. I have no fears of them."

He started to lift the jug to take another swig. She wrapped her small arms around it and wrestled it away. "No more drinking. You have to find this Apache."

Jesus closed his eyes. Already she sounded like a wife. One little drink would not hurt. Besides, he might start trembling again. She fled with the bottle and he was forced to resign himself that was all he would get.

Perhaps he could reason with her—later. When she returned, she began to gather her things and he knew her intentions were to go along. His head felt light and he blinked his eyes; they felt gritty.

"Get dressed so we can leave," she ordered.

Damn. He wondered if he had done the right thing going back to her after all. He felt terrible; he had a splitting headache, a bad stomachache and was within a hairbreadth of vomiting everything inside. He dressed and struggled with a bowl of leftover cold beans she handed him. Then she went out the door and brought up the three horses that Major Bowen bought the day before.

He finished the bowl and picked up the first saddle and

pad. She took the other one outside while he saddled the bay. Then she left for the well with a large olla on her head to get water. He wondered where he could find something to drink. Only a little to clear his head, that was all he needed.

He put Sam T.'s saddle, the one Bowen chose for him, on the big sorrel. Two good horses, sound and well enough shod for the trip he planned. The second bay was the packhorse, but he showed Texas blood like the others. Thicker, with more muscle than the run-of-the-mill *caballos* most Mexicans and Indians rode. The sorrel was a hand taller than the rest. The Major warned him that Sam T. would need such an animal.

Jesus put the pack saddle on the bay. When Tia returned, she began to fill the panniers to bulging with things. He noticed her packing when he set the crossbuck on the third horse and cinched it down.

"You can't take everything with us," he said over his shoulder.

"Just what I think we will need."

He shrugged. What could he do with such a strong-headed woman? He didn't want to argue, he wanted a drink. She soon had the canteens full of water and hung on the saddle horns. Packs tied down on the horses, he finished cinching his bay.

"Why don't you stay here?"

She ignored his question and shoved his new Winchester in the boot. "We better ride out before we draw suspicion."

"Oh, yes," he said, recalling the major's words about the secrecy around their mission.

Mounted and headed north beside the Santa Cruz in the cool morning air, he wondered what he had forgotten. She rode the spunky sorrel and kept it beside his bay.

He hoped this man Sam T. didn't get too mad about him letting a woman take his horse. The major said Sam T. had been a captain in the war with him. No matter; he trusted his ex-commander's choice of men.

Jesus studied the purple mountains and shook his head in disbelief. No whiskey; this would be a long day. He drew a deep, ragged breath. This woman had turned into a devil on him. Then he glanced over at her shapely brown legs, too short for the stirrups. Oh, she was such a wonderful spirit in bed, though. With a hopeless head shake, he looked at the brim of his new straw hat for divine help.

"Can we find him, this Too-Gut?" she asked, looking across the saguaro-clad hillsides.

"If he is alive, we can." Then he laughed aloud.

"What is so funny?"

"Two days ago, I was daydreaming in that pit. If I had some horses and supplies I would go to the Sierra Madre."

"We are going north?" She frowned with a bewildered look at him.

He shook his head. "It doesn't matter where we are going. I am not working in that pit anymore, am I?"

"No, but only if you don't get foolish and go back to drinking."

Jesus shook his head. Women did not understand anything.

In late afternoon, an Indian woman they met on the road gave them some vague directions. From her instructions, they rode up a canyon choked with mesquite. Jesus rose in the stirrups to try to see through the lacy branches. Then he spotted a brush wickiup covered with old scraps of tarp. He dismounted heavily and handed her the rein. His head pounded and he wondered if Too-Gut was even at home.

He squatted on his heels. The wonderful soft black boots felt good on his feet.

"Aren't you going to ask if he's home?" she whispered from the saddle.

"If he's home, he will come out when he gets ready. It is impolite to bust up to a man's door."

She shrugged.

A young woman came out. She looked like a hawk. Not pretty, but her eyes shone like liquid coal and gave him a hard once-over. Then he saw the copper-skinned Too-Gut slip outside with a rifle in his hand. His name came from the great stomach that hung over his breechcloth.

The Apache blinked his eyes. "Jesus?"

"I have work for us to do."

"I don't work for the army." He shook his head so hard that his bangs even lifted.

"No, Major Bowen needs some trackers."

"Trackers?"

"Yes, and he will pay us two dollars a day. He needs to find some outlaws."

"Good. We can find them." A sly grin spread over his brown face. "When?"

"Four days. Meet me south of Tucson on the river."

Too-Gut nodded.

"Will they give you a permit to leave the reservation?" Jesus asked.

"You got some whiskey?" Too-Gut had ignored his question. Jesus knew the man had heard him.

"No, I don't drink—anymore." Jesus turned and looked at Tia. She nodded her approval. Then, stiff-like from the long ride, he rose to his feet.

"Gawdamn! You go to church now?" The Apache laughed until his belly shook. Then he sobered and nodded thoughtfully. "I see you in four days."

"Will you need a horse?"

The Apache held up two fingers. "The ones here are too weak to ride far."

Jesus wondered about buying two more horses. The major said he could buy what they needed. He hoped the major approved. Two also meant the girl was coming. He raised his eyes to the sky for help. That would be a picnic, two females along with them. His mouth felt dry. If he only had a drink. He worried that without a pass from the agency, Too-Gut would be considered a bronco Apache with a price on his head.

How would the major and this Sam T. take that? Maybe he should have stayed in the adobe pit. There were less worries there.

"Be damn good to work again," Too-Gut said and slapped him on the shoulder. "You have pretty woman too. Next time bring some damn whiskey."

"In four days, I will meet you on the river. Do you need any food?"

"You got some tomatoes in a can, huh?" Too-Gut turned his face to the side, waiting for his answer.

"Some, I can give you. That's all you want?"

"Plenty good." Too-Gut waved the girl forward to come take them from Jesus. "Plenty good stuff."

Jesus dug them out of the pannier and gave her six cans. Too-Gut nodded his approval. They parted, Tia and Jesus headed west.

"Can we ride off this reservation tonight?" she asked, nervously scanning the saguaro-studded hills.

"Why? We can camp anywhere we like. I never saw no Indian police today. They don't know we're here."

Tia looked around worriedly, then she chewed on her lower lip before she finally spoke. "I don't want an Apache to take me. I'll be glad to get back to my casa."

"We can ride a ways," he said, studying the low-hanging sun. Good, that meant she would stay at home. He drank some tepid canteen water and wished for whiskey.

Sam T. strode down the hillside street toward the small creek that gurgled through the town's center. He heard someone mention Walnut Creek as the name of the stream. Mrs. Tremble's food was sustaining and he wanted a walk worse than anything, but planned to learn what he could with a visit to the street of saloons the men in the boarding-house called Whiskey Row. City planners had put all the bars in one block to make it easier to control things. He understood the philosophy of such thinking. Any hell-raising was confined to one area and the more genteel could avoid it, if they wanted it that way.

A buggy with a spanking-good black horse went by. A man in a business suit who sat upon the seat with a whip in his hand nodded sharply in passing. In the twi-light, Sam T. watched him drive up the hill and turn into the prestigious whorehouse gate. Someday he needed to inspect that opulent palace.

Sam T. crossed the bridge and watched three cow-boys ride up. They dismounted, hitched their ponies and rushed into Mahoney's bar like they were dying for drink. With a search around in the growing evening, he could see several horse down the street were hitched, and some rigs too, before the various establishments.

He parted the batwing doors of Mahoney's and saw the threesome he'd observed earlier, one on each side raising the arms of the third cowboy. Some sort of cele-bration, from the looks of it.

"Look, boys, this is Buddy's last night out to howl. Sat-urday night, he's getting hitched to the boss! Whoopee!"

"All right, drinks for the groom," Mahoney said, holding up a bottle and glass to pour him one.

"What about the best man?" one of the cowboys asked.

"Hell, he can buy his own," Mahoney said. "He's getting off scot-free."

Everyone laughed out loud and moved in to clap Buddy on the shoulder.

"Howdy, Captain," Mahoney said, coming down the bar.

"Howdy, Sarge. And I'm paying for my own tonight. Guess the cowboy's got him a wife?"

"Ah, the lady owns the Bar TF. She'll be a handful for that lad. She's a spoiled daddy's girl and never been married. Bet she's pushing thirty-five. Ah, she ain't bad to look at. But she's been running that ranch since they came here. Her daddy got himself laid up from a horse wreck and he still can't walk or ride."

"Buddy is good-humored enough about it." Sam T. pointed toward the prospective groom with his glass, which Mahoney filled for him.

"Sure'n he better be. She can horsewhip him, if he ain't." Mahoney laughed aloud. Then he lowered his voice. "Mamie VanKirk is some woman. Be lots of fun to be at their wedding, though. Wish I could go, but that's my biggest night here."

"I imagine it is. That's a public place?"

"Oh, sure, Saturday night out at the Chino Valley Schoolhouse. It's where the families and couples go dance. Draw big crowds too."

"I might have to see that," Sam T. said and studied the amber whiskey in his glass.

"You'd be welcome," Mahoney said.

Sam T. wondered if Julia would be there. Maybe if he was still in town he could rent a rig, drive out to the fort and offer to take her. No, he better not. How would folks take it? Not good. Best he not do that; she had a husband. He wished that woman was off his mind. When would

the major get back? His return might have more to do
with what Sam did next anyway.

"You and the major going to do some mining together?" Mahoney asked.

"I guess," Sam T. said, to be agreeable and keep off the
subject of what he would eventually do in the territory. He
finished up the evening more informed on the town and
business in general.

The next morning, Sam T. took his breakfast at the
boardinghouse. He learned a little more about the fellow
boarders. There was a bank teller, some store clerks, two
carpenters. He could tell they were anxious to learn about
him. All eyes were turned when he explained, "Major
Bowen and I are looking at some mining properties."

That sounded like the best thing he could come up
with and the nods of satisfaction down the way pleased
him. Maybe the major would be back in town and he
could learn everything about this secret marshal business. Strange that Bowen never mentioned it was undercover work in his telegram; obviously it was. He
looked over his coffee and studied the wallpaper's pat-
terns. The major would tell him all about it when he
returned.

Midmorning, he climbed the hill and walked to Bowen's
house. When he passed the bordello, he didn't notice anyone spying on him from the upstairs window. At the bungalow, Mary looked up from her gardening and pushed
a stray wisp of hair from her face to smile at him.

"Morning, Sam. Did you sleep good last night?"

"Sure did, Mary. Mrs. Tremble is nice lady. Thanks
for pointing her out to me."

"He's in there. Grouchy as a bear, but he'll be glad to
see you," she said, raising up from her knees.

"What's upsetting him?"

She smiled and shrugged. "He'll have to tell you." She went ahead of him through the living room.

"Sam T. Oh, good, you made it," the major said and rose from his place at the table and shook his hand.

"I don't really have an office." Standing astraddle the straight-backed chair, Bowen looked around. "We can sit here fine. We've used worse."

Gerald Bowen had accumulated some more lines in his face since their last meeting, but he still looked like a typical, straight-backed West Pointer. Sam T. selected a chair beside his, and Mary took his hat.

"Thanks, ma'am," he said after her.

"You two want coffee or whiskey?" she asked.

"Need whiskey, but we better start on coffee," Bowen said in a disgusted tone. "Glad you're here, Sam, but I have to tell you this may be the biggest mess you and I ever tried to handle."

"Mary said it was undercover."

"Worse than that." Bowen held up a hand as if to wave the notion away. "There's outlaws all over this territory and no statewide law enforcement agency. It all falls into the lap of county sheriffs." Bowen explained his problem and added the latest reluctance of the governor to continue through with the project.

"When I got back early this morning, I had this waiting for me." Bowen waved the paper and then handed it to Sam T.

Dear Gerald,

After due consideration, I am afraid at this time the formation of the Marshal unit may not be the best idea. I know you have spent considerable time and hired men to come implement this plan. Everyone will be compensated for their ex-

*penses as well as you, but some things have arisen,
both in Tucson and in Washington, that make it
imperative we don't begin this operation at this
time. I know you will understand.*

*Respectfully
Yours,
John Sterling*

"So what happens next?" He handed the letter back
to the major. Had he come all this way for his expenses?
Perhaps he was going into the mining business after all
and it wasn't a lie he told them at breakfast. Shirley's
sharp words niggled him. *Think about your future.*

"I'm going up there and confront him." Bowen stood up.

"Now, dear, don't lose your temper. You and John have
been good friends," Mary said, holding the coffeepot in
one hand ready to serve them.

"Get your hat, Sam T. We're going to the governor's
mansion."

"Yes, sir." Sam T. shook his head privately at Mary
and snatched his hat off the tree, two steps behind the
shorter man going out the front door. "Oh, we'll need that
coffee later," he said.

Bowen explained on their walk about Sam T.'s salary and what they would pay the two ex-scouts and
how Jesus would have things ready for him when he
arrived in Tucson. Then he shook his head in deep frustration. "That is, if we can convince Sterling to do this.
He's got the spine of a woman at times." Bowen's lips
formed a wry scowl and he continued, "This outlaw gang
leader that's been raping and pillaging southern Arizona is called Lamas. He's probably in Mexico by now,
though."

"That mean if we settle this with the governor and get
started, we can't even go after him?"

"Sam T., I've never known something like a border to ever stop you before."

"Just testing the water, sir."

A thin black girl ushered them into the mansion. Bowen addressed her by name and she showed them to the governor's office.

"Sah, this Major Bowen and this man like to see you?"

"Oh, yes, come in, Gerald." Sterling looked up from his paperwork. "That will be all, Daisy," he said and dismissed the girl. She curtsied and left them.

"This must be Sam T. Mayes." The governor rose and took his hand. "I am sorry about the inconvenience." Then Sterling shook his head, looked hard at Bowen, then at Sam T. "Close the doors. I've got more news, and it isn't good."

"What is it?" Bowen asked, while Sam T. shut the double oak doors.

"That damn gang robbed the Halsey stage out of Nogales yesterday, took a mine payroll, shot a prominent Tucson citizen by the name of Tom Stauffer. Massacred the stage-stop people and took Stauffer's wife as a hostage. I've wired Mexican officials to try and stop them if they went across the border."

"That's the reason Sam T. is here," Bowen said disgustedly.

"You know we could have a serious international incident over this if we sent lawmen across that border."

"You pay a ransom for her and you'll have a dozen more kidnappings," Sam T. said and drew a cigar out of his vest pocket. Bowen was right; this man could squirm out of a lot.

"Listen," Bowen began, "we have the gang leader's name and the whole thing is set up. Let Sam T. ride down there, pick up those two ex-scouts of mine and go learn what he can about this gang."

"We can't afford to have an incident on the border."
Sterling looked at both of them for an answer.

"You can't afford to have this gang continue to pillage
either. Your U.S. marshals aren't doing anything and that
sheriff down there is collecting taxes!"

Sterling poured some whiskey in a tumbler and downed
it. Then he straightened. "You're right, we better do something. Mayes, whatever you do—Oh, it doesn't matter."
He dropped his chin and shook his head in defeat.

"Sam T., raise your right hand," Bowen said. "John's
going to swear you in as an officer of the Supreme Court
of the Arizona Territory. You're going to be a marshal."

"Do you promise to uphold the laws, both territorial
and federal?"

"I do."

Sterling dropped back in the chair and poured himself another glass of whiskey. Then, as if he had not
thought of it before, he drew two more glasses out of his
desk. "We better drink to this. It may be my last official
act as governor."

"Quit worrying about that," Bowen said with an impatient head shake for the man. "We now have a spy in
our midst."

"Oh, dear."

"He works for Senator Green."

Sam T. suppressed his amusement when Sterling
slapped his forehead with the palm of his hand. "Not
Green."

"Stop being so theatrical. I'll find the lowlife that's
feeding him information. You check your staff—close."
Bowen used his index finger to rap on the desktop.

"I will, but how much does he know?"

"That the price of sheep's going up."

"What's that mean?" Sterling frowned, displeased.

"That's what I told the one who trailed me around in Tucson. I don't think he knows a thing about our business. But I think we have a spy."

"It does get involved. Marshal Mayes, good luck. I personally think you need an army. Gerald thinks you can handle it. I hope we all survive this."

"Thank you, sir. I'll be as discreet as I can be." They drank up, then Bowen excused himself and Sam T.

They had started walking down the hill when Sam T. broached the subject of when he should leave for Tucson.

"Sunday. That should give Jesus time to find the Apache Too-Gut," Bowen said.

"Good. My trunk with my things in it will be here by then. Guess I'll go to the big wedding Saturday night."

"Who's getting married?" Bowen asked

"Cowboy named Buddy and some ranch woman named VanKirk."

"That's the silly women in the corset on the stage."

"Oh?" He glanced over at the major for a reply.

"Damnedest thing. She must have bought those new clothes in Tucson for the wedding. They had her snugged up way too tight in this corset. And it became a life-or-death ordeal and she had to get out of it."

"And you helped her?"

"Yes, of course. I was very gentlemanly about it."

"Yes, sir, I am certain you were."

Bowen gave him a peevish look. "We best not discuss the matter of the lady's corset around Mary."

"Oh, I sure wouldn't think of it," Sam T. promised.

"You'll have to find out about this Stauffer woman they kidnapped when you get down there. I'll fill you in on all that I know about the gang. Which isn't much."

"I hope they don't ransom her." Sam T. wished, for the woman's sake. Casting a glance at the big house when they passed it, he shook his head and tried to rein in his patience, keeping up with the Major's quick stride. His new job had started off very unconventionally.

Ella Bordeaux used her finger to stir back the lace curtain so she could see the two men striding back up the street together. She already knew the new man was going to do some mining business with the major. Luckily that wimpy little teller Bates gave her the information on the big man when she was in the bank earlier. His name was Mayes. She also had a copy of the telegram from Judge Tripp in Tucson to the governor. The Border Gang struck another stage, stole a mine payroll, killed several people and kidnapped a socialite from Tucson society. A Justine Stauffer.

She recalled the night before with the telegrapher. When Sassy brought him upstairs to her apartment, he shifted so nervously from side to side, she wanted to laugh at his obvious discomfort.

By the poor boy's own disclosure she learned his salary was only twelve dollars a week with the Western Pacific Telegraph Company. Why, at that rate he couldn't even afford to visit Lily every other month. When Ella learned that was all he earned, she had him sit down and served him some cognac.

"A young man like you could earn more money if he was sharp enough about business."

"Yes, ma'am." He sat there very alert with the drink in his hand.

"You handle all the messages that go to the governor and others?"

"Yes, I do."

"Then when a message to them comes in, is there a copy, an extra copy of it?"

"You want me to give you a copy?" he whispered.

She winked at him. "And in return for those copies you can come every Tuesday night and snuggle up there in the bed with little old Lily until dawn."

"Oh, Jesus," he gasped and about spilled the drink in his hand. "Every Tuesday night I could stay here for that long? For that long?"

"If we can do business, of course." Ella examined her nails and waited for his reply.

"I'd give my left—I mean, sure, I can do that. What ones you want?"

"Copies of the governor's and Major Bowen's for right now."

"You won't tell no one?" he asked.

"Of course not. Do we have deal, Brad?"

"Oh, yes, ma'am."

"First you better drink the cognac," she said, motherly-like, to him. "Then we need to get you down there, so you can jump in her bed, boy. She's been ready for over a half hour waiting for you to get here."

"It starts tonight?" He blinked his eyes in disbelief.

"You're dealing with an honest woman, Brad. You do your part and I'll do mine."

"I could go to prison for doing this, you know." He set the glass down after draining it

"I'll never tell and you won't, so who will ever find out?"

"Yeah. She's really waiting?" He tossed his head in that direction.

"Yes, go ahead."

She watched him disappear as anxious as a dog after a gyp in heat. Oh, well, she had the communication matter covered.

Ella stepped back from the window now. That plan worked easier than she had expected. Earlier this afternoon, Brad had brought the telegrams over himself after he delivered the governor his copy. Maybe Daisy B. knew something more about those three men's latest meeting. Later she'd send Sassy after ice cream with her to find out. It made her feel much better to have things under her control.

If she could only figure out Senator Green's telegram of the day before. What kind of sheep business was Bowen in anyway?

CHAPTER 9

With his fingers laced behind the back of his head, Lamas sat in the straight-backed chair. His legs extended, he studied the tips of his polished boots and listened to Sanchez's report.

"A man called Narrimore has put the word out in Nogales that he would pay a thousand-dollar ransom for the white woman."

"How much did he say?" Lamas turned his ear to be certain he heard the man correctly.

"Word around Nogales is that he will pay a thousand dollars for the Señora Stauffer."

Why? Lamas wondered. Did that gringo want this white woman for himself? Perhaps this rich hombre had felt her silky flesh and enjoyed her subtle body as much as Lamas himself had. He could hardly have enough of her. Her naked presence stole his breath—no woman in years had done this to him. Maybe he would grow tired of her in time, but at the moment, the very thought of her luscious body made his guts roil. Perhaps too, this man's offer might be a trap.

Sanchez went on about how this Narrimore had many

tough gunmen to back him up. Yet, Lamas schemed, there
might be a way to collect the thousand dollars from this
rich gringo, then slip in and filch the treasure back from
under his nose. Perhaps he would not even give Narrimore
this high-breasted woman. Not for any amount. Then too,
maybe he would find a way to take the money and run.
That would be a great trick.

Sighing with gusto, Lamas contemplated the talk in
the cantinas if he could pull off such a sly thing. People
would laugh and say, *Lamas is a desert fox. He has taken
the gold and kept the woman. The rich gringo must be
grinding his teeth in frustration.*

Yes, that would be a wonderful trick. Idly, Lamas
poured some mescal in a goblet that sat atop of the long
table. He lifted it to his smiling lips and Black entered
the room.

"Lamas, I'm going north for a couple of days."

"Have a drink, Ezra." Lamas offered it with a big grin.
"I need to discuss a matter with you." He turned back to
Sanchez. "For now, I don't know what I will do about her.
Here is some money. Go visit your woman. I know where
I can find you." He put four ten-dollar gold pieces in the
man's brown hand.

"*Gracias, Don Lamas.*" The man put on his sombrero
and hurried off.

Black pulled up another chair and straddled it backward facing him. After he poured himself a drink, he
pushed his Stetson back and looked attentively at Lamas,
who said, "A rich man named Narrimore from Tucson—
he spread the word in Nogales he is willing to pay us a
thousand dollars for Señora Stauffer."

Black whistled. "Hell, she's more valuable than we
thought. When do we collect?"

"In good time. Perhaps, amigo, he would pay more?"
Lamas suggested slyly.

The Texan nodded and sipped his drink. "That's possible."

"When you go north, find out all you can about this Narrimore."

Black lifted a brow in inquiry before a comprehending smile flicked across his sun-browned face. "Lamas, you old fox, you've got a plan, ain't you?"

"*Sí.* There are people in Mexico City who would pay much for such a smooth-skinned lady, no?"

Black nodded. "Kinda like selling the same horse twice, huh?"

"You keep your ears open, Ezra, and be careful. The stage driver, he is still alive." Lamas shook his head in disgust. Word was that Grundy too had survived his wounds. They had not left witnesses before.

Black rubbed his stubbled jaw. "Reckon they've got our descriptions out by now?"

Lamas shrugged. Deep in his thoughts, he absently sipped his mescal. At last he frowned. Who would arrest them? The fat cow of a sheriff at Tombstone and his deputy? No, not those two. "You be careful going up there. This man Narrimore has some hired guns."

"Yeah, I'll be careful," Black said absently. "Do you have some money?"

Lamas expected the request. He drew ten twenty-dollar gold pieces from his vest pocket and tossed them on the table toward Black. "You try that Indian girl, amigo?"

Black shook his head mildly as he rose. "No. I'll be pushing off now. And I'll check out Narrimore's men and see what I can find out about him."

It disappointed Lamas the Texan did not strongly deny the business about the Indian girl. He liked to needle the big man and get him testy. But Lamas had seen the flash of desire in Ezra's eyes when they stripped Justine

Stauffer to the waist at the stage stop. Then, before any of them touched her, Lamas had surprised himself that day by preventing his men from raping the woman. Usually he allowed them to use a captive female any way they wanted. But this one, this lily-skinned señora, was to be his. She was too fine for anyone but a leader. Besides, he had been generous with his men. Hadn't he just given Ezra two hundred dollars? Hadn't he allowed Sanchez to go home to his wife and children, taking with him enough pesos for plenty of food and drink? Even Sarge and Jimmy were given money for the cantina. But the Stauffer woman was for him alone—for the time being. He drew in a deep breath, then sipped his mescal. There must be a way to get that gringo's money without releasing the woman to him. Lamas was not ready to give her up—yet. He wasn't finished with her.

Lamas remembered the rifle shipment for Marques. He jumped up and hurried down the hallway, his boot heels clicking on the tile floor. He had forgotten to tell Black to check on the rifles at the warehouse. The don would be anxious to know when they would arrive. "Black, wait!"

Justine Stauffer lay fully dressed on the bed, her eyes open wide and her fists clenched at her sides. A wave of humiliation and anger swept over her, causing her to tremble as she recalled the Mexican's hands upon her. Even though Lamas permitted her to take a bath after he had possessed her, she still felt defiled and dirty as though she would never be clean again. But the worst part—she groaned and clenched the bedcover in her fingers—the absolute worst part was that her body had betrayed her. Lamas, as despicable as she considered him, was undeniably an experienced lover. He knew how to draw every ounce of response from a woman.

Squeezing her eyes closed against the bitter memory, Justine gritted her teeth. Hatred boiled inside her like a festering sore. Hatred of the arrogant leader of the gang, hatred of her dead husband, and hatred of herself. The blazing emotion gave her strength and a new determination to escape her captors. She was not defeated yet.

One good thing: Lamas brought one of her carpetbags of clothes to this hacienda, so at least she had a clean dress to wear. What happened to the rest of her luggage, she might never know. She rose and carefully smoothed the material. Then, with precise movements, she reached for the hairbrush on the washstand. Since the only door to the bedroom contained a peephole, she feared that some lecherous eyes spied her; she remained fully clothed at all times. Ruthlessly, she dragged the brush through her tangled curls, plotting and discarding plans for escape. She recalled how, in a moment of sheer desperation, she became pliant in Lamas's arms and whispered promises of passion if only he would release her. His response, deep throaty laughter, caused her, even now, to redden with shame.

Lamas had not sent for her so far this day. Perhaps he would release her. Perhaps he had gone to negotiate the ransom that he had smugly told her he meant to obtain. Maybe he had given his men permission to use her as he had. Oh, dear God, the idea didn't bear thinking about. She glanced around the simply furnished room. The high windows were open but barred, and the heavy oak door was bolted from the outside.

A small whimper drew Justine's eyes to the other bed in the room. The young Indian girl Angela lay on her side on the bed. She jerked convulsively in her sleep and put out a hand as if warding off an attacker. Before dawn, that young Jimmy had awakened Justine when he roughly returned the girl to the room. No doubt Angela was reliving an experience similar to her own. Justine sighed in sympathy. The poor Indian girl possibly experienced a more terrifying situation. She was the plaything of the other men: the pockfaced Jimmy, the swarthy Sanchez, Sarge, and the tall cowboy, all of whom no doubt had been free to use the girl as they wished.

Pained by the girl's discomfort, she watched her twist in the bed. Justine rose and moved to her side. Gently she tried to rouse her.

Angela jerked at the touch of her hand; her eyes flew open, her dark face twisted with fear. Justine smiled at her, wishing the girl had a better command of English since her own Spanish was lamentable.

Angela scrambled up in bed and backed against the headboard, her legs tucked beneath her. Like a trapped animal, she looked quickly around the room. The scent of flowers floated through the open window on a soft breeze. Justine breathed in deeply. Smelling the presence of blossoms in this outlaw's hideout was a bitter irony. She glanced at Angela. The girl cried silently, the tears streaking her olive skin. Justine, although sympathetic, envied the girl's ability to release some of her emotions in tears. Her own eyes felt dry as the desert and gritty like they were coated with coarse sand. Her lips were cracked and dried. Lamas must have drained every ounce of moisture from her body. She flicked her tongue across her lips, then she moved to the pottery olla that hung by the window.

Beads of moisture gathered around the base of the hanging water jug. Justine used the gourd that was placed on the washstand and dipped some of the cool water into it. After drinking her fill, she tilted the olla and refilled the gourd, then carried it across the room to the girl.

"*Agua*," she said softly, inviting Angela to drink.

The girl took the vessel hesitantly, keeping her eyes on Justine's face. She drank deeply, then wiped her mouth on the back of her hand. "*Muchas gracias.*"

"*De nada,*" Justine said, using her limited knowledge of Spanish. But Angela took the words as an indication that Justine spoke the language. She opened her mouth and released a stream of excitable, unintelligible Spanish.

"*No comprendo.*" Shaking her head, Justine sighed in disappointment. Angela gave up and smiled as if to say, *We are in this together; somehow we will manage.*

Justine's chest tightened with pent-up emotions. How would they manage? Everything appeared so hopeless to her.

Saturday night, Sam T. attended the wedding of Buddy and Miss VanKirk. It proved to be a festive occasion at the Chino Valley Schoolhouse. After the short ceremony, everyone danced in the packed building. Several couples from Fort Whipple were in attendance. Sam T. searched the crowd for Julia's face.

After properly introducing himself to a lieutenant and his wife Flora, he danced with the officer's wife. While they waltzed to the fiddler, he led the young woman into a tactfully phrased conversation about Julia, the woman he'd met on the train. Flora had met Julia upon her arrival at Fort Whipple, but did not know her well. She also said Julia's husband was still at Fort Apache across the territory to the east. That was enough; he didn't dare pursue the matter, feeling a little empty that the girl never came out that night with the other officers and their wives. After the set, Sam T. bragged on Flora's skilled footwork, thanked her for dancing with him and returned her to her husband.

It was early the next morning in Prescott when he

waited to board the coach to Tucson. His war bag loaded in the boot, he and the major stood at the side by themselves and discussed the last details.

"Jesus should be there to greet you in Tucson. I sent a telegram to his girlfriend. Her name's Tia Rubio. If you can't find him, perhaps you can locate her. Good luck, Sam T. Don't get yourself killed fighting an army of bandits, and like we discussed, the less publicity over their arrests we have, the better the governor will like it."

Sam T. nodded and he recalled some earlier instructions "Do I need to see Judge Tripp while I am in Tucson too?"

"Yes, he's the strongest official we have backing the marshals program."

"I'll do that. The other new man you hired is due here soon?"

"Yes, John Wesley Michaels. He's suppose to arrive this week."

"Is Sterling going to let you hire him?"

"He better. I think we now have an understanding with the governor. This territory needs a full set of marshals. Take care; looks like they're loading passengers."

"Oh, I saw Miss VanKirk last night at her wedding. To be real honest, Major, I don't believe she wore her corset."

"I know she didn't."

"Oh?"

"She threw the damn thing away somewhere below Maricopa Wells."

Sam T. laughed when he shook the man's hand. It was sure neat to have something on the major. Always so straitlaced and he had to undo the woman's underwear. Oh, he'd loved to have been there and seen it.

"Sam T. Don't take any unnecessary chances."

He sharply saluted the man. "No, sir." Then, still

amused about the major's corset incident, he climbed in the coach.

His arrival in Tucson the next morning in a cloud of dust and a loud "Whoa" from the driver looked uneventful enough. He climbed down, stiff and sore from the jolting twenty-four-hour ride. He'd had very little sleep and the food served along the way reminded him of pig slop. When he stepped off the coach in the early morning shadows, he spotted a short wiry man under a wide sombrero with crossed cartridge belts looking everywhere for someone. He felt certain the man must be Jesus Morales. He reminded Sam T. of a proud banty rooster.

"Morales?" he shouted.

"*Sí,* Señor Mayes. Did you have a good trip?" the ex-scout inquired, looking relieved to have found him. He quickly reached out and shook his hand.

"Not too bad." Sam hefted his war bag on his shoulder and looked around. "Where's the Apache scout?"

"Señor." Jesus frowned up at Sam. T. "There is a small problem." He sounded very secretive and glanced around the street as if making sure they were not being overheard.

"Well, what is it?" Sam T. asked, feeling that if he continued having setbacks he would never get on the trail of these outlaws.

Jesus whispered, "He is a Cherry-cow."

"What the hell does that mean?"

"Some call them Chir-ic-ah-huas. Means a tribe of Apaches. Most call them Cherry-cows."

Jesus stopped Sam T. on the sidewalk, then he made certain they were alone save for a passing freight wagon before he said, "The agency at San Carlos won't give him a pass to leave the reservation, because Geronimo took a lot of his people to Mexico. They are afraid men like

Too-Gut would follow him down there if they gave him a pass."

Sam nodded. "This man—why the major said, he was a former scout for the army."

"*Sí*, he and I were both scouts for the army."

"Hell, that doesn't make any damned sense," Sam growled irritably.

"I do not make the laws, Señor. We must be careful. The army has sent a lieutenant and some troopers from Fort Thomas to search Tucson for him. Those men are here now." The scout cut his dark eyes around to check.

"Oh, Lord!" Sam muttered. More delays and stumbling blocks. He hoped Mrs. Stauffer was still alive. A week had passed since she had been kidnapped. "Well, Morales, where's the Apache right now?"

"We'll go meet him tonight. Come, we must get some supplies. I have a horse for you. The major said you would need a big horse. I think the one he picked will do. You are very big man, señor."

"Call me Sam T."

"Ah, *sí*."

Sam cocked an eyebrow and smiled wryly down at the smaller man. "Well, let's get those supplies." Jesus had to hurry to keep up with him as they headed down the boardwalk.

"Could I carry that for you?" Jesus offered to take his war bag.

"No, I can manage it all right."

They passed a cantina and several loafers out in front spoke friendly to Morales. Sam T. understood enough border Spanish to know that they good-naturedly teased him about some woman.

"I hope you and Morales get one of them *tigres*," one of the men said, mostly in English, to Sam T.

Sam agreed with a bemused frown. What in hell was all this about a *tigre*?

Half a block away, Jesus spoke quietly. "I told several people that we were going to Mexico to hunt the jaguar."

"That's right," Sam said aloud. A good cover. Was it the man's idea or the major's? Didn't matter; they were going tiger hunting, all right—for the two-legged variety.

In a large store, Morales ordered the list of supplies, which Sam paid for with money that the major had advanced him. Dried beans, rice, bacon, canned goods, matches, flour, soda—the list looked complete enough to outfit them.

"We will come tomorrow very early for these supplies," Morales told the storekeeper.

Outside the store, in a fast walk, Sam asked Jesus about a packhorse.

"No problem, Sam T. He is with the other horses."

"How many more do we have?"

"A packhorse, also one for Too-Gut, and one for his wife."

"Morales, his wife is going along? Are you crazy?"

"Oh, no. You will see; it will be all right. Come on, I know a cantina ahead that has good food to eat," Morales said with a grin.

"A wife?" Sam repeated.

Jesus shrugged as he led the way. "She is not very pretty, but she can cook and watch the horses."

"I need to go talk to Judge Tripp first."

Jesus didn't say a word as they walked on.

"The major said for me to talk to him before I left. Something wrong?"

"No, we can go there. The courthouse is this way."

Good thing nothing was wrong. Sam T. would have to get used to this man's ways. He liked Morales. Some people in the world he liked, some he tolerated, some he disliked. So far the man at the moment ranked in the upper third.

Tucson was a town of plastered buildings. Commerce was the number one activity, Spanish the primary street language. Sam overheard bits and pieces of conversation, but understood only a little of it. He had learned that Tucson had once been the Confederate territorial capital, and sentiments still ran deep. It would do an ex-Union officer to keep an eye out; some old graybacks had not forgotten that conflict.

Jesus waited outside the courthouse. Sam T. left his war bag with him. He wondered if the judge would be there that early. Inside the cool building, he spoke to a clerk behind a desk in the lobby. The building was so empty their words echoed in the halls.

"Judge Tripp, please."

"Nature of your business?"

"He's expecting me."

"Name?"

"Sam T. Mayes."

"Oh, yes. The head of the stairs, first office on the right." The man looked up with his reading glasses on the bridge of his nose to examine him.

Sam T. thanked him and went up the hardwood staircase.

The door was open and a gray-haired man stood at the window in the second room.

"Judge Tripp?"

"Yes?"

"Mayes is my name, sir."

"Ah, wonderful. Bowen told me all about you. Come in. Coffee?"

"Certainly," Sam T. said.

Seated in a leather chair before the judge's desk, he listened to the man's version of the Stauffer murder and kidnapping. "A very attractive and well-liked lady in this city. Justine Stauffer was a member of the society circle here. I pray you can find her safe and alive. I managed to get a tintype from her mother. Actually under a false pretext. I didn't mention you were coming, of course."

Sam T. thanked him. He studied the picture while Tripp went on talking about all the criminal happenings and how pleased he was about the marshals' formation. She was a strikingly attractive woman, perhaps too glamorous to be mixed up with these cutthroats and to survive.

"You know the leader?" Tripp asked.

"We have his name."

"The stage agent, he gave Taggett at the Halsey stage office a description of them. The poor man was still alive yesterday."

"Where's this agent at?"

"Verde City is the stage line's headquarters."

"We best go there first. I'm going to do all I can for this lady." He started to hand the tintype back.

"No, Sam, you keep it. May help identify her, God forbid." Tripp shook his head.

"We'll do the best we can."

"I know that. Oh, yes, I have two dozen John Doe warrants made out for you to take along. That should get them locked up in some jail until you can do more." He handed the sheath over, then stuck out his hand. "God be with you, and if you need something, contact me. I want this marshal business to work."

"You are one of the rare ones," Sam said and thanked him.

"No, there are lots of good God-fearing folks out there farming and ranching want this mess cleaned up."

"That's what it's about." Sam T. took his leave and hurried down the stairs and out of the courthouse.

"What did he know?" Jesus asked, standing up.

"We have a picture of Mrs. Stauffer," Sam T. said, checking around before he handed him the tintype.

"Oh, she is very pretty." Jesus returned it with a serious nod.

"Let's hope she stays that way," he said and pocketed the picture. "Now, about some food?"

The cantina that Jesus chose to eat in was almost deserted in the morning hours. When they entered, Sam's broad build drew a few curious stares.

"Oh, Jesus," a pretty girl exclaimed. Jesus caught her in a hug, then they chattered in Spanish like magpies.

"Mona." Jesus released her. "This is Señor Sam T. Mayes, who is going to Sonora to hunt *tigres*."

She smiled up at Sam; her eyes openly admiring his face and build. "Jesus is a very good guide, señor. You will have a good hunt down there."

Sam T. returned her smile. When she walked away, he noticed that Jesus' eyes remained on her.

"I ordered some food and beer," he said at last.

"Good," Sam said and settled in the chair. His left hip still carried a bushwacker's bullet embedded too deep to ever remove. It throbbed enough so that he shifted his weight on the seat. Perhaps Shirley had been right. He should have stayed at his office job. There would be plenty of long days in the saddle ahead of him. Tripp's support sounded sincere enough. All this delay and the problem with the Apache . . . his new job might require more patience than he could muster. Maybe the food and beer would put him in a better mood.

Lamas received his monthly invitation to visit Don Ramon Estaban Marques's hacienda. Though still weary from the raids and each night enjoying the luscious Justine in his bed since he'd returned to the hacienda, he decided after reading the invitation he must go at once

and see the don. It would not be wise to insult *el patron*.
Don Marques would be his key to unlock the doors of
the hacienda owners' society to him. Besides, he had
not seen the man in two months. He hoped Black had sent
back some word of the rifle shipment. But Arizona was
a long way from the factory—they could still be on a ship
coming around the horn, for that matter.

Leaning against the doorjamb, Lamas watched Pedro
the gardener watering the flowers and plants. If he went
to the Hacienda Marques, who could he leave in charge?
Black was gone to the Santa Ritas in Arizona, where
he slept with the widow woman. Sarge was off in the
little village of La Paloma on a drinking binge at the cantina. Sanchez was busy getting his wife pregnant again.
Which only left Jimmy.

Most likely the kid would still be sleeping off a night
of drinking and lovemaking with the Indian girl. But if
someone rode up and threatened his home, the gardener
would run off screaming and the women in the kitchen
would cower in a corner. Jimmy was only a shade better
than nothing, but he could guard the captive women so
they didn't escape.

Striding absently to the open gate, Lamas looked to
the distant purple mountains. He knew this old hacienda made a perfect fort, isolated in the greasewood
and organ pipe cactus of the desert. Who would come
here to bother him? He shrugged off the thought of in-
vaders. No one wanted to face such a powerful man as
himself.

With a sigh of resignation, Lamas went to the back
bedroom to awaken the lazy boy.

"Wake up!" Lamas stood over the sprawled naked
form of the kid. Red nodules dotted the youth's thin
shoulders and back. His white skin's coloration looked
sickly pale against the dark blanket on the bed.

"What's wrong?" Jimmy grumbled as he rolled over on his back.

"I must go see someone for a few days. You are in charge."

"In charge?" the kid groaned. He raised up on his elbow and blinked his sleep-filled eyes. "Oh, in charge." Abruptly he was wide awake, his eyes no longer glazed, but sparkling with anticipation.

Lamas cursed silently; his glare narrowed on the kid's face. He knew the dull-witted boy suddenly realized what being in charge could mean.

"If that gringo woman has one scratch on her when I return. . . ." He leaned over, his index finger pointing at the kid's face like a saber. "One bruise on her, or you even touch her, I will kill you when I return. *Comprende?*"

"Huh? Oh, sure." Hurriedly Jimmy wrapped the blanket around his waist and swung his legs off the bed. "I wouldn't do—"

"Be certain that you do not touch her!" Lamas cut him off.

"Hell, Lamas, I got that Indian girl to myself."

Indecision over leaving flashed through Lamas's mind. He knew that the kid was a liar. He might even have to kill him when he returned from *el patron*'s, but what else could he do?

"I am leaving immediately. Come outside."

Pedro had saddled his good black horse. Lamas carried a canteen of water and some food for the journey packed in his saddlebags He left orders with the gardener and the two Mexican women to feed the prisoners and see that they did not escape. He did not feel comfortable with the boy in charge, but perhaps nothing would happen.

Jimmy was dressed and yawning by the porch post when Lamas mounted up. He looked down at the kid. He felt it would be a waste of time to warn Jimmy of the rules once again. He must ride and get back as quickly as possible.

"*Adiós*. Take care of my hacienda, Jimmy!"

"'Bye." The kid waved, but did not move from his position on the porch.

In the small bedroom that formed their dungeon, Justine lay on top of the covers. Her mind was blank. She had grown numb with fatigue from thinking of ways to escape. As she clutched the blanket, her heart tossed fretfully. She wanted to find sleep so that she could awaken from this nightmare.

"Señora," Angela whispered. "Lamas vamoose."

Justine looked up into the girl's brown eyes. "Angela and Justine vamoose too," she said pointing to the girl, then herself.

Angela nodded eagerly, her eyes sparkling with excitement. She was ready to escape.

Now that the leader had left, Justine wondered who had been put in charge. The tall cowboy, perhaps? He would be a tough one to trick. But she thought he had ridden off earlier. So hard to keep track of time or dates, despite her plans to do so. The rat-faced Sanchez? No, she had not heard him in the halls for days either. A vision of the filthy Sarge caused her to shudder. How long since she heard his coarse gravelly voice in the hallway or outside in the past several days?

Sighing to herself, she sat up on the bed. It did not matter who was left in charge; she and Angela were going to escape. Somehow. Just how she wasn't sure, but an opportunity had to present itself.

As if in answer to her prayers, Justine heard the door being unlocked. She glanced quickly at Angela, but the girl shook her head.

Jimmy entered the room with a smug grin on his

pocked face. From his look, she knew the answer to who was in charge. With his butt, he pushed the door closed behind him. He stared at Justine and his lips formed a smirk. This time she felt certain he had not come for the Indian girl.

"Well, fancy lady, guess who left me in charge?" He moved to the end of the bed. "Either of you try anything, Lamas said to kill you. Understand?"

Angela edged to get behind him. Justine knew she needed to draw his attention from the girl. She prayed that Angela had some plan in mind.

"Take off your clothes, Mrs. Stauffer!"

"I will not."

In a swift movement, the kid strode to her and jerked her off the bed. Choked by the wad of fear in her throat, she froze. Whatever he had in mind for her, from the look of wild excitement in his eyes, he would not be gentle. He appeared to be waiting for her to struggle, to give him a reason to overpower her.

"W-wait," she whispered, putting out a hand against his heaving chest. "I—I'll do it. Don't tear my dress. It's all I have to wear." A wave of revulsion swept over her at the persuasive tone in her voice. She forced a smile to her lips and allowed her long lashes to sweep over her eyes. If only Angela would hurry and do something. Determinedly she resisted the temptation to look beyond the kid's shoulders and see what the girl was doing.

Jimmy laughed huskily and took a step backward. He licked his lips at the prospect of what came next. Justine began to slowly unbutton her dress in front. She wished the girl would hurry; her fingers trembled on each button. Jimmy's breathing grew heavier. Justine knew his lust soon would overcome his anticipation, and then . . .

She squeezed her eyes shut tight. Next she felt him reach out and push the material aside, exposing her breasts.

A dull thud and a splash of water caused her eyes to flash open. Angela stood behind the glazed-eyed kid. The dripping olla hung from the girl's hand. Jimmy weaved on his feet, then with a low grunt slumped forward on the bed.

"Ha!" Angela exclaimed. She looked grimly at Justine and nodded. Justine froze for a moment, then Angela began gesturing wildly, indicating they should tie Jimmy up. In haste, Justine closed her blouse to cover herself and did half the buttons.

Quickly gathering her scattered wits, Justine helped roll the wet man over and pull the sheet from under him.

With reluctance, she removed the revolver from his holster.

"Señora, here." Angela said insistently and she pointed at the cartridge belt around his waist. The girl quickly made strips of the sheet.

Swept with nausea, Justine looked at the man's white face and plastered hair. She cringed at even the thought of touching him. Finally she undid the buckle and pulled off the belt. Angela bound his hands behind his back with strips of the sheet and gagged him with his own kerchief. The Indian girl certainly had no intention of letting a revived outlaw follow their trail.

Angela drew a knife from the kid's sheath. The sight of the weapon sickened Justine; then she told herself the knife was a necessity. But a knife and a handgun seemed small protection against a gang of cutthroats should they catch up with them.

Angela sprang to her side and pushed her toward the door. There was urgency in her movements that galvanized Justine into action.

After easing open the thick door, the women looked out in the shadowy hallway. There was not a sign of anyone. Justine signaled Angela to step into the hallway and to keep watch while she replaced the bolt on the outside of the door. Then, easing flat against the cool walls of the house, they moved toward the back door. Voices came from the kitchen and halted them in their tracks. Justine placed her hand over her heart, trying to still the violent pounding. With her other hand, she tried to hold steady the holster so the cartridge belt would not rattle.

The voices faded, and the two women took their chance. Running on their toes, they hurried to the back passage. At the door they stopped. Angela grabbed two floppy sombreros off a peg and shoved one at Justine.

Justine put it on clumsily, then glanced back, expecting to see the menacing faces of Lamas's servants. She swallowed a hard knot in her throat. No one followed them. A wave of relief swept over her, but Angela's tug on her arm brought her back to sharp awareness.

The stable was a ramshackle affair of crooked poles and a brush arbor roof. As the women raced toward it, Justine feared she would hear a shout from the gardener. But there was no sound of a human outside.

Hastily, Angela picked two gentle-looking horses to saddle. A few moments later she lithely swung aboard the smaller horse. Justine fought to retain hold of the gun belt and at the same time struggled to get on her animal. It didn't work. She followed it around in a circle. At last she was forced to put the belt over her head and loop it over her chest and under her arm in order to mount the horse. She smiled grimly at last in the saddle. It was stupid to be so worried about losing the gun belt when she had never even fired a gun in her life. But she knew they had to have some kind of defense.

For a moment, she wondered what the Indian girl

planned next. Angela dismounted, opened the gate bars and went inside the pen. Holding her own horse by the reins, she waved her arms at the others. They broke out of the opening to escape the corral. Justine reined in hers to assist the girl. She quickly realized the plan. No horses—no pursuit. The herd stampeded through the front compound gate and under the archway. Like a jockey, Angela rode low on the neck of her pony close after them. She screamed ear-shattering war cries to spur the horses on faster. The two of them raced north with all of Lamas's horses pounding ahead of them.

Sam T. and Jesus finished their meal of peppery rich food and settled back to drink their coffee when four soldiers burst into the cantina. A clean-shaven lieutenant, wearing a stiff-brimmed felt hat and a starched uniform, led the men. A customer pointed him in the direction of Jesus and Sam T.

"We have trouble, señor," Jesus murmured with a look of dread in his brown pupils. Sam turned his head to see the officer stop abruptly at their table.

"Jesus Morales?" the officer asked. "We're looking for an ex-army scout. He is a Chiricahua by the name of Too-Gut."

Jesus shrugged. "What has he done?"

"Done? He's a bronco Chiricahua," the officer repeated grimly. "That is reason enough. Now, I did not come here to be put off. I have it on good authority that you know where this man is."

Sam T. sized up the lieutenant. In his early twenties, and no doubt fresh out of West Point. His arrogant manner irritated Sam T.

"Lieutenant," Sam said, "just hold on a minute. This man is an officer of the court. You better back off."

The young officer raised a haughty scowl at Sam.

"I suggest, sir, that you stay out of this. It does not concern you."

Sam T. rose to his feet, his tall frame towering over them. With his eyes narrowed in warning, he jabbed a finger in the officer's direction. "You listen good, Lieutenant. You are out of your jurisdiction here."

"Who are you, sir?"

Scowling with impatience, Sam T. gritted his teeth. "An officer of the court, Sam T. Mayes."

"Mr. Mayes"—the officer stressed the "mister" part and his lip curled back to emphasis his meaning—"this is a military matter."

"No, it's you who doesn't understand. This man's a civilian, not military." He jerked a thumb in Jesus' direction, not taking his deep-set gaze from the lieutenant. "Morales is my deputy."

The young officer swung sharply; his heels clicked together and he commanded, "Sergeant, arrest this man."

Feet apart, Sam swept back his coat and gripped the bone handle of his Colt. "As you were, Sergeant! Now, Lieutenant, you listen to me. I told you this man works for me, and if you don't want a full military funeral, I suggest you back off. Now!"

The officer's face paled. "Who is your superior?"

"Major Gerald Bowen, army retired. He's in Prescott."

"You can be certain, Mr. Mayes, that I will wire him. I'm sure Major Bowen will support me in this matter."

Sam T. shrugged. He didn't care who the lieutenant wired. "That's your privilege." He leaned forward slightly and stared down into the lieutenant's eyes. "For now, back off."

His face red with either anger or embarrassment, the officer turned to his noncom. "Sergeant, move the men out."

Sam T. sat down and watched them file out the door. He wasn't sure that the lieutenant wouldn't reconsider and be back in a few moments if his anger got the better of his discretion.

"Now I see why the major hired you," Morales commented with a grin. "Did you know that lieutenant would back down?"

Sam T. shrugged. "I figured he would." He had gambled on the man's inexperience and won.

"We will have to be more careful," Jesus said. "The military wants Too-Gut."

"That doesn't make a damned bit of sense," Sam T. muttered and lifted his cup of cold coffee. "According to the major, Too-Gut was a loyal scout. Why does the army want to treat him like he's a criminal now?"

"I do not understand either, but it is a crazy law, no?"

Taken back by the injustice of the matter and what little he could do to resolve it, Sam T. lowered his cup. "Maybe we'd better move on and find this Too-Gut."

"You are right. Come on." Jesus stood and led the way out of the rear of the cantina as he talked. "We will ride south; Too-Gut will see us and join us. We will not have to look for him."

"Morales, these outlaws are holding Mrs. Stauffer. It's been over a week now. We can't afford to dally around here very long. I hate to think what they might be doing to her." War bag on his shoulder, he followed the man into the alley and the bright sun. No sign of the soldiers.

"I have learned some things about this gang the last few days." Jesus checked around to be certain they were alone. "They are led by this Lamas and many of his gang are simple farmers and small ranchers from below the border. But I hear he also has some very mean men that ride for him, besides these peons."

"Any more names?"

Jesus shook his head. "People are afraid to say much more."

They stopped at the end of the alley and checked the street both ways. Sam T. saw no sign of the military and felt relieved. They turned and hurried up the dirt street filled with stray chickens and screaming brown-skinned children at play.

"What will we need to catch them?" Sam T. asked after a quick check over his shoulder. He saw nothing out of place.

"We will need all the help we can get."

"I agree we need this Too-Gut, if he's a fighter."

"Oh, he's a fighter. I think we should get the horses and leave right now."

"Yes. We better do that," Sam T. agreed. "I'm real concerned for this Stauffer woman's safety."

"If we wait until the sun sets, those soldiers would have a harder time to find us."

"How late is that mercantile open?"

"Oh, I forgot. We will need to get the supplies." Jesus shook his head in disappointment.

"We can ride through the alleys and be certain we don't meet them. You know this town better than they do."

"I have a better idea. We can send Tia to get the supplies. They don't know her."

"That's your lady friend?"

"You will meet her." Jesus beamed with pride.

"Good." Sam T. checked again and breathed easier when nothing was behind them. They hurried on toward the south side of town.

Tia's place was a small hovel on a few acres of irrigated land. The horses stood in a pole corral behind her casa, munching on fresh hay. He spotted the sorrel over the others. From a distance he appeared to be a good, tall horse.

"*Buenos dias*," the short, attractive woman said from the doorway.

"Tia, this is Sam T.," Jesus said.

"I am glad to meet you."

"My pleasure, ma'am," he said, putting down the bag and wiping his sweaty forehead on his sleeve.

"We need you to take the packhorse to the mercantile and get the supplies he bought," Jesus explained. "The army is looking for Too-Gut. We had one run-in with them already."

"It'll be better if they don't follow us," Sam T. added.

"No problem. Do I need to pay for the supplies?" She looked at both of them for the answer.

"No, they're paid for. I'll write the man a note," Sam T. offered.

"I'll go saddle the packhorse," Jesus said and hurried off.

"Sam T.," she said in a low voice when he was gone. "Don't let Jesus drink." Her frown of disapproval punctuated her words.

He nodded to the short woman that he understood. One more thing to add to his problems. She never explained herself, but tossed her head and walked around back where Jesus was fixing the packsaddle. He shouldered his bag and followed her.

Jesus wasted no time piling the crossbuck on the bay horse and cinching it up. "The red one is your horse." He motioned toward it.

"Got a name for him?" Sam T. asked, circling the sorrel with a critical eye.

"No."

"I'll call him Big Boy, then." He caught the rope

halter and peeled back the horse's lips for an examination of his teeth; he decided he was five or six years old. Good stout horse; the major did all right. He bent over and checked the shoe on the front foot. Then he recalled the note Tia would need from him and went for his war bag.

He wrote for the merchant to release the supplies to Tia and told him that they needed to leave sooner than expected. She left in a trot, leading the bay down the narrow lane for the road.

They went over their gear. Sam T. let out the stirrups on his saddle and unloaded his war bag. He tied the bedroll and slicker behind the seat, put his Winchester in the scabbard. Then he stuffed the extra shells, writing paper, pencils, a clean shirt, some socks and underwear in the saddlebags. Mentally taking inventory, he remembered the warrants and added them.

"How far is Verde City?" he asked, straightening with his hands on his hips, trying to stretch his stiff back.

"Only a few days ride—south."

"At the Halsey stage office they have descriptions of the gang members. What else can we do?"

"We can bribe some people who know on the border." Jesus made a strong bob of his head to reassure him this plan would work if the stage agent was no help.

Tia returned in a short while with the packhorse loaded. No one had followed her. Out of breath, her enthusiasm still shone on her face.

"See any soldiers?" Jesus asked.

"They never saw me." She smiled smugly and he led the horse around the back to put with the others. "I will fix some food."

"Maybe we better be leaving," Sam T. said, feeling uneasy about the time lost.

"No, you must eat first."

"I won't argue." After the bad food on the stage ride and the prospect of campfire cooking ahead, he agreed with a nod to her. "We'll eat before we leave."

Jesus returned in a few minutes and convinced him it would be better to leave under the cover of darkness. They unsaddled the packhorse, took a siesta beneath a palm-frond ramada and ate some of her rich spicy food before sundown.

"When you return, we will have a fiesta," she promised them, then stood on her toes and kissed Jesus good-bye. Sam T. agreed they would need a celebration on their return. He mounted Big Boy, reached out, took the pack-horse lead and, with a wave to her, started down the lane. His scout led the other two horses for the Apaches and followed him. In the west, the fiery sun set behind the saw-edged mountains.

The men rode in silence along the shallow river. The road wound under great gnarled cottonwoods that lined the way.

"How far are we going tonight?"

"Not far," Jesus said vaguely.

Sam sighed inwardly. He'd have to rely on Jesus and gamble that the major was right about him being trust-worthy. Time would soon tell about the man's judgment.

In the starlight, the jagged silhouette of the distant mountains looked brooding. Around them, the desert hillsides stood studded with giant-armed cactus that tow-ered like menacing threats under the starlight.

After an hour's ride, Jesus brought his horse to a halt and called out something in Spanish. Sam reined in beside him. There was no answer to Jesus' shout. Then in the distance he heard an owl hoot. Jesus answered with a similar call.

"Sam T., Too-Gut is coming."

"Yeah, that's what I figured," Sam said. His hand

instinctively rested on his gun butt, while he peered around in the dim light.

A short figure, wearing an unblocked hat, emerged from the night. He spoke in stilted English. "We wondered if Morales had forgot us."

"Sam T., this is Too-Gut."

The man came forward. Sam dismounted, flicked a match and held it up so that he could see the Indian's face. Satisfied, he blew it out.

"Sam T., the major is a good man." The Apache reached out and squeezed Sam's hand in both of his. They were callused and his fingers were strong. "If he says to ride with you, then we go."

"The major tells me you're a good man as well," Sam T. said, convinced of the man's sincerity.

"You see soldiers?" Too-Gut asked.

"*Sí*. We had a run-in with some tonight. So we better ride," Jesus said, his voice filled with concern.

Sam T. peered into the darkness behind the Indian. "Who is that?" he asked, recognizing another figure in the silver light as female.

"Da-yah," Too-Gut grunted.

Sam T. recalled Jesus' earlier words about Too-Gut's wife. He sighed inwardly. He had hoped she was not along. Nothing else to do; he spoke softly, "Mount up."

They rode down the King's Highway at a jog until after midnight. Jesus led the way across a shallow ford.

"We could camp here," he offered on the other side.

Sam T. agreed and dismounted wearily. His hip ached and he hoped that the stiffness would pass, if he ever became accustomed to riding long distances again. He undid his bedroll and dropped it on the ground. When he turned back, the woman wordlessly took the reins to his horse.

"Sleep, Sam T. We will guard this place," Jesus assured him.

"I'll take a turn," he said.

Too-Gut laughed. "No need, Sam T. Apaches never sleep."

Grateful for their assurances, Sam knew for certain he could fall asleep without even trying. Besides, it was time for him to test the major's confidence in these men. He spread out his blanket and, with the Colt in his right hand, settled on the hard ground to sleep. His eyes closed and he fell into an uneasy slumber.

In the cool of the morning, Sam T. studied the distant Santa Rita Mountains. A flock of buzzards circled a short distance down the shallow Santa Cruz River. Their low, tight formation indicated something dead.

"The buzzards are finding breakfast, no?" Jesus commented when he joined Sam.

"Where's Too-Gut?" The Apache had not been seen since Sam arose. His woman acted busy making a fire and cooking, but he'd not seen her mate. She was a small woman in a many-layered brown skirt and simple blouse, and he ventured her to be in her teens. Not pretty, with a hawk nose and eyes like dark precious stones, but all business.

"Who knows?" Jesus shrugged his shoulders under the ammunition belts like it was no problem. "Perhaps he has gone hunting. Do not worry, Sam T., Too-Gut will be back."

Yeah, Sam thought, that's easy for you to say. What the hell do I know about Apaches? The sight of that many buzzards unsettled him too. They were probably after an expired rabbit or maybe a dead wild horse or steer. Hell, it could be anything. There was no need to get worked up about a bunch of vultures. But where the hell was his scout?

Sam turned and walked back toward the campfire. Da-yah squatted beside the small fire and watched over a bubbling pot of beans. The smell of strong coffee from the other container tickled Sam T.'s nose. He watched the woman tilt her head and scan the distant land, as though searching for something. Then he turned to see what she was looking for.

Too-Gut came into view on horseback, hurrying his way down the steep, sandy bank. He splashed across the shallow river and used his rifle stock to spank the horse up the other side to join them.

"Sam T., two men are down. One is dead. Come quick!"

"Here," Jesus said, "take my saddled horse." He handed Sam the reins and turned to the Apache. "Do you know these dead men, Too-Gut?"

"No." The Apache reined his mount around and led Sam back the way he had come.

Keeping his feet free of the short stirrups, Sam followed with a grim impression of what to expect. He'd seen corpses eaten by buzzards before. The great black birds flushed off the branches at their approach. When they rode into the clearing, Sam did not need Too-Gut's pointing finger to spot the men.

"One is still alive. Barely." Too-Gut pointed his rifle barrel toward a man seated on the ground, his back against a tree.

Sam T. dismounted quickly, taking Jesus' canteen from the saddle horn. He hurried to the wounded man's side. Death was no stranger to Sam, and the man's sunken eyes and grayish skin told him the wounded man's time on earth would soon expire. Kneeling beside him, Sam T. noted the dried black blood on his shirt, centered by a moist spot of fresh crimson.

He propped the man against his shoulder and tilted the canteen of tepid water to his lips. The man's mouth was cracked and caked with the desert's dryness as though he had been sitting against the scrubby tree a long time.

Slowly Sam T. trickled water into his mouth. The copper smell of the wound tried to overpower him. After the man had weakly drunk, he nodded his head in thanks.

"Who did this?" Sam T. asked quietly. He glanced around, noting that Too-Gut waved his arms at the brazen vultures to ward them away.

"A day ago . . ." The dying man's words were so weak that Sam had to strain his ears to make out what he was saying. "We were camped out on . . . the road. They jumped us. Two masked men. Marched us here—shot us—took the wagon." A violent burst of coughing broke up his words. He gasped for breath.

"The wagon? What was it carrying?" Sam asked.

"A hundred new rifles."

"For who?"

"A merchant in Nogales," the man gasped out. "Arman—"

"The men who shot you—?" Sam T. started to question him before he realized the man was dead. Gently he eased him to the ground.

Rising stiffly, Sam T. shouted to Too-Gut, who searched the ground for any tracks left by the killers. "Can you make out anything?"

The Apache rose and pointed westward. "Two men and a wagon went back across the river."

"Follow the trail." Sam T. glanced around at the corpses. He hated to leave them to be carrion for the black scavenger birds.

Jesus burst through the brush on his sorrel. "Who are these men?"

"Freighters who were carrying a wagonload of rifles for someone called Arman something."

The Mexican dismounted and glanced in disapproval at the dead man by the tree.

"Sam T., what do you think happened here?"

"I think we have some cold-blooded killers who stole a load of rifles." He motioned toward the lifeless man. "He said it was a day ago, but he was delirious." For a long moment he considered what they should do next. "Need to do something with them."

"*Sí*. It is bad to leave them for the buzzards."

"We should bury them," Sam T. said, speaking his thoughts aloud. He knew it would be better to hurry and get on the trail of the killers, but he found it distasteful to simply leave the corpses out in the open.

Jesus scuffed the hard ground with the side of his boot sole. "This is caliche; we cannot dig in this hard ground. It is better to use rocks to cover them."

Sam T. nodded in agreement. He turned as Too-Gut rejoined them. "Well?"

"Wagon, horses go south."

Sam T. looked around and scowled. He let out a deep breath and said quietly, "We'll bury them in one common grave. A wagon can't get too far ahead even if they've got a day's start." He looked at his men, anticipating an argument, but there was only a grimace of distaste on Too-Gut's face and weary acceptance on Jesus'.

A rock mound had been formed over the corpses when Da-yah appeared. She spoke in a low undertone with her husband.

With a smile, Too-Gut turned to Sam T. "Woman do this. We go eat food."

"Come on, Sam T.," Jesus invited. "The food will be getting cold."

Sam looked doubtfully at Da-yah. But her blank expression gave nothing away. She had obviously made her decision. He gave her a slow smile of gratitude, which she acknowledged with a slight inclination of her head.

He followed the men back to camp. He worried about the load of stolen weapons and their final destination. Besides, they had two murderers to chase down. Another delay. At the rate they moved, he would never find that Stauffer woman or the gang of cutthroats.

Maybe Shirley had been right; he might have been better off in his desk position. No; he shook his head wearily. He liked the challenge of his new position. It was just the damned setbacks that irritated him. Maybe he wasn't doing his job right? What would the major want him to do?

Removing his Stetson, he ran his hand through his thick brown hair. The major would want him to get the rifles back from these outlaws if he could do it quickly. He would just have to hope that Justine Stauffer was still alive.

The men gobbled down the beans and washed away the taste with bitter coffee. Sam could see the impatience of his assistants as a tangible thing. He knew exactly how they felt, for he shared the same irritating frustration.

"We'll have to find that wagon," Sam said, noting the buzzards still circled.

"You mean before we go to Verde City?" Jesus asked, his dark brown eyes locked on Sam's.

"Yes, we better stop and try to catch these bandits. Too-Gut can trail them."

The Apache nodded. "Leave big tracks, write direction on the ground." A big smile exposed very white teeth against his copper skin. "We catch them quick."

"What about Da-yah?" Sam asked.

"She will come," Jesus assured him as he stood up.

Sam T. set his plate down on a rock and took out a

small cigar. He peered through the blue smoke of the match. "Where can a man sell rifles?"

"To Apaches," Too-Gut said.

"You think Apaches did that?" Sam T. gestured toward the area where the buzzards were hung in the sky.

"No, but there are still Apaches around here." Too-Gut waved his thick arm to the east and to the mountains that rose up far across the desert.

"I thought Crook had all the Apaches on the reservations," Sam T. commented, ready to remount the red horse.

"One they call Geronimo is still on the loose. Some say he has much Mexican gold."

Sam T. shook his head. "Why would an Apache want gold?" He looked at Too-Gut for an answer.

The Indian grinned. "White man not take beads for long guns." His words drew grim laughter from Sam and Jesus.

The men rode together in a companionable silence, tracking two killers. At midday, Too-Gut dismounted and crouched low to inspect the ground. Sam clasped his hands on the saddle horn and waited. The fact that Da-yah had not yet joined them bothered him.

When Too-Gut walked back to them, Sam tried to read his expression. "What's the problem?"

"Wagon went off the road." He pointed into the mesquite and catclaw.

Sam squinted against the harsh sun. He wiped his forearm against his sweating brow and cursed soundlessly. Now what was he supposed to do? He looked at his Mexican scout. "Jesus, how far can they get in that direction with a wagon?" He pointed, indicating east.

"Not far."

"Well, lead off."

They found the abandoned wagon in a dry wash. It

was empty. Sam walked around it, glaring in disgust at the bleached boards. He slapped his palm against the sideboards. "We're too late."

Jesus shouted from the dry wash, "They loaded the guns on packhorses here."

The sound of drumming hooves on their back trail drew Sam's attention. To his relief, Da-yah came into view, leading the packhorse. One small worry off his shoulders. Now he had a new one to take its place. The thieves could move faster with the packhorses than they did with a wagon. There was no telling how far ahead they'd gone. He asked Too-Gut's opinion.

"They maybe were here this morning," the Apache commented. Not waiting for a reply, he moved ahead, inspecting the trail of the packhorses.

Sam felt torn with indecision. He could follow the thieves or he could continue south to learn the woman's fate. "Damn the lawless Arizona Territory," he cursed under his breath.

"Jesus, we'll ride after these men for one day, then we have to turn south. My job is to get Mrs. Stauffer back and try to bring in the Border Gang. This setback is not going to help us."

"*Sí*, Sam T." Jesus nodded in agreement. He spurred his horse up the sandy wash in the direction that Too-Gut rode. Sam T. turned to Da-yah.

She smiled widely for the first time and spoke in fair English. "You don't worry, Sam T. We catch them fast." She rode past Sam, jerking on the lead of the reluctant packhorse. He shook his head in disbelief over the whole matter. He only wished he were as confident as his assistants.

By twilight they crossed a high range and coursed up a wide canyon between two sets of hills. Too-Gut was scouting ahead, while Jesus rode with Sam T. and Da-yah.

"Tomorrow, if we haven't found these killers," Sam T. said with a sigh, "we'll have to forget about them for a while."

"They have to rest. They will be at a place called Miguel's Cantina," Jesus said matter-of-factly.

Sam glanced at him in surprise. "What sort of place is it?"

"One for bad hombres." Jesus' solemn face punctuated the seriousness of the location.

"What makes you think they're going there?"

"Because, Sam T., there is no place else to go." Jesus turned in the saddle and gestured at the cactus-studded land in the low twilight. Sam supposed Jesus was right. He would just have to trust the Mexican's judgment.

Later, a crescent moon rose. The three of them squatted on a ridge that overlooked the cantina. The yellow lights of Miguel's flickered on the dark floor of the valley below. Too-Gut had already been down there and inspected the place.

"Packhorses there, Sam T. Eight of them. Have wet backs, but the guns are gone."

"Did they take them inside?"

"No boxes inside. Only three men and a woman," Too-Gut said

"Miguel has a Papago wife," Jesus said, to explain the woman there.

"And the men inside the bar—what are they doing?" Sam asked, shifting a little in his uncomfortable squatting position. Maybe someday he'd get used to this business of sitting on his heels.

"One is perhaps Miguel. The other two have big time. Very drunk," Too-Gut said with a smile in his voice.

"Where in the hell are the guns?" Sam wondered aloud.

"Maybe," Jesus said slyly, "the drunk men will want to tell us, no?"

Sam nodded, pushed up and stretched his back. Puzzled by the events of the day, he turned and absently took his reins from Da-yah. He mounted the sorrel and waited for his assistants to do the same. Then they began the descent down to the cantina.

"Let me go in there first," he said. "They won't suspect me. I'll tell them I'm lost." The others agreed with a nod.

Sam T. drew up alone in front of the cantina and dismounted heavily. Too-Gut and Jesus lingered behind so they could station themselves strategically around the cantina.

"Good evening, señor," a voice greeted him from the dimly lit doorway when he hitched his horse.

"Hello."

"You are lost, señor?" the man asked in a heavy Mexican accent.

"Maybe. But I could sure use a meal and some whiskey," Sam said pleasantly.

"Ah. Come into Miguel's," the man invited.

When Sam T. entered the low-ceilinged adobe structure, he immediately noted the two men at the bar. They stopped drinking and eyed him suspiciously.

"What's your business here?" the taller one demanded. Sam T. realized that, even drunk, these men would be deadly. He calculated that Jesus and Too-Gut had had enough time to be in place.

A woman shouted from the back of the cantina. The men whirled and drew upon her.

Sam T. dropped to his knees, the .45 in his hand. His gun kicked and the roar of pistols blasted the room. Sam's bullet caught the taller outlaw in the chest and sent him sprawling backward onto a table. The outlaw's bullet smashed into the glass behind the bar. Miguel gave a shout of pain that for a second took Sam's attention from second outlaw. Deciding to run, the shorter one headed for the back, but Too-Gut's rifle cut him down before he reached the rear doorway.

Sam T. watched the man crumple to the floor and knew he was no longer a threat. Acrid gun smoke rose in a gray cloud enveloping the room.

"*Madre de Dios!*" Miguel shouted. Sam T. turned and noticed that the cantina owner had been shot in the shoulder. He crossed the room and glared down at Miguel. "Where are those rifles?"

"I am a poor man, señor. I know nothing of any rifles."

"You see that Apache?" Sam T. said, gesturing with his thumb at Too-Gut. "He's a Chiricahua. I'll let him have your mangy hide, and he'll get the damned truth out of you. So you better get to talking fast."

"I did not know these men who brought the packhorses. Miguel minds his own business," the cantina owner whined and hugged his wounded arm.

"I want a name."

"I do not know, señor." The man's eyes were pleading as he protested.

"Too-Gut," Sam shouted, "get over here!"

"Oh, Mother of God," the man gasped. "I don't know these men. Many strangers came and took the boxes from them." He flung his hand out at the dead men. "Then they rode away."

"And who are these dead outlaws here?"

Miguel shrugged and averted his eyes from the prone outlaws on his floor. "One is Jeff. One is Salty. They rode here today. I have only seen this Jeff before. A week ago he came in here."

"From which direction?" Sam demanded.

Miguel bit his lip, glanced at Too-Gut, then answered with a gulp. "South."

Sam T. looked questioningly at Jesus, who shook his head.

"He is very much afraid, Sam T. I think he is telling all that he knows."

"Check their pockets." Sam pursed his lips. Two dead men in exchange for two more was a poor average. And it was worse when he had no leads. A load of rifles was on its way to who knew where, and if that wasn't bad enough, the rifles were loaded on fresh horses. He would never catch them and save Mrs. Stauffer too.

Scowling in disgust, Sam T. moved behind the bar and took down an unbroken bottle of whiskey. He used his teeth to uncork it, then took a long swallow from the neck.

"There is a note in this man's pocket," Jesus said.

"Let me have it." He took another drink of the bitter whiskey, the fumes stinging his nostrils. Then he sat the bottle down and reached for the piece of paper that Jesus extended to him.

It was badly creased at the folds, and sweat had caused the ink to run. Sam turned the paper up to the light. All he could make out was one word, *more*, and he wasn't too sure that was right. Besides, the word didn't make any sense.

"I can't read the damned thing. It's too messed up. How much money they got on them?"

"Maybe two hundred dollars." Jesus dropped the twenty-dollar gold eagles on the bar. He picked up the bottle of whiskey and sampled it. "Whew! This is bad whiskey."

Sam T. agreed with a nod, thinking of Tia's words. "Don't drink any more of it. Where's Miguel's woman? Maybe she can doctor him. It looks like he's only scratched."

Da-yah nodded, disappeared and came back shoving a thickset Indian woman into the room.

"I will get the man to talk plenty," Too-Gut said, making it more of an offer.

"No, no. I think he's said all he knows. Here," Sam T. said, handing Too-Gut the bottle, "have some bad whiskey." The Apache took the bottle, drank some and then grinned big like it was good.

Jesus made a face at the Apache's thirst of the firewater and shook his head. "What now?"

"We need to head west. We'll never catch those gunrunners with their fresh horses."

"Sí. It will take all night to get to Verde City," Jesus said, taking the bottle from Too-Gut.

Sam picked up the coins from the bar. "Two hundred dollars for a wagonload of rifles and four men's lives. Come on, let's get out of here. Miguel can bury these two outlaws."

Sam T.'s shoulders slumped when he walked outside to his horse. He would need to send a report of this incident to the major. Perhaps Bowen could alert other lawmen about the stolen rifle shipment.

Already he and his assistants had lost a valuable day. It was a precious amount of time for a kidnapped woman to have to wait.

CHAPTER 10

Lamas studied Don Ramon Marques across the heavy table. *El patron* was a man in his mid-fifties, his silvery hair meticulously slicked back. He wore many thick gold rings on his thin fingers, and his jacket was a beautifully embroidered velvet garment.

Smiling to himself, Lamas lifted the goblet of wine. Who would have thought, when he was a boy in the village, that he would someday feast as an equal with such a powerful man as Don Ramon?

"Any news, my friend," Marques asked, "about the shipment of those rifles?" He paused and sipped some wine before he continued. "I will be most grateful for their delivery."

"*Sí, Patron*," Lamas said noncommittally. "My man has gone to Nogales to check on them. Delivery of freight sometimes is slow."

"I understand. I am grateful for your hard work on my behalf."

Lamas wondered if the man knew about this gringo with the big ransom in Nogales. He considered how he should phrase his question.

"Ah, Don Ramon, do you know of an American called Narrimore?"

"Ah, yes, my friend. He is a very rich and powerful Americano from Tucson. His name is Daniel Narrimore."

"What does he do?"

"Gold and silver mining. He has some claims in Mexico. Very rich man. I have been to his fine house in Tucson."

Lamas expressed no surprise at the information. So the man who offered a reward for the woman owned many mines. It was all very interesting; Lamas mulled on the matter. That large a ransom for the woman looked so tempting. He must plan it carefully.

He smiled and raised his goblet. "I will soon have those guns for you, Don Ramon."

"Ah, good. We are all good friends, amigo. Of course, I will pay you well." He raised his glass. "To our friendship."

When a servant entered the room, Marques looked at him impatiently. "Well, what is it?"

"Someone wishes to speak to Señor Lamas."

"Who is it?"

"A peon."

"Let him wait." Don Ramon scowled at the man. "We are in the middle of our meal."

"*Sí, señor.* But this man, he said it is very important." The servant looked pained and concerned about the matter.

It might be important. Lamas placed the linen napkin from his lap beside his silver plate, then smiled at his host. "Excuse me, Don Marques. I will speak to this peon and send him on his way."

Lamas's heels clicked across the tile floor as he hurried toward the entrance. What stupid one was here to disturb his meal with the *patron*? He would kill the dumb bastard for such an intrusion.

When he entered the vestibule, he saw his gardener Pedro. His hat was in his hand, his face downcast. Something bad was wrong at the hacienda. Lamas did not like the looks of this. The gardener waited silently until Lamas had dismissed the don's servant.

"Señor Lamas, you must come at once! The woman, she has escaped."

"Escaped! You lie. How could she escape?" Lamas asked under his breath. That stupid Jimmy had let her get away. He would pay with his life.

"I am sorry, but they rode away yesterday."

"Yesterday! Ride your horse like the wind, Pedro. Go get Sanchez. Tell him—" Lamas stopped abruptly, reading in the man's face that there was something more he had to say. "What—what else is wrong?"

"I have only a burro; the women, they have stolen all your horses too. Every one, they took them all." Pedro made a wide sweep with his white sleeve to demonstrate.

"Stolen all my horses!" Lamas shouted. He would stake that Jimmy to an anthill, pour honey on him and laugh as the ants devoured his flesh.

"You take my horse. I will borrow one from Don Ramon. Go ride and tell Sanchez to come to my hacienda quickly." He watched his servant hurry away.

Shaken by the news, he shook his head in disbelief. All of his horses gone? Struggling to regain his composure, Lamas turned and walked slowly back to the dining room. He forced a smile at his host.

"Is something wrong?"

"My man, he worries." Lamas shrugged, taking his place at the table. "Someone has stolen some of my horses."

"Oh, is that all?" Marques burst into laughter. "Even from Lamas they steal."

"Yes. Even from me." Lamas forced himself to join in the mirth. "Even from me they steal. But I have sent this man to get my best tracker. Justice will be swift."

"Yes, amigo," Don Ramon agreed soberly. "Horse thieves must be handled quickly and severely. Sit and eat. There will be time later to catch these felons."

"Certainly," Lamas said unconcernedly, although inwardly he seethed with angry impatience. There would be time enough to catch them, he tried to reassure himself. Later, he would ask His Excellency for a horse, although he knew it would cause more laughter at his expense.

He lifted his goblet, his eyes on the regal-looking man across the table. Mary Gonzales, you village *puta*, with the clap, he mused, if only you could see me now. I, the village *bastardo*, have become a leader of men, and now I eat with great men of power. And I too have beautiful clothes such as Don Ramon's. He smiled smugly as he looked down at the red silk shirt he wore, the cuffs and pockets outlined with black silken threads.

Sipping his wine thoughtfully, Lamas continued to allow his mind to wander. It lingered on the white woman and her naked body. Why did he crave her more than any woman he had before? Why was she the first woman to satisfy him? He'd made love to hundreds of women. He tried to dismiss the matter, but the image of her form remained branded in his mind. No escaping from that fact. How had she gotten away? Where would she go? By herself she would be easy to recapture. But if the Indian girl guided her, it might be a much more difficult task. Sanchez would find them. If anyone could locate them, it was the Yaqui.

* * *

The desert grew chilly in the hours just before dawn. Justine crouched in a dry wash, her arms wrapped tightly around her body like a cocoon, trying to maintain the little body warmth she had. Her legs had grown numb from stooping so long, but she dared not sit on the desert floor. She knew that there were snakes and insects around. Insects frightened her as much as the reptiles. Once, years before, she had been stung by a scorpion that crawled from under her bed. Her foot became swollen to the size of a melon and pain filled her for days. Now, remembering the incident, she hastily checked the area around her feet.

Angela had not returned. Hours ago, it seemed, the girl had gestured for her to stay put while she went off on her own. Justine surmised that she intended to search for water. The only fluid they had was from a barrel cactus Angela had slashed open the previous day with Jimmy's knife. It tasted bitter, Justine recalled, but the mushy pulp sustained them and their horses.

"Señora Yusteen!" Angela hissed.

Justine turned in the darkness, her heart racing at the sound of the voice. "Did you find water?"

Every cramped muscle in her body protested when she rose to her feet. Her spine felt as though it would never be straight again. Erect at last, she hurried toward the sound of Angela's voice, dragging the reins of her stubborn horse behind her.

Angela acted engrossed in the towering bluffs. Then she signaled for Justine to follow her. The narrow pathway through the sparse brush led deeper into the canyon, with dizzy-high cliffs above them. The pink light of dawn crept slowly over the towering walls.

Justine stopped short of the source and blinked. The only indication that water was in the basin were the damp rocks surrounding it. Fed by a small trickle from the foot of the stone face, the small pool looked so inviting, she could hardly believe it existed.

Whimpering with joy, Justine sank to her knees and lowered her face to sip from it like a cat. Irritably she pushed back the gun belt that dangled from her neck, the pistol digging into her ribs. She relished the cold sting of the icy water on her sun-baked cheeks. The water pained her swollen throat and she had difficulty swallowing; then it ran down her insides, sinking into a hard knot in her empty stomach.

Her thirst quenched, Justine sank back on her heels and grinned up at Angela. Thank God for the girl. Angela could have left her shivering in the dry wash for Lamas to find, but instead her new friend had returned for her. Sighing, she struggled to her feet and stepped out of the way so that her horse could drink his fill. Then she held the reins of both horses while Angela drank again.

Shifting the irksome cartridge belt, Justine looked around at the granite bluffs. There was a jackrabbit sitting beside a nearby rock, obviously waiting its turn at the drinking pool.

Justine looked hungrily at the rabbit, but knew it would not be wise to shoot the gun, not even for food. The sound would only draw attention to their presence. She sighed, wishing they at least had a canteen to fill with water, but even that small luxury was denied them.

"Yusteen. Vamoose!" Angela turned and gestured toward the north.

Justine nodded wearily. It was time to ride again. The calves of her legs complained as she mounted, and her back ached as she tried to straighten in the saddle.

Single file, the women rode out of the canyon and headed across a broad stretch of desert. Justine was long past pangs of hunger. She was weak from the lack of food, and the water she drank sloshed nauseatingly in her rumbling stomach.

She turned in the saddle to look behind her. There was nothing in the distance. Nothing but the hot wind to sweep the low brush and saw-edged mountains. Perhaps Lamas would not follow them. But she knew that was a frail hope. The man would follow as surely as night followed day. He was too proud, too arrogant to be beaten by a mere woman. And she also knew there was a smoldering attraction there—with him—toward her. Even in the stubbornness of her condition she had begun to realize the change. Animal-like, perhaps. Their bizarre relationship had grown into something different than the raw rutting by him the first time. She only knew for certain that the whole dimension of this outlaw Lamas scared her. With her heels, she booted the horse on faster to catch up with Angela.

Lamas raced Don Marques's horse back to his hacienda. Whipping and spurring, he crossed the many miles with no concern for the poor animal's condition. It had been reckless to go so fast under starlight, but fury overwhelmed any caution. He dismounted the lathered horse and left it grunting for its breath at the front gate.

"Leta! You dumb bitch of a housekeeper, where are you?" he shouted, charging up the dark hallway.

"*Sí, Patron?*" a subdued voice called out of the darkness.

"Where is Jimmy?"

"Gone."

"What do you mean, gone?"

The middle-aged woman stood in the lit doorway, wringing her hands in fear. "He ran away after we untied him."

"Untied him?"

"He was tied up in the women's room."

Lamas drew a deep breath. The stupid boy had done exactly what he had been warned not to do; he had messed with the gringo woman. And that whore and the Indian girl had obviously outsmarted that dim-witted, pimple-faced bastard.

"When we took the meal to the woman's room," the housekeeper explained haltingly, "He—he was on the floor. The women were gone. So I untied Jiminez. He swore at us when we ungagged him. I was very afraid, señor."

"Yes, you have good reason to be frightened, you stupid old bitch!" Lamas unleashed his temper on the woman. "Go find me some mescal at once." Still filled with rage, he headed for the dining room, his heels clattering on the floor. There was nothing he could do until daylight. Sanchez and the others would be back at the hacienda by then. He kicked out at a floor vase, sending it crashing against the wall. Next time, you gringo whore, he vowed silently . . . next time, I shall chain your shapely ass to the wall.

He sank down on a chair and closed his eyes. He would get that bitch back. She was worth a lot of money. Besides, he was not finished with her supple body. A vision of her smooth skin against his darker skin was enough to send a violent flash of frustration through him. Sanchez would track them down. And he would have his leader's permission to cut the Indian witch's throat. She was the one who had led the white woman away. No doubt she cast a spell on that stupid Jimmy too. Señora Stauffer was no match for the harshness of the desert, but the squaw was. Perhaps she would even be a match for Sanchez. No, no. Lamas shook his head. His rat-faced tracker would hunt them down. And then . . . then Lamas would laugh in the face of the defeated señora.

Yes, he would laugh.

* * *

Miles north in Arizona, Sam T. rose with the coming dawn. He and his assistants had stopped to rest the horses. Da-yah was cooking beans on a small fire. She wore a dress made of many men's shirts. Squatted at the small, smokeless fire, she studied her cooking pot intently.

"The major will get us papers?" Too-Gut asked. He leaned against a cottonwood tree, his unblocked hat shading his face. He wore a faded blue noncom's shirt that came halfway to his knees. His thin pants were tucked down in calf-high Apache boots. Sam T. noted the old repeater in his arms. The gun was like an extension of the Indian, never out of reach.

"If he can."

Too-Gut nodded. "Major plenty big man. Army jumps when he gets mad."

Sam pursed his lips and shook his head regretfully. The major had given him no special document that would allow the Chiricahuas to stay with him. In fact, Sam's own authority as a civilian barely stretched enough to send the shavetail lieutenant away when he threatened Jesus.

"Major is good man," Too-Gut said. "Him send paper soon. San Carlos is like a shithouse. Bad place to live. Why can't we stay in the mountains?"

Without an answer, he shrugged. Sam T. silently hoped that the Apache was right about those papers. He had never seen this San Carlos, but if this man complained, it must be the pit of the world.

Jesus returned from watering the horses at a spring. "Where should we go next?"

"How far away is Verde City from here?" Sam asked.

"Couple of hours."

"Good, I want to go there and talk to that stage agent. Judge Tripp said he might be able to furnish us some

descriptions of these men. We could use that. Right now
we could walk by them and never know anything." He
studied the ocher-colored pipes of stone on the side of
mountain base. A hot, barren country full of stickery
plants. The two scouts and Da-yah acted as comfortable
in it as the lizards that darted about on the dusty ground.
He thought of something else. The hell that poor woman
must be having if she was still alive.

If those men had harmed her . . . He sighed. Of course
they had harmed her. Men who cold-bloodedly shot robbery victims held small quarter with hostages. Only if
they hoped for a big ransom, would she remain safe.

Sam T. and his three assistants rode south. Jesus
reminded him of Frederic Remington's pen-and-ink
drawing in the *Harper's Weekly* of a Mexican bandit. The
barrel-chested Too-Gut and his woman made strange-
appearing deputies. But he was satisfied that they were
veterans of the land, and law enforcement was not too
disconnected with their military experience.

"Does the stage agent know much about the gang?"
Jesus asked when they mounted up.

"Well, according to Judge Tripp, if the man's still alive
he can give us a complete description of them." Sam T.
reined Big Boy around and booted him out with Jesus'
bay. "Judge said he understood the stage line paid big
bounties to informers and they might know something
more."

"I didn't ask the man," Jesus began, "but if we find this
whole gang, will the major send us help?"

"Jesus . . ."—Sam T. paused a long time before he
finished—"I'm afraid we're it." The scout's small sound
of acknowledgment told him enough—he understood.

They rode on in silence. By midday they were back
beside the Santa Cruz River, north of Verde City. Sam T.

was grateful for the few cottonwoods along the stream. They provided some shade from the blistering sun.

"Verde City is just over the rise," Jesus said.

"We'd better leave the Apaches here. There might be another army patrol," Sam T. said.

"Too-Gut, you stay close by," Sam T. said. "Jesus will come and get you when we're ready to move on."

Too-Gut nodded, then he and Da-yah crossed the nearly dry stream. The woman jerked on the packhorse that was lagging behind her. Sam T. watched them go and felt a surge of sympathy. They were people without a home.

Sam T. shook his head, set spurs to the sorrel and followed Jesus toward town.

They rode up the main street. Verde City was a small cluster of adobe buildings with a hotel, a house of ill repute, two saloons that were two stories tall and a smattering of small stores. Halsey and Talbert's Stage Office looked to be the hub of activity. A wheelwright worked respoking a wagon, a blacksmith fitted a team with shoes. His hammer rang as he forged new shoes, and the smell of burning coal filled the air.

"Could I help you?" a friendly man asked, waving a cigar from the doorway of the stage office.

"We have a mutual friend, I believe," Sam T. said and dismounted. "Judge Tripp? My name's Sam T. Mayes, and this is Jesus Morales."

"How do. Any friend of the judge's is welcome here. Come on in. I've got whiskey and some damned bad coffee inside. Oh, yeah, my name's Taggett. Marsh Taggett."

Sam ducked when he followed Taggett through the low doorway. Jesus' rowels clanged as he came behind Sam. The dusty office was low-ceilinged and Sam had to keep his head bent to prevent scraping it with his hat.

"Whiskey or coffee?" Taggett offered.

"Coffee's fine. For both of us."

Taggett looked at Sam and raised his brows. "Mayes, this batch of coffee is damned bad."

"Coffee's fine," Sam repeated. Jesus nodded in agreement.

The three men sat in the cool room, sipping the bitter brew. Taggett reviewed what he knew about the stage robbery.

"This Lamas . . ." Taggett said, looking at Jesus, "do you know him, Morales?"

"He is a very mean one."

Sam T. listened silently. Jesus had not mentioned to him that he personally knew the outlaw. The fact bothered Sam until he realized that most likely Jesus had said it simply to keep Taggett talking.

"Well, this Lamas and his gang went back across the border after the robbery. Mrs. Stauffer and the Indian girl were alive then."

"You're sure?" Sam demanded of the stage line manager.

"Yes, but that was several days ago. Someone saw both women and they didn't look too abused. Grundy's stepdaughter Angela and the Stauffer woman from Tucson."

The words "too abused" conjured up an ugly image that filled Sam with helpless rage. Those outlaws had to be brought to justice. A border was no excuse to allow criminals to do as they pleased.

Taggett's grim voice captured Sam T.'s attention again. He listened carefully to every scrap of information that Taggett gave them. He became impressed with the man's knowledge of these elusive criminals.

"Lamas has a hacienda in Sonora. They call it Los Palmos, means 'palms.'" Tagget waved his index finger at them to make his point. "It's well guarded. You can't ride within fifty miles of it. Men have tried and their bones are bleaching the ground down there now."

"What about the men who ride with Lamas?" Sam T. asked. "Have you learned anything about them?"

"Yeah, a little. Grundy told me before he died that one was a tall Texan called Ezra Black. He's a horse thief. A Texan who's handy with a gun and he likes women. Someone saw him in Nogales this week."

"Jesus?" Sam turned to him. "Do you know Black?"

"Only by sight. I have seen him in Tucson, maybe a few times. But I didn't know he was a gang member."

"See, that's their secret," Taggett said and shook his head in disgust. "They meet and strike and don't stay together like that damn Clanton bunch does. You two get really greedy for more bounties, you can go clean them Clantons out."

Sam T. nodded to indicate he heard the man and shared a private look with Jesus. Taggett thought they were bounty hunters—good.

"Does Black know you?" Sam T. asked Jesus.

"No. I am not a famous person."

"Good." They laughed before Sam turned to Taggett. "Well, what about the sheriff?"

"Saguaro County doesn't have a real sheriff," Taggett said grimly. "Oh, they've got one, but he spends all his time in Tombstone worrying about his mining interest or his politics."

"Sounds as if you aren't too impressed with the man."

"Impressed? With our stages being robbed, two mining experts shot and a society woman kidnapped? Hell, Mayes, that driver died and so did Grundy, and it ain't easy to find someone to run that stage stop between Nogales and Coyote Wells. And that tub of lard Sheriff Wainwright and his grubby deputy haven't done one damned thing about it. Not one thing."

"Wonder where Stauffer was headed," Sam mused aloud.

"Word has it that he was on his way to see Sheriff Wainwright. I'm not so sure about that."

"If he was going to Tombstone, why did he come this way and not the Benson route?" Jesus asked.

Taggett frowned and rubbed his chin. "Good question, unless he was avoiding being seen. I looked through some papers that were found scattered around the stage stop after the robbery. They were a report on a Tombstone mine. I gave them to Wainwright's deputy to pass on to him, since they had the sheriff's name on one of them."

"I see," Sam T. said slowly. He didn't actually understand all the implications, but for the moment he let the matter pass. "Taggett, you know anything about a gun shipment?"

Taggett frowned for a moment. "No, but we do sometimes haul that kind of freight."

Sam decided to let the matter drop. "Well, I appreciate your help. Jesus and I need to get moving."

"There's a two-hundred-dollar reward for the gang from my company," Taggett said. "Twenty-five a piece for those gang members. But a hundred for Lamas."

Sam rose from the chair. Rewards seldom brought in criminals. They did produce information occasionally, but usually from some informer hoping for a percentage. He looked down at Taggett with a sudden thought. "Has there been any word about a reward for Mrs. Stauffer?"

"Strange you mention that, Mayes. Someone from Tombstone put out some feelers. He's offered a thousand dollars for her safe return."

"Who's he? A family friend?"

"Beats me, Mayes. Could be a friend. He's a rich and powerful man. Name's Dan Narrimore."

"Why would a friend offer that much money?"

Taggett shrugged. "Narrimore's a slick one. If he intends to pay that kind of money, there must be something in it for him." Taggett stood and followed them the door. "You two aim to take on the whole Border Gang?" His voice was filled with skepticism.

Sam looked at him through narrowed eyes, stung by the man's doubts. "We'll handle it."

"I will say you got guts." Tagget shook his head like he wasn't certain that was a good idea. "Nice to meet you both. Good luck."

As they rode back to where they had left the Apaches, Sam T. was mired in thought. The closer they got to the Border Gang, the farther away they seemed. The day was practically gone. They'd have to make camp for the night and start with first light. Even the big sorrel needed some rest. The pony Jesus rode had to be spurred to move.

"How far to this place of Lamas's?" he asked Jesus.

"I have never been there." He shook his head.

Sam searched the growing twilight. He had a feeling they were being watched.

When Jesus gave a sharp quail's whistle, Sam T. realized that the Apaches were returning. He seriously considered how he and his three assistants could go up against a whole gang of killers. Looked like, before long, he'd see how strong a force he had gathered for the role of Territorial Marshal. On the other hand, he'd be damned if he was going to give up.

Justine Stauffer had never eaten rattlesnake. She was not sure that she could force it past her tongue. Yet the desert beans that Angela had gathered proved a meager offering for her hollow stomach. She needed some kind of sustenance.

Earlier, Justine's horse shied from the sidewinder's buzz. Instantly the brown-eyed Angela handed Justine her reins and slipped from her horse. Within minutes, the snake was smashed with a rock, dressed and packed away for their evening meal.

Marveling at her companion's skill, Justine handed back Angela's reins and once again they headed north. There was still no sign of pursuit. They had traveled a great distance on their spent horses. Whenever possible they stopped under a rimrock's shade to rest them, then walked on foot for miles, leading the weary animals. Angela constantly checked the ground they passed over, brushing it several times with a branch of smelly grease-wood to erase their tracks.

The only signs of life were lizards and an occasional jackrabbit that they didn't dare shoot for food, lest the sound of the shot give their location away to any pursuers.

Twice they stopped so that Angela could cut open a barrel cactus. Justine was grateful for the alkaline-tasting mush. She knew had it not been for girl's skill in the desert, she would have long since perished.

Later in the evening Justine squatted to watch Angela start a fire. It took a long time, since they had no matches. The Indian girl patiently used a length of material torn from her ragged skirt hem as drive belt to twist a stick back and forth, until finally the friction at the point caught some tiny tinder on fire.

Forced into this animal-like existence, Justine scowled at her gritty skin and sour-smelling clothes. The insides of her thighs were rubbed raw from riding astride the horse, and her neck was sore from the heavy cartridge belt that she wore like a necklace. When she imagined what she must look like, she had to force back tears of self-pity.

Angela cooked the rattlesnake slowly. The wonderful aroma of the cooked meat made Justine dizzy. She gratefully accepted the hot food from Angela's fingers. Chewing slowly, she tried to shut her mind to the source of meat she was eating. To her amazement, Justine found the meat sweet and flaky. It flooded her mouth with saliva. She waited eagerly for her next bite.

A coyote howled in the distance. Only two days previously the same sound would have driven Justine to panic. But now she shrugged, deciding the animal was probably after a desert rat or rabbit. She did not begrudge him his food. Never again, she vowed, would she look down upon beggars or bums. And when she finally escaped this mess, she never wanted to be dirty or hungry again.

"Good food," she complimented Angela.

The girl grunted and nodded cheerfully. She punched Justine on the arm and muttered some Indian words.

"Yes," Justine said as if she understood. "We make one helluva pair."

Then they both began to laugh. It started with a giggle, then a chuckle that ran on to hysterical amusement. Justine plopped her bottom on the ground and shook with mirth.

Finally, weak with laughter, she rubbed her fists into her eyes. At least the tears of mirth soothed her burning pupils. She wished there were a way to repay Angela for her kindness and help, but she knew there wasn't.

The coyote howled again and its mate answered. Justine settled her back against a warm rock. She dared not lie down on the ground, even though she had finally given in enough to sit upon it. The desire to curl up with her head on her hands was strong, but the image of the snake prevented her from taking that chance. A cold chill swept over her as she recalled the coiled serpent, and for a moment nausea rose inside her. To think she had eaten the snake! She hugged herself for warmth and dropped off into an uneasy sleep. It was only their second night out in the desert.

Lamas became furious. He stalked the house, peering out to the east for signs of the returning gardener and Sanchez. Where in the hell were they?

At dawn he saddled Don Marques's horse and searched about for his own horses. But he found no sign of them. The borrowed gelding had drawn up lame. Lamas blamed himself. His wild ride home on the animal the previous night no doubt did the damage. He headed back on the limping horse, which only added to his fury.

"That Jimmy will pay for this!" Lamas vowed. After he brought the Stauffer woman back, he would go find the stupid boy. Then he would dig a hole neck deep, making sure that it was near an anthill before he placed that blessed Jimmy inside it. A faint wisp of dust appeared in the east. Lamas squinted; perhaps it was a dust-devil wind. No. Someone was coming at last. He could see the rider. It was Sanchez. Grinding his teeth with impatience, Lamas looked across the heat-wave-distorted desert. Now, you white witch, he promised silently, I will catch you and you will pay for the the trouble you have caused me. No one, no one makes a fool of Lamas! His eyes gleamed as he envisioned himself stripping Justine's white body. His hand would land heavily on her round behind, and then . . .

Sam T. and his small posse rode out of Pima County into Saguaro County. Morales led them over a cut in the range of hills. Sam T. wanted to meet Sheriff Wainwright, the man in whose jurisdiction the crime had been committed.

"You said you haven't been to Lamas's hacienda Los Palmos?" Sam asked Jesus as they rode single file up a narrow canyon

"No. Perhaps Too-Gut has been there. It is a very dry land to cross."

Sam T. turned in the saddle and looked at the Apache. "Too-Gut, have you been to this man Lamas's place? They call it Los Palmos."

"Los Palmos. Way down in Sonora?" He made a wave with his hand like he meant in the south. When Sam T. nodded, he continued, "Once, when I was a young brave. The Apaches traded with the old man who owned the place then."

Sam turned his attention back to guiding his horse down the narrow trail. Over his shoulder he asked, "Can we ride there after I see the sheriff?"

"Two hard days," Too-Gut said.

They stopped to rest along the San Pedro River—a shallow, wandering stream that afforded some shade under the rustling cottonwoods, a green oasis in the brown grassland. They watered their animals.

"We wait here," Too-Gut said. "If you need help, we come fast."

"All right. We won't be long. I want to head there as soon as we return." Sam T. started to mount when the Apache shouted at him, "Get a rifle for her." Too-Gut pointed his own long gun at Da-yah. Then a smile crossed his copper face. "Don't worry; she won't shoot you."

Jesus laughed aloud. Sam T. looked from Too-Gut to Jesus.

"I wasn't really worried about her shooting me," he said dryly.

"We know. What Too-Gut meant, Sam T.," Jesus explained, "is that Da-yah is a good shot, and we'll need all our guns if we go to this Lamas's place."

"Yes. I agree," Sam said. If he had misgivings about the bland-faced woman in battle, it still was no excuse to refuse to get her a weapon. "I'll buy her a rifle."

"Good." Too-Gut grunted. Da-yah ignored the conversation concerning her.

Sam T. set out in a short lope with Jesus beside him. He hoped a talk with the lawman in charge of the stage holdup investigation might help settle some more things about the gang. He also had to buy a woman a rifle. He sighed wryly. His new job certainly had a lot of intriguing sideshows to it. At least it wasn't as dull as his desk job.

Tombstone was sleeping midday. A quiet, dusty town with only the sounds of mine machinery pounding and elevator cables whining. Rows of parked ore freight wagons all over. The main street otherwise looked deserted. A cur dog barked a welcome.

Sam T. and Jesus drew up in front of the jail. A man lounged in the doorway. Dressed in a yellowed Union jacket with galluses to hold up wash-worn canvas britches, the man spat on the boardwalk.

Sam raised his eyebrows in mild disapproval at the man's careless appearance. Obviously he was not the sheriff, since his tarnished badge read DEPUTY.

"Sheriff here?" Sam asked.

The man squinted up at them, then turned away insolently to spit. "Who's asking?"

"An officer of the court," Sam said bluntly as he dismounted.

"Well, you're looking at the law in this county."

Sam was not impressed by the statement. "I want all the details on the stage robbery and kidnapping."

"And just what are you going to do about it?" The man's tobacco-stained lips curled in a sneer.

Sam was less than three yards from the man, and it

was only by exerting absolute control that he did not grab his collar and shake him until his yellow teeth rattled in his head.

"Have you done anything about the crime?" he asked pointedly.

"Hell, there ain't nothing I can do. They're in Mexico. Seems they don't honor this badge over there in Sonora." He pointed to Jesus. "Just ask him."

"Have you heard of a request for a ransom?" Sam persisted his questioning.

"I've heard lots of things."

Sam T. looked down at the boardwalk and clenched his teeth. Patience, he knew, was not his strong point and he was having a hell of a hard time reining it in. Drawing a deep breath that should have been a warning to the man, he raised his head.

"Mister, I've been here a good while and I haven't heard a damned thing worth my time. Now, what do you know about these outlaws?" He took a step closer, towering over the slovenly man.

"You're kind of bristly, ain't you?" the man said with a put-on smile and squinting against the sun.

Sam heard Jesus shifting in his saddle. Obviously the scout expected him to flatten the deputy at any minute. Sam continued, "You just leave personalities out of it, Deputy, and start talking about these outlaws."

"What the hell? You ain't going to do no more than I did. I told you that them bastards are in Sonora. They're probably having a good old time drinking tequila, and by now they've sold that woman to white slavers. Just what in the hell do you expect me to do about that?"

"This woman's husband. What was his business coming here?"

"That's the sheriff's business."

"What do you mean?"

The deputy spat off to the side and resumed his position in the doorway. "He told me that him and Stauffer had private business."

"Where is the sheriff now?"

"Gone."

"Damn it!" Sam T. swore and raised a fist, his eyes blazing. Anger billowed inside him so that he almost choked on it. "If you don't find some civil words, I'm going to jerk that tongue out of your brassy mouth. Now, I'm asking you again. Where's the sheriff?"

The man sobered instantly, realizing Sam T. was dangerously close to losing his temper. "I told you, mister, he's gone on some business, I guess. But when he's away, I'm in charge."

"Yes, I can see that," Sam said with an edge of sarcasm. "What's your name?"

"Dormer. Clyde Dormer."

"I'll remember it." Sam started to leave, stopped and turned. "When do you expect the sheriff back?"

"Couple of days, I reckon. You can check back then."

"We will, Deputy, we, will." He unhitched his horse. "Jesus, we've got supplies to get." His scout nodded at him and reined his horse away.

"Hey!" Dormer called after them. "You and that greaser plan to go down there? Don't tell anyone that I didn't warn you. You'll be buzzard bait. Them buzzards down there are hungry too."

Sam T. ignored the man, but grunted in disgust at their having wasted all that time. When he glanced over, Jesus looked about to laugh. They rode up the street.

"That man rattled you pretty bad, no?"

"Did it show?"

"Show?" Jesus slapped his large saddle horn with the palm of his hand. "*Sí*, it showed."

"His kind of law irritates the hell out of me. No wonder

this territory needs marshals. Let's get that rifle and some supplies. What do those Apaches like?"

"Whiskey."

"Forget that."

"Candy?" Jesus suggested. "I forgot that it is against the law for Indians to have whiskey."

"It's not that," Sam T. explained. "We'll need clear heads to find those outlaws. We can drink whiskey afterward." He wondered if there would be an afterward. If Dormer was right, then that poor woman was already on her way to Mexico City. That thought did not soothe his disposition.

Before Sam T. and Jesus left town, Sam made a trip to the telegrapher's office. He sent off a wire to the major, requesting papers for his two loyal Apaches.

CHAPTER 11

The insides of Justine's thighs were on fire from chafing against the saddle leather. The muscles in her arms turned rock-hard, and despite the floppy straw hat, the sun still scorched her face. She dismounted stiffly, clung to the saddle, until her sea legs grew steady enough to support her weight.

Four ugly buzzards circled above her. She averted her gaze from the big birds and spotted Angela. The Indian girl had ridden up a barren slope to scan the country beyond them.

Justine shaded her eyes with her hand, too weary to even think about their pursuers. She dropped down and sat on the ground, with her hands spread out to support herself. Her horse blew out a weary breath that sent a whirling spiral of dust up Justine's nose and into her mouth. She spat it away with indifference.

There was no more snake to eat, and only a few shriveled prickly pears and alkali-tasting cactus to sustain them. The warm pulpy plant soured on her empty stomach, nearly gagging her. Only the moisture she had derived from it made the chewy substance worthwhile. In a moment of desperation, she smeared the pulp on her scorched face and received momentary relief on her burning skin.

"Yusteen!" Angela shouted and motioned with her arm. "Andelay."

The girl pointed east and seemed anxious for Justine to join her on the rise. Wearily she pushed to her feet and clumsily mounted her horse. She dug her heels into the tired pony's side, wondering what was wrong now. What did Angela want to show her that was so important it couldn't wait until she had rested for a moment? She was surprised her stamina had lasted this long. If they didn't find some kind of sanctuary soon, Justine thought with a sigh, she wouldn't know what to do.

When she joined Angela, the girl grinned at her. What for?

"*Agua*," Angela said.

"Water?" Justine croaked. "Where? Where's the water?" She wanted to drown herself in it and put an end to this miserable fugitive existence.

Angela led the way down the slope. Beyond the next hill, Justine blinked her eyes in disbelief at what she beheld. Before them stood a crumbling wall and behind it rose glorious green trees. The closer they drew to the verdant island, the harder she prayed it wasn't another mirage. Dear God, don't . . . When she opened her sore eyes again, she expected it to have dissolved from her vision. No, it hadn't. It was an abandoned hacienda.

Although the walls were fallen-down stretches of rock and adobe, the place appeared to be a real oasis. The pool was a square-shaped tank skimmed over with a light layer of green moss.

Undaunted by the scum, Justine dismounted quickly and stumbled toward the water. Impatiently, she struggled to push the gun belt over her head and remove her shoes. Without hesitating, she plunged fully clothed into the water, creating a great splash that dampened the surrounding rocks and dry ground. The water felt warm, like a soothing cradle of comfort for her shattered body. Justine luxuriated in the cloudy liquid, allowing it to saturate her clothes. She cupped her hands and bathed her heated face; then, making a spout with her hands, she sprayed the tepid water over her hot head.

Angela led the horses to the water's edge and stood watching in amusement at her companion's antics. A delighted smile spread across her brown face as she nodded her approval over their discovery.

"Come on in, Angela," Justine invited with a throaty laugh. Playfully, she splashed the girl. Angela giggled and stepped back.

"*Uno momento*—" the girl pleaded and pointed to the grass in back where she was taking the horses. Justine agreed, then turned back to the luxurious pleasures of bathing.

After the horses drank their fill, Angela led them through an arched wall toward the green trees.

At last, weak with exhaustion, Justine crawled out of the pool and sat on the rock wall that surrounded the hacienda. The sun immediately began to dry out her clothes and hair. She ran her fingers through the long tangled curls and wished for a comb. Half asleep and relaxed, she gazed around at the weathered hacienda. Taking care to spread her skirt over her knees, she held it away from her legs so it would dry quickly. It seemed odd that anyone would abandon a wonderful hacienda like this. At one time it must have been a delightful place. Even now some of the graceful structure remained intact, indicating people of good breeding once inhabited the welcome oasis.

A frown drew her brows together. Where had Angela

gotten to? It had been some time now since she had taken the horses around the building toward the shady trees.

Reluctantly, Justine rose, pulled the still-damp dress material away from her skin where she sat on it and moved toward her weapon, which she had left by the pool. The hated gun belt lay beside her shoes.

The sound of approaching horses startled her. She searched around for Angela. But there was no sign of the girl. Her heart pounded in apprehension. Justine moved quickly toward the gun belt.

The drum of the hooves drew closer. To her attuned ears, it sounded like an army of bandits descending upon her. Moaning in fear, she fell upon the revolver and wrestled it from the holster. She had no idea if she could actually pull the trigger. But a vision of Lamas's face, obsessed with his desire for her body, overwhelmed her. If it was Lamas riding to the hacienda, she could imagine herself putting a bullet through his black heart.

With hands that trembled uncontrollably, Justine held the wavering Colt at chest level. Where, oh, where could Angela be? Three men rode into view. Justine squinted her eyes, trying to see their faces beneath their dusty hats. She knew immediately that Lamas was not among them. None of the riders looked faintly familiar. For that she offered up a small silent prayer, but did not lower the gun.

"Mrs. Stauffer! Thank God, you're alive!" the tall man in the lead said, with what sounded like heartfelt relief. "Dan Narrimore sent us to find you. The name's Sid. This here's Pete and Red," he said, jerking his thumb behind him at the other men.

"D-Dan sent you?" Justine echoed. Perhaps she was hearing things. Had the man said Dan Narrimore? Was he actually her savior? She lowered the gun barrel and looked in shocked disbelief at her rescuers.

Sid dismounted in a fluid motion and ran toward her with his arms out. Why did he look so worried . . . ?

"Thank God. Thank God." She reached for this wonderful cowboy's hug, but her arms were too short and she piled on the ground in a black swirling dust devil.

Lamas was furious. He shaded his eyes against the sun. The wide sombrero on his head did little to shield him from the scorching blaze. The horse beneath him stomped a hind foot impatiently. The gelding was one he borrowed from Sanchez, since Don Marques's fine horse had gone lame. A whole day had been lost by going to Sanchez's place to get this mount. Sarge was still not back from his drinking binge. Black was out of his reach. Lamas felt the women drifting farther away from him all the time. There were still no signs to indicate their passage. The stupid women picked the driest direction to travel. Buzzards would probably be the only thing to mark their demise.

No doubt he had lost a thousand-dollar ransom. Still, he refused to give up the chase. The memory of his hands upon Justine's silky skin consumed him in a fever that fried his brain. He was not finished with that bitch.

In the distance, Lamas could see Sanchez returning; the Yaqui had ridden ahead in search of more tracks. Perhaps he found something this time.

"They have passed this way, amigo," Sanchez reported.

"You found signs?"

Sanchez shrugged and looked toward the north. "Perhaps they made it to the old Roble hacienda. It is many miles to go without water, but that squaw may have found a way."

"Quit talking in riddles! Do you think they could make it there or not? If these women are still alive, I want them back!"

"*Sí*. If they are still alive, I will find them for you."

"Your mangy hide may depend on that."

Sanchez did not acknowledge the threat. He turned his horse and set out in a fast trot toward the north. In no hurry, Lamas rode after him, wondering if the women could really make it so far without food or water. Perhaps by nightfall he would have her in his blankets again.

Sam T. found the scrub-juniper- and yucca-studded high desert of the border interesting. Tall grass brushed the belly of Big Boy, and a fat whitetail deer spooked at their approach. He and Jesus rode the stage route along the border en route to Nogales. The foursome had split several hours before. The Apaches went south to scout Lama's hacienda.

Too-Gut assured Sam T. the two of them could scout Lamas's headquarters easier and with less chance of being detected than four could ride up and do it. Too-Gut and Da-yah could slip in close enough to learn the fortresses's strengths and weaknesses. After finding out what they needed to know, the Apaches were to meet Sam and Jesus at a prearranged place southwest of Nogales. The plan made good sense, so they split up.

Jesus thought he and Sam should check in Nogales for any news of Mrs. Stauffer. Perhaps someone was already on their way to ransom her. Maybe there would be more information on the Border Gang there too. It was a time-consuming plan, yet, when Sam weighed his small law force against Lamas's, he realized it would be wiser to wait on the Apaches' report concerning the strength of Lamas's army. They had to have some idea what they were up against. The many unknowns about this situation niggled him as the two rode along.

"Sam T.," Jesus spoke hesitantly as they began to cross a narrow dry wash, "is your badge good in Mexico?"

Sam shrugged. Deep inside he had the same reservations that Jesus shared, but he wasn't going to admit it. "It doesn't really matter, Jesus. We're going to get that gang and bring them back for trial."

"*Sí.*"

When the two rode into Nogales in the late afternoon, the border town bustled with freighters.

"We can go over to my friend's cantina," Jesus suggested.

"We'd better put these horses up first; they're getting a little run-down."

"I know of such a place. Come."

Sam T. ignored the chatter of begging children who ran along beside their horses. Jesus' coarse Spanish words sent them scurrying away.

"There is a certain lady I know who will help us," Jesus said.

Sam smiled. "Oh?"

Jesus looked at him and blinked, then he laughed. "Yes, she is in the business, but that is not what I meant, amigo. Rosita knows everything that happens. She will have some information for us on those outlaws."

"Well, just remember all we need is information," Sam reminded him.

They drew up before a small wagon yard. Jesus was laughing under his breath. "*Sí*, Sam T. Only information this time."

After leaving their horses with the livery, they walked down a narrow street to a cantina. Jesus stepped inside. Sam T. followed, ducking his head to avoid the low rafters.

A buxom woman of about forty shrieked a welcome to Jesus. Spanish words seemed to tumble over themselves as she and the Mexican scout hugged each other. Sam stood by silently, glancing around at the patrons.

When Jesus had finished greeting his lady friend, he introduced her to his boss.

"Rosita, this is Señor Sam T. Mayes."

She smiled, her eyes admiring his tall form and broad shoulders. "My pleasure, Señor Mayes. Come. Rosita has tequila, beer, whatever you would like." She led them to a small table in the corner, then spoke curtly to a thin-faced bartender to bring them some beer.

Seated between the men at the table, she studied Sam's face for a moment. "You are not here for pleasure, no? What do you need?" she asked in a soft whisper.

Jesus looked around; then, keeping his voice low, he asked, "Were is the gringo called Black?"

"He rode out."

"When?"

"I don't know. Maybe two, three days ago. I last heard that he rode out in a big hurry."

"Why?"

Rosita shrugged, then her eyes blazed as if remembering something unpleasant. "If you want to know, then go ask that little bastard Jimmy. He is over at the Rojo. I won't let him in my place."

"He is a gang member too?" Jesus asked.

"Sure. Worthless—" The curl of her lip showed her contempt for him.

"Are you sure?" Sam T. asked. He felt his pulse quicken at the prospect of so easily capturing a member of the gang. To have someone to interrogate too enthused him.

"Of course I am sure. Rosita knows everything that happens in this town." She swung her arms behind both of them and then hung her fingers familiarly on their shoulders.

Sam T. sipped on his glass of beer, looked at the woman over the rim. He frowned thoughtfully. "You know anything about a shipment of rifles?"

The woman's brows rose in surprise. "Rifles?" She pursed her lips as if trying to remember. Slowly, she nodded her head. "*Sí*. A dealer ordered them for a secret customer. A hundred new Winchesters. But they have not arrived."

Sam T. shrugged. His expression clearly telegraphed to Jesus that he did not want to say any more about the rifles to her.

"What about a ransom for the Stauffer woman?" Sam asked, abruptly changing the subject. "You heard anything about that?"

Rosita nodded. "Yes, there is a thousand dollars reward for Señora Stauffer's safe return."

Sam frowned, wondering if the woman had misunderstood him. "Did Lamas send that word?"

"Oh, no, señor! A man in Tombstone offered the money to anyone who found her—alive."

"Who is the man?"

"His name is Narrimore. He had some pistoleros out there looking for her."

Sam recalled that the stage line operator Taggett said that Narrimore had offered a reward. He wondered what this man Narrimore wanted with Mrs. Stauffer. Family friend? And what would he be doing with hired guns? If Narrimore's men located Justine at the hacienda, they might try to shoot it out, getting the woman killed in the process.

"What about this Jimmy?" he leaned over and asked Jesus. Options kept rollng over in his mind. What would be the best way to arrest him and interrogate him about the gang? They had to be inconspicuous and not rile up the Mexican authorities.

"I can find him, Sam T.," Jesus said confidently.

"Fine. But when you do, you come get me. Don't try to take him on your own."

"*Sí.*" Jesus stood up and put on his sombrero. "One thing. I could use a few pesos for a beer or two."

Sam looked at him with a small smile. He rose and dug two silver dollars out of his pocket. "You watch yourself. No whiskey."

"*Sí.* We will meet at the stables later." Jesus jangled the coins in his palm, then stuffed them into his pocket.

"No, you can meet him here later," Rosita interrupted. "This man looks tired and I have a bed this big hombre can use. To sleep in."

"Yes, good idea," Jesus said with frown of concern.

"Jesus," the woman said sharply, "your patron is safe here."

"Since you two have decided," Sam said, "I won't argue. I'll shut my eyes while he finds him. Don't make it too long."

Jesus agreed with a nod.

Sam T. mused on the inviting thought of a real bed. His hip would appreciate the rest. Rosita held no appeal for him, but he was grateful for her hospitality. He looked at the waiting pair and then nodded.

This job as territorial marshal was not working out as smoothly as he had anticipated. Perhaps after a few hours' sleep he could assemble all the facts and put the information about this case in some sort of perspective. He had faith in Jesus finding the gang member. Maybe they would get some answers from this Jimmy. Surely this outlaw could tell them if Mrs. Stauffer was still alive. Perhaps Sam would have to wait for Too-Gut's report on the hacienda to learn anything else. Who were those rifles intended for? Better yet, who had them?

Sam followed her down the narrow hallway lit by small candle lamps. There was not a hell of a lot he could do for the next few hours besides sleep. She turned the knob, opened the thin wooden door and stepped back for him.

"Sleep good, big man. No one will disturb you."

"*Gracias,*" he mumbled. She caught his arm and kissed him on the cheek.

"That was for hiring Jesus."

Sam T. blinked at her. His nose full of her perfume and musk, he studied her.

"He needed such work. You are a good man, Sam T." She clapped him on the arm to go ahead.

He agreed, and there seemed no need to tell her about Major Bowen, who deserved all the credit. His dulled thoughts were on the inviting bed in the room and shutting his eyes.

Justine hugged the thick woven cotton blanket around her, shivering in spite of the small fire that Sid and his men had built. The orange-blue flames licked up in tongues, but did little to drive away the cool night air. Scooting closer on her butt, Justine wondered if she would ever be warm again.

A shadowy figure, armed with a rifle, squatted on his heels across from her. The yellow light illuminated Sid's long mustache. Despite the show of force by these men, Justine felt anxious for them to be on their way. If only Angela would come back. There had been no sign of the Indian girl and Justine worried about her.

"Ma'am, we have more blankets," Sid offered, obviously having observed her shivering.

Knowing he was talking about their own blankets, she smiled feebly and shook her head. "No, thank you. I'll get warm soon."

"Sure. I hate to bother you, Mrs. Stauffer, but we can't find that Indian girl you were telling us about. It's making the men a mite nervous. The girl knows that we're your friends, don't she?"

Justine cleared her throat and forced herself to sound confident. "I'm sure she does, Sid. She saved my life, you know."

"Yes, ma'am, but me and the boys would feel better if you'd call to her. Try to make her understand that we ain't going to hurt her."

Sighing wearily, Justine rose. She knew Sid was right. She was glad Dan had hired him. The other two men, Pete and Red, had been very considerate of her comfort too. Earlier they had fixed some beans and coffee, which tasted like ambrosia to Justine's jaded palate. It was really absurd of Angela to hide out in the desert when she could be by the fire, eating decent food for a change.

Irritated by her friend's obstinacy, Justine moved beyond the fire circle and called out, "Angela! Angela, come!"

The vast star-flecked desert swallowed her words, losing them in the chilly night air. She tried repeatedly to reach the girl, but there was no answer.

"I'm sorry, Sid. She must have taken off somewhere. Are the horses still out back?"

"Only one, ma'am. Could she have gone back to her people or something? Mrs. Stauffer, you got any idea how far back Lamas and his men are?"

Justine lowered herself back on the ground beside the fire. She had no idea how many days and nights she had been on the run. They all ran together in her tortured mind. Regretfully she shook her head, hoping Sid didn't think she was stupid.

"Don't worry about it," he said. "You try and get some rest. You're safe now."

Safe. It sounded like a foreign word. Only in Dan's strong arms would she ever feel safe and warm again.

After arranging the saddle beneath her head, she wrapped the blanket tightly around her and glanced across the fire at Sid. Even though she felt grateful for the presence of the three men, they posed only a small force against the savage rapist Lamas and his men. Such a fragile defense to hold off his ruthless outlaws.

She closed her eyes, thanking God in her prayers for sending Sid and his men to the hacienda. Soon, soon she would be with Dan.

Immediately Justine fell into a heavy slumber. She was walking through the desert again, nothing but barren scrub land for miles. Far in the distance, on a low horizon she could see Dan. He was wearing a white vest, the familiar panama hat perched on his black hair. She moved toward him, but the desert transformed into quicksand and began pulling her down. Tears rolled down her face and she lifted her arms, pleading with Dan to save her. At last he began to move toward her, his figure shimmering through the heat waves that rose from the desert floor. Justine blinked the tears away to see his face. Only it wasn't Dan. It was the grinning, dark face of Lamas.

A pistol appeared in her hand as if by magic. With cold calculation, Justine raised the gun and aimed for his heart. The revolver kicked hard when she fired it. She watched in a mixture of joy and horror when a hole appeared in Lamas's bared chest. Crimson blood flowed through the thick black hair, running in rivulets down his muscle-corded stomach. She lifted her eyes and smiled into his blazing black visage. He lunged for her. She stood immobile. Her limbs were frozen, holding her prisoner. When Lamas fell to the ground, the desert sand began to swallow him. Justine moaned softly in her sleep.

A cold wind jolted her awake. She blinked her eyes. Sid squatted by the fire. And Lamas, she realized, was still out there somewhere—alive.

In anticipation of what would happen next, Lamas wet his lips and peered into the darkness to better see the woman on her knees before him. He squatted down on the heels of his kidskin boots and smiled at the tied-up bitch. He nodded his approval at Sanchez, who stood beside her, the rifle cradled in his arms. At last, his man had captured and delivered one of them.

He knelt down and reached out, snatched a handful of her long hair and jerked her face close to his. "How many men are with the gringo woman?"

They'd never get an answer from this one. She was an Indian. Neither threats nor torture would open her stubborn mouth. Perhaps he would quickly use her body, then slit her throat. He looked around in the night. There was no time or place for that here. Which was a shame. Besides, she would only fetch a few pesos in some flea-ridden whorehouse. She and that other *puta* had cost him dearly. His brood mares, stallion and all the ranch horses were gone and now he was out in the desert, dirty as when he was an outcast boy in the village where he was born. This slut had caused him enough trouble and discomfort. He glared down at her, the moonlight on her face displaying her blazing, contemptuous eyes.

Angela flung back her head in defiance and spat in his face. The slick warm wetness ran down his cheek unchecked. His chest heaved with rage and a small tic in his jaw muscles fluttered.

"Kill her," Lamas said softly.

Sanchez's rifle butt smashed her head like a ripe melon. In an instant, Angela was dead.

"Damn whore!" Lamas stood up.

"Sarge will be here soon," Sanchez said.

"Taking him long enough." He walked away from the lifeless body. Where in the hell was Jimmy? he wondered impatiently. Perhaps Sarge had already found the stupid boy and fed him to the ants. No, he would wait. And when they did stake him on an anthill, Lamas vowed with relish, he would sit on his heels and watch with great pleasure as the insects devoured him.

Tomorrow, he would take back the silky-skinned woman too. He could already savor the pleasure of whipping her milky skin until the blood ran freely down her bare buttocks. On the back of his hand, Lamas wiped what remained of the dead girl's spit from his face. The night wind picked up and blew off the sombrero latched at his throat. He lifted the hat back on his head.

Sleep well tonight, Señora Stauffer, he thought. Tomorrow you will pay.

Jesus entered the Rojo Cantina. Cigarette smoke hung so thick it curled around in clouds under the low roof. Under the yellow candle lamps, the thick haze engulfed the serious gamblers, who played cards on a green felt-top table. He eased to the bar and felt in his pocket for the money Sam T. had given him. Two dollars, an entire week's wages working in the adobe pit. He scanned the bottles of expensive liquor behind the bar. His tongue floated at the notion of tasting real tequila, salt and lime again.

"Hey." A young painted *puta* slipped up and hugged him around the waist. "Buy me a drink, amigo."

He looked down into her eyes. She was too thin, too young. He wondered about Tia. He missed her. It forced him to recall the week he stayed at her place getting ready for Sam T. They were good times. This wisp of a woman—yes, she would be the one.

He put his arm around her familiarly and whispered in her ear, "Let's find a booth."

The girl's eye widened. "Sure. My name is Ruby."

"Yes, Ruby," he whispered. "Bring the lady some whiskey," he said to the bartender, and with his hand on her waist, they went to the darker side of the cantina.

She slid in the booth and he followed. Someone was busy in the next one. All he could see was the wooden divider when he sat down, but he could hear the other couples breathing hard and their squirming told him enough. They would soon leave for that one's crib.

"What is your name?" she asked, getting up on her knees and slipping his hat off. With care she smoothed his hair and fussed about his face with her hands.

"Jesus." He drew out the dollar to pay the barmaid for her drink.

"You don't want anything, señor?" the girl asked.

"No." He shook his head, then accepted his change and put it on the tabletop before him.

"Ah, Jesus . . ." Ruby moved to get in front of him, so her knees straddled his legs. "You want to feel my tits?"

He leaned forward to whisper in her ear. "Where is this outlaw they call Jimmy?" His hands idly ran up and down, feeling the sides of Ruby's hips under the material.

She narrowed her eyes and peered closely at him. "Who?"

"The outlaw Jimmy."

She checked around to be certain they were alone, then she leaned over and cupped his ear in her hand to whisper, "Across the street at the Monte, passed out in a room. Don't you tell him I said so. He is a gang member of Don Lamas's. They would kill me so fast."

She straightened and looked into his eyes to plead for her request.

"Your secret is safe with me. I am going to pay you two bits for your kindness."

"Oh," she moaned disappointedly. "I could show you such a good time in my bed." She tossed her head toward the back.

"I have business. Another time."

She swept her limp hair back and kissed him hard on the mouth. *Putas* don't kiss men. He knew she was sincere in her heart. No time for her; he needed to find this Jimmy and then go wake Sam T. Perhaps Jimmy could be "persuaded" into telling them much about the Stauffer woman.

At last, Ruby reluctantly moved aside so he could slide out of the booth. When he stood up, he gave her the two bits and pocketed the rest. They exchanged strained smiles. Jesus made his way across to the Monte. With a dollar and thirty cents left in his pocket, he went into the lobby.

The night clerk stood behind the counter, busy reading the newspaper. He never looked up. At the desk, Jesus cleared his throat for the man's attention.

"Yes?"

"What room is Jimmy in?"

"Why?" The man looked ready to fall asleep on his feet.

"Fifty cents of this is yours for an answer." Jesus slapped the dollar on the counter.

"In back, room seven in the courtyard." He motioned with his head that direction, then reached for the dollar.

"Fifty cents," Jesus reminded him and covered the clerk's hand with his own, pressing down to make his point.

"Yeah, I can count." Their gazes met and Jesus released his hold.

"I need a passkey too."

The clerk nodded and reached underneath to produce one.

With his change and the key in his pocket, Jesus went out in the night and stood on the porch. The Chinese lanterns strung along the porch of the Rojo lit the night. The place beckoned him. Not for the young girl, Ruby—but for the yellow gold in those bottles gleaming so bright behind the bar. He rubbed his whisker-bristled mouth with the palm of his hand and licked his dry lips.

How could one little drink hurt him? He had the money. Sam T. was napping at Rosita's. He had the room key. Damn, he could taste it. His heart quickened at the prospect of having a stiff drink. A vision of that hellhole, the adobe pit, reminded him quickly of his duties. Did he want to throw away everything he had? Jesus physically tore himself away and started climbing the cobblestone street going up to the hill. He better go wake up Sam T. They had work to do.

The laughter of the whores and the sound of the music in the night behind him did not make this any easier. Tia, we should go find a priest when I return. He thought of the girl back at Rojo's and compared her to Tia. Not for him. You can be proud of me, woman. He hoped Sam T. fared better in getting some sleep than he did with his personal problems. Jesus drew a shuddering breath and hurried on his way.

In the early morning light, Sam T. and Jesus crossed the hotel's sprawling courtyard. Somewhere, a rooster crowed. Both men searched around for anything out of place. Jesus crowded close, used the pass key and then eased the door open. Pistol held high, Sam T. looked around one last time, then followed Jesus into the room.

The sleeping outlaw lay naked, sprawled face down on the bed. Sam T. quickly shut the door. Good enough; they had him.

"Wake him up," Sam hissed.

Jesus holstered his pistol and picked up a pitcher of water from the bedstand. He sloshed the kid with the water, then quickly lifted the new-looking gun and holster from the bedpost.

"W-what the hell?" The dripping outlaw flopped over and blinked his eyes at the sight of them.

"You've got thirty seconds to decide if you're going to live or die. Where's Mrs. Stauffer?" Sam T. demanded.

"Who are—"

Sam cut off his question. Gripping the boy by his hair, Sam shoved the barrel of the Colt into the kid's cheek. "Talk or die!"

Jimmy's Adam's apple bobbed erratically. His eyes nearly crossed as he looked at the pistol against his face. "S-she's gone."

"Where?"

"I don't know, mister. She and that Indian bitch run off. Hell, Lamas ever catches me, he'll kill me over it."

In disgust, Sam shoved the kid back on the bed. Jesus moved to the kid's side and held a glistening knife to his throat.

"Tell us everything," Jesus ordered.

Jimmy gulped, his eyes wide in terror. "No—no need for that knife. I'll tell you what you want to know."

Sam stepped back, opened the door to check the courtyard. No one in sight. He closed the door and leaned his back against it. With the Colt still in his hand, he pointed at the outlaw. "I'm listening."

Jimmy cleared his throat and tried to sink down in the bed to get away from the threat of Jesus' knife. "They caught me off guard."

"Who?" Jesus insisted.

"Those bitches—they tied me up and run off with all of Lamas's horses and then rode out."

"And just where was Lamas all this time?" Sam asked with heavy sarcasm.

"He was off somewhere. Cripes, mister, I don't know. I managed to catch one of them loose horses, then I rode like hell out of there before Lamas came back. That crazy Mexican will kill me for it when he finds me."

"Where are the other gang members?"

"Hell, how should I know? Probably out with Lamas looking for them two damn bitches in the desert."

"So the women got away?" Sam went over the matter in his mind.

"Yeah, that high-assed Stauffer bitch tricked me. That's why I'm here. If Lamas ever catches me—"

Sam T. wanted to bust him in the mouth, but he contained his anger. It was good news the women had escaped. Perhaps Too-Gut and Da-yah would manage to find them before Lamas did.

"Get dressed. You're going across the border."

"What for?" the kid demanded.

Sam's eyes narrowed. "You can go peacefully with us over there or we'll deliver you to Lamas. What'll it be?"

"Just who are you guys?"

"You never mind, boy," Sam growled. "Just get dressed; we ain't got time for explanations." He tossed the boy's clothes to Jesus.

There were more important things to do than spend time on this worthless piece of shit, Sam mused grimly. Mrs. Stauffer was somewhere between them and Lamas's place. By this time, she could either be safe or lost in the desert or recaptured by Lamas. The latter alternative was one that Sam didn't want to dwell on.

A scream that ended in a gurgling sound awoke Justine. She jerked up, her heart thundering against her breast. She peered in the darkness beyond the red embers of the fire. Her skin prickled in fear; she sensed death, looking at the crumbling hacienda.

Shots rang out in the night. Fiery tracers from a gun barrel flashed in the darkness. Then there was silence, a heavy, uneasy stillness that filled Justine with icy fear. A rush of desert wind swept over her face, bringing a chill. She leaned back on her elbows, uncertain whether she should fling back her blanket and run or lie there as if asleep.

Sid appeared suddenly and crouched by her side. He spoke in a low, urgent whisper. "Either Lamas found us or it's the Apaches. But the way them Apaches hate the night, I can't believe it's them. Whoever it is, they've got Red. I'm sorry, ma'am, but we need to ride out of here."

"Can't we—I mean, won't we be in more danger riding in the dark?"

"Ma'am, I ain't sure. All I know is somebody's found us and they ain't friendly. Now, don't get me wrong, I ain't afraid of facing any man, but this night fighting is different."

A man approached. Justine sucked in her breath, her eyes widening.

It was Pete. He knelt down on the other side of the fire. "What are we going to do, Sid?" he asked with an edge of impatience.

"Get out of here come sunup," Sid said.

"Yeah," Pete muttered. "If we live that long."

"Just keep your eyes peeled."

Justine threw back the covers. Fully dressed, she still shivered in the cool night air. Withdrawing the heavy six-gun from her holster, she slipped the cartridge belt over her shoulder. How much longer, she wondered, until dawn? She didn't want to risk speaking, in case it gave away her position to Lamas or whoever was out there.

Surely Angela had not killed Red. No, Angela would have realized by now that these were good men. Yet she had run away. Perhaps the Indian girl did not trust anyone.

The warmth from the blanket on her shoulder did not offer Justine any comfort. She hugged the material around her, trying to slow her pounding heart. Staring through the wall of darkness, she prayed that Lamas was not out there somewhere, ready to take her back to his hateful hacienda. She would never submit to him again. He could beat, even threaten to kill her, but never again would he pleasure himself with her body. Oh, dear God, she prayed, let help come soon.

Lamas dozed against a rock that still retained some of the past day's warmth. At the sound of leather soles approaching, he opened his eyes and peered keenly into the darkness.

Sanchez's small figure was silhouetted against the dying campfire. "One is dead; I cut his throat."

"Good, but they will be on their guard now. Sleep a few hours and we will take them in the morning."

"*Sí*, Lamas."

Strike and withdraw like a swordsman, Lamas mused to himself. Tomorrow the woman would be his once more to fondle and ravish. To punish too. When he tired of her, perhaps he would take her to Mexico City. She would bring him much gold there. And if he could trick the rich gringo Narrimore out of his reward . . . There must be a way. He was a good planner. He drew in a deep breath, then wrinkled his nose in disgust. A strong disgusting odor of sweat and horse clung to his silky shirt.

"Did you hear the quail call, *patron?*" Sanchez asked softly.

"Yes. Why?"

"There are Apaches all around us." The Yaqui, with his rifle in hand, squatted beside Lamas. He swiveled on his toes to search for them.

"What?" Lamas hissed. He moved slow-like until he too squatted beside his tracker. A cold chill ran up his arms under the shirt's material

"*Sí.* The rooster quail does not call so late at night."

Lamas held his pistol ready. The Apaches would die if they came upon him. He was ready for them. They would find out that they had not chosen some easy prey.

"Sanchez!" Lamas whispered. "I hear horses."

Sanchez did not reply at first. Then he spoke. "*Sí,* Don Lamas. Those were our horses. The Apaches stole them."

Lamas stood up, kicked at a pebble and ground his teeth. Those red bastards would pay for this. The retreating hoofbeats faded into the night. He cursed them repeatedly in Spanish. First the women had stolen his horses and now Apaches were stealing them. Was there no justice? He was a man of means and station in this country, not some common peon. It was not right! They would all pay for such insolence.

"Now we must finish off those men and take her," Lamas said, realizing the dilemma they were in. He straightened and brushed the dirt from his britches. "We need their horses to ride."

"*Sí,* Lamas. I'll go kill another one," Sanchez said, obviously trying placate his leader.

"Do it and be quick. It will be dawn in a few hours." He waved the man on.

Lamas narrowed his eyes with frustrated rage. When he got revenge on all those he hated, there would be many bodies to feed the vultures. After this was over, they would wax fat on the corpses he would leave behind.

Sam T. paced across the dry wash for the twelfth time. He threw a sharp look at Jesus, who stood in the shade of a scrub tree. With Jimmy incarcerated in the Nogales jail in Arizona, they awaited Too-Gut's return.

The surprised town marshal in Nogales accepted Sam's John Doe warrant. He did not demand any further explanation and agreed to keep Jimmy in custody until Sam called for him. But the arrest of the young outlaw was a pitiful step compared to what he still had to do to end the Border Gang'S reign of terror. Sam felt that he was getting nowhere.

"Someone is coming," Jesus hissed. Apparently he had heard horses from his position on the bank of the wash.

Sam peered through the early morning light and saw Da-yah coming on horseback through a thicket. She led two unfamiliar horses.

"Sam, come quick," she said, bounding out of the saddle. "Too-Gut is watching the bad ones. Two men have the white woman, but the Indian girl is dead."

"What? Who killed the girl?" Sam T. asked, jerking tight his girth on Big Boy to get ready to ride.

"Lamas must have," Da-yah said flatly. "The men with the lady are white men. Cowboys."

"Who are they?"

Da-yah shrugged. "I don't know."

"Good men or bad men?" Sam T. asked, mounting up.

"One with her is plenty good." She nodded to make her point. "He takes care of her."

Jesus rode toward her and took the two spare horses' leads for her. Sam T. waited for Da-yah to remount.

Good news at last. Mrs. Stauffer was still alive. Too-Gut was near her, but what could he do alone? Who, Sam T. wondered, were the good cowboys? There was no sense in asking questions; they had some riding to do.

"How far?" he asked Da-yah. Rocks clattered beneath their horses' hooves as they scrambled up the steep bank to the desert floor.

"Hard ride. Maybe half a day."

He finally felt better about the situation than he had in some time. At least now he could take some positive action. Da-yah knew where Mrs. Stauffer was, and Too-Gut would do all he could to protect her. That poor woman must have been through hell by this time. Sam urged the big gelding on to keep up with the tireless Apache woman.

Hot air rushed over his face as he pushed Big Boy. The smell of creosote in the desert was heady. The thought of their closing in on these outlaws had cleared his senses.

Ella Devereaux's secret meeting with Senator Green was to be held a short ways off the road to Iron Creek. She waited beside the surrey in the bright sun. Out of habit, she jerked up the front of her dress and corset. Birds sang nearby and the gentle wind made the temperature pleasant. A good place to meet, in this meadow, far enough off the road to escape the curious eyes of on-lookers. In her dress pocket was a copy of the telegram Green wanted.

ARRESTED FIRST BORDER GANG
MEMBER—JAILED IN NOGALES—SAM T.

This was all the proof Green needed that Sterling and Bowen had set up a secret force of lawmen quite to the contrary of the legislature's wishes. She walked back and forth through the small blue flowers and grasses in her soft dogskin slippers. Where was that potbellied Green? It must be past two o'clock.

A few minutes later, he appeared on horseback, and when he drew close, he bounded from the saddle. She raised her eyebrows at his athletics, then took the blanket from the buggy seat and the hamper of food and drink she had brought along.

"Hi, Ella," he said and hurried over to walk beside her.

"How have you been, Arthur?"

"Busy. You did get that proof and bring it with you?" he huffed.

"Yes," she said and handed him the basket to hold while she spread the blanket on the ground.

"You always are so lovely," he cooed. "My, my, food and whiskey, and, of course, lovely you."

She turned and winked mischievously at the man. Arthur must be in his fifties, she decided. Ella once observed his tintype of a wife who looked humorless enough to have a pole up her ass. Certainly Mrs. Green did not appear to be a picnic person.

The blanket spread, she took the basket from him and knelt to arrange things. She began to unload the various articles. Fried chicken wrapped in cloth napkins. Hot bread still warm to her touch. Butter in a secure bowl. German potato salad—

"May I read it?" he asked, like a small kid seeking candy from his mother. At her nod, he eagerly joined her on the blanket and she drew the yellow sheet from her pocket for him.

"Yes, yes," he said, sounding impressed, reading it to himself beside her. Then he threw his arms around her and began shouting, "I've got him! I've got him!"

"It is what you wanted?"

"Oh, hell, yes, let's celebrate."

"Sure," she said and looked down in mild shock as he began to undo his pants. Oh, no, her idea to celebrate was . . . The hard ground under the blanket held little appeal for her. She'd better get ready. Obviously the little man beside her on his knees, shrugging down his trousers, was ready for his part.

CHAPTER 12

Dawn appeared as a tiny slip of pink on the distant, saw-toothed horizon. Justine held the horses' reins and waited. She felt uneasy; they planned to leave shortly, but she wanted to go on. To her relief, when she glanced up, she saw Sid carrying two canteens over his shoulder and hurrying to rejoin her. His eyes continually scanned the surrounding area in search of any threatening forces.

"Come on, Pete," Sid said over his shoulder. He placed the canteen straps on the saddle horn and called out to his partner again.

There was no answer from Pete. A look of annoyance crossed Sid's face. He glanced at Justine and shrugged. She noticed that he grew more apprehensive with every moment.

"Come on, let's ride," he said impatiently. "Go ahead and mount up, Mrs. Stauffer," he urged when she hesitated.

"But where's Pete?"

Sid shook his head. "I'm not sure. Will you please get in the saddle, ma'am?"

A rifle shot sprayed hot sand over them and hastened Justine's movements to mount her horse.

Sid swung in the saddle and twisted around to fire his pistol in direction of the assailant. The shots spooked their animals. Justine's bolted forward and jerked her hard against the back of the saddle in the first leap. She fought for control with the reins.

"Come on, ma'am. We've got to get the hell out of here!"

In the confusion of her horse whirling around, she spotted Sanchez's familiar face at the gate of the crumbling hacienda wall, his rifle leveled on Sid.

She started to scream when two more shots from the other direction caused her to twist around to see who else was shooting. The rounds sent Sanchez fleeing back inside the hacienda. Who fired them? Obviously a friend or someone on her side. No time to see who.

"Come on, let's ride," Sid shouted, riding up beside her. He began to whip her horse to make it run. They raced away from the hacienda. The cactus and greasewood flew by her in a blur as she and Sid fled across the desert. She prayed that they were leaving that black-hearted Lamas behind them. Maybe he was dead. But that was a frail hope. It would require more than an ordinary bullet to kill the evil bandit. If only, she thought with desperation . . . if only they really were escaping Lamas. Her eyes blazed in hatred so fierce that she could hardly see. Then, seized with panic, she screamed for the horse to go faster.

Lamas discovered Too-Gut's picketed horse and rode him down the dry wash. He could hear sporadic firing coming from the hacienda. Sanchez was keeping the Apache pinned down with rifle fire. Lamas had already decided he and the Yaqui would ride out after the woman and leave the Apache afoot. How did one damn Apache cause this much trouble? Who was he?

The sound of an approaching horse caused him to rein up abruptly. More Apaches? he wondered in disgust. Pistol in his hand, he waited, ready to pull the trigger the minute the rider came into view.

Sarge drew up on the sun-bathed ridge above him. At Lamas's wave, he drove his horse down the steep bank and reined him beside the leader. Sarge's lathered mount blew loudly through its wide nostrils.

"I heard shots." Sarge motioned his arm in the direction of another rifle crack.

"One Apache." Lamas scowled in disgust.

"One?" The noncom shook his head in disbelief.

"He is very cunning."

"I have some more bad news," Sarge said quietly.

"What now?"

"Jimmy is in the Nogales jail. A big man in a brown suit and a Mexican who was with him picked Jimmy up and marched him across the border."

"Across the border?" Lamas frowned as another rifle report shattered the air above them.

"Yeah. I heard about it last night. Your gardener Pedro told me you wanted Jimmy for letting the women get away."

Another round of shots, closer this time, forced Lamas to break off their conversation. "Come on, we'll ride around and get Sanchez. We will go get some help. The Guiterez brothers in Tucson have many men that we can hire. We will find out who this brown-suited hombre is and kill him. In Tucson, we can find out about these men who have arrested Jimmy too."

"You mean to go back north?" Sarge asked in disbelief. "What about that Apache out there?"

The man had asked a good question, but he had better
things to do than to mess around all day to kill one stinking old Apache. What Lamas needed much worse were
more guns and men, if he was ever to get the Stauffer
women back from all these bastards—Apaches, pistoleros, and this big gringo, whoever he was. Lamas had
never seen the likes of so much trouble before. Enough
of all this—his mind was made up, he would ride at
once to Tucson and hire the primo badmen, the Guiterez
brothers to help him get her back.

"To hell with him," Lamas said at last. "Go get Sanchez and let's ride." He frowned as they parted. He hurried the horse up the hill for a look around. Apaches! And
now some big man who had the nerve to ride into Mexico and take prisoners back to Arizona. What next? Was
the Apache who had been shooting at Sanchez a relative
of the dead Indian girl? Who knew? Well, Sarge would
get Sanchez and they'd leave that red devil afoot. Sanchez could catch one of those dead cowboys' horses
to ride.

Lamas swore under his breath. Those bastards would
pay for this. He would get the white woman back later.
No one treated the great Lamas like this and escaped
punishment. He would get them. He swore it on his
mother's grave.

Sam T. knew from the position of the sun that it was close
to midday. The sorrel had not weakened despite the hard
pace he had held him to. Their three animals were lathered and breathing hard from the long push they'd made.
Da-yah pointed her rifle toward the green oasis of the
hacienda ahead of them. Sam T. nodded in acknowledgment. Was it too much to hope that Mrs. Stauffer
would still be there? Alive?

Sam, Jesus and Da-yah rode single file down the dry

wash. On the other side, Too-Gut appeared, waving his rifle. He came down the steep slope in a jog. The Apache looked alone and unscathed. Sam T. nodded in relief and he reined the sorrel up in front of the scout.

"The outlaws go north. Take my horse. Woman and one cowboy ride east." He used the rifle to point out their directions.

Good. For the time being she has escaped them, was Sam T.'s first thought. What to do next perplexed him. He indicated to the scout that he'd heard the words and signaled with a motion of his head to go on to the ruins.

Too-Gut bounded on behind Da-yah and they rode to the old hacienda.

"A cowboy had her?" Sam T. questioned when they arrived. Too-Gut nodded. Sam booted his horse in close to look at the dead red-haired man; his bloody torso was sprawled awkwardly on the ground. The man's high-crowned hat lay at a distance from his body. His throat had been cut. The outlaws had left another victim. Sam T. gazed beyond the wall to the north. Nothing in sight, but he knew the killers were not far away.

"Sam T.," Jesus asked, "what should we do?"

"Right now walk these hot horses. If we don't, they'll get stiff. I have to hope the woman is safe. We're going after those killers."

"Too-Gut," Sam T. asked, "how many men were here?"

"Two bad hombres. I am sorry, Sam T. I should have killed them," the Chiricahua apologized. "Oh, and another in army clothes joined them here."

Sam T. shook his head. "No, you did your best. At least the woman managed to escape. We'll get them sooner or later. You've done well."

Too-Gut's gaze rested on the flat country to the north. Sam T. saw the resolve in his brown eyes.

"Don't worry, Too-Gut, we'll get them."

"Yes," the Apache agreed. "Then the major can get the papers to let us work for you."

Sam wanted to say something reassuring, but he had no real answer.

"I'm sure he'll try." There was nothing he could do for them at the moment. He watched Da-yah lead the horses back and forth to cool them. Sam T. felt anxious to take up their trail When the horses cooled off, then they could set out again on the outlaws' trail. This time they were close.

Sam T. began to worry about Mrs. Stauffer's well-being and decided Jesus should follow Mrs. Stauffer's trail to make certain she was safe. He and the two Indians would track down the outlaws. They separated. Jesus rode east to track her and the cowboy's trail. Sam, Too-Gut and Da-yah headed north after the gang.

The desert lay flat to the north It was bordered by jagged mountains so distant they shimmered in the rising heat waves like mirages. Sam T. watched Too-Gut study signs. Lamas and his crew had left no obvious clues, but the Apache had little trouble keeping on their faint trail. Sam drew abreast of the tracker and scanned the dull area ahead of them. Too-Gut pointed his rifle northwest.

"See their dust?" Too-Gut asked.

Sam T. squinted, but was unsure whether he saw a small wisp of dust or if it was a distortion. "No," he finally said. "But that's why I have an Apache scout."

Too-Gut smiled. "They will camp in the mountains."

"Is there water?"

Too-Gut shrugged as if that were unimportant and dismounted onto his bowed legs. He squatted, the rifle across his knees. Da-yah came and took his horse away.

"We rest here," he said. "They will grow careless if they think we are not after them."

Sam T. looked one more time in the direction of the outlaws. Why was Lamas riding north? He had better odds of survival in Mexico. At his current direction of travel they soon would be in Arizona, and arresting him there would be no problem. What was the man's logic? Some criminals had none—Lamas was smarter than that.

Justine's horse ran until it couldn't go any farther. It slowed to a trot, then a walk, until finally it simply stopped. Sides heaving and lathered with foam, the horse's deep coughs rattled the stirrups.

The creature's legs buckled, and it dropped to its front knees. Justine quickly dismounted and looked at the beast in shocked sympathy. She glanced behind her, expecting to see Lamas appear out of nowhere.

"Get up here, ma'am," Sid said, bringing her out of her dazed stupor.

"It's no use." Her eyes flooded with tears. She wanted to do something for the rasping animal, but knew there was nothing that could save the dying horse. She stood, trembling helplessly, dismay and confusion clouding her mind.

"Come on, lady," Sid insisted and reached down to help her on the back of his horse.

Justine gazed up at Sid's dirt-streaked face. His persistence and determination instilled some strength in her. Despite his assistance, she was unable to mount on the first try.

"Try one more time," Sid urged. "We're going to make it.

Again she scrambled, and finally in a tremendous effort she hauled herself up behind him. For a moment, they simply rested on his horse. Then the animal began to move beneath them. She placed her hands on Sid's shoulders to steady herself.

"Are you all right, Mrs. Stauffer?"

Justine swallowed dryly, then in a hoarse whisper assured him that she was fine.

Late in the afternoon, they rode into the outskirts of Nogales. The sounds of civilization instantly revived Justine's weary spirit. Here they would surely be safe from Lamas and his wild gang.

In front of the hotel, she dismounted stiffly and looked back at the hills closing in behind them. Was she really beyond his grasp? she wondered.

A young boy stood beside Sid's horse. "Señor! Señor!"

Sid shook his head as he dismounted. "We don't need any help." He smiled at Justine. "Do we?"

"No, not now," she said with a smile of relief. The outlaws could not get them.

Sid wrapped the reins around the hitch rack in front of the Santa Cruz Hotel. Justine swayed on her feet and wrinkled her nose at her filthy dress. Exhausted to numbness, they shared a private look at each other of *Thank God*.

"My gawd! Sid's found her. Go tell Narrimore!"

Justine looked up in surprise at the men gathering on the hotel porch.

"Sid, where are the others?" one of the men asked.

"Dead."

Justine heard his words, but they became a roar of water in her ears. The last of her energy had drained away.

The men rushed forward and assisted her inside the hotel. Their kindness and consideration filled her with gratitude. Was she hungry? the man asked. Thirsty? She shook her head. Sleep was all the comfort she needed.

To sleep in a warm, comfortable bed would be the greatest reward for all her sufferings.

It was dawn when Justine awoke in the hotel room. Her eyes and her throat felt parched. A glass of tepid water from the pitcher on the washstand quenched some of her thirst. She attempted to wash her face, but her sun-fired skin was too sore, the soft cloth felt like sand against her cheeks. She looked around the room, sighing with contentment at the rich maroon and gold furnishings.

A knock came at the door, and she was able to summon up a reasonably bright smile.

Upon opening it and seeing the man standing in the hallway, Justine sucked in her breath sharply. Tears of joy filled her eyes.

"Dan!" She fell into his arms, burying her face against his shoulder. He pecked her on the cheek, then disentangled her arms from around his neck.

Justine watched him move to the window. A sense of hurt and bewilderment flooded over her. Something was wrong. Was this the same man she remembered? His Prince Albert jacket, ruffled shirt and wavy black hair beneath the stylish flat-crowned hat were the same. But his handsome face wore a hard, determined expression that she had never seen before

"Where are your husband's papers?" he asked flatly.

Justine blinked her eyes. "Wh-what?"

His face darkened. "I need the final reports on the Silver Lady Mine."

"Dan? I—I don't know what you mean."

"Stop stalling. I want those papers, Justine!"

She sank down onto the bed, her head reeling with confusion and humiliation. Through troubled vision, she looked at the man she thought she once loved. He was a total stranger. Oh, God, what had happened to him? To her? Was she still in the thrall of some kind of nightmare?

"Get ready to travel. You're going to my ranch."

"But I—"

"No buts. Walker will take you. And perhaps on the way you'll remember where those damned papers are at." Scowling with contempt, he strode past her and out the door.

Shocked into speechlessness, she stared down at her rough hands. Had Dan rescued her to use her for his own purposes? Her face reddened with shame. Dan Narrimore cared nothing about her. All he was interested in was Tom's report on the mines. She had no idea where the papers were. The last time she had seen them was at the stage stop. It seemed like a lifetime ago. Perhaps it was. Her life was not the same and probably never would be again. Lamas might have taken the reports and thrown them away, or maybe they were left lying on the ground with the rest of the unwanted baggage. Who knew? Shaking her head in dismay, Justine flinched when someone knocked on the door.

A man opened the door and stuck his head through the opening. "Are you ready, ma'am? We need to go out the back way."

She rose. Justine had not the strength left to oppose anyone. The cowboy led the way down the stairs, through the rear of the hotel and into the alley. She was silent as he helped her into the waiting buckboard. Then, sighing deeply, she raised her eyes.

At the end of the alley stood a Mexican, wearing belts of ammunition. She gasped, her face drained in fear. Surely he was one of Lamas's men. Then, she wondered if she had spoken her thoughts aloud.

"What is it, ma'am? You look like you've seen a ghost," Walker said with mild concern.

Swallowing hard, she forced her gaze back to the end of the alley. The Mexican was gone. She blinked her eyes. Had she imagined the man? "It's nothing," she told Walker.

He raised his brows, but never spoke. Then he clucked to the team and they were on their way. She looked around. The Mexican was nowhere to be seen. When the buckboard pulled up the long hill out of Nogales, she gave one last look over her shoulder. Nothing.

Sarge's horse turned up lame. Lamas was furious. Bad luck dogged their every footstep. He knew the horse would never last the trip. They halted to allow Sarge to inspect the horse's pad.

"Stone-bruised," Sarge said with disgust.

"Is anyone coming?" Lamas shouted to Sanchez, who was ahead of them on the lookout.

"There is no one coming."

Lamas leaned back in his saddle. To ride one of their other horses double might cripple it. How expendable was the man? If they ran into a posse he would be very necessary. Otherwise . . .

"Listen, Lamas, we can split up here. I'll head northeast and when this horse gives out, I can walk and hide my tracks." Sarge shook his head like that made no difference. "I'll get another horse somewhere and meet you. Hell, there's lots of places up there I can get one."

Lamas considered the plan and then nodded in agreement. That way the man would not slow them down. Besides, Sarge was tough; walking wouldn't hurt him. "You be in Tucson at the Guiterez brothers' in four days or we won't wait for you."

"I'll be there."

"Here is some money. Buy a good one." He handed

the man four double eagles and checked his own shift-ing horse. "See you in four days."

"And keep your eyes and ears open," he reminded the man. "I want to know about this big man in the brown suit. I do not trust such a brazen hombre."

Sarge wiped his gritty face on his sleeve. "I've got connections. I'll find out who the hell he is."

Lamas turned and motioned for Sanchez to lead out. He gave a last look at Sarge headed northeast on the crippled horse. Lamas was not sure that the man would make it. But Sarge was desert-tough, a veteran of the Apache warfare. Maybe he would meet them in Tucson.

Lamas reasoned that if they were being followed, the trackers just might follow Sarge, allowing him and San-chez time to escape. Lamas kicked the horse he had stolen from the Apache. He regretted not cutting the Indi-an's throat. Later he planned to ask Sanchez again who he thought the Indian might be. Maybe the Apache worked with the men who had rescued that gringo whore.

The vision of Justine riding hell for leather from that abandoned hacienda filled him with red-hot fury. When he reached Tucson he would hire the Guiterez brothers. They knew each pistolero in Tucson who would gut his own mother for a gold coin. Just the kind of men he needed. He would ride at the head of his new army and find all these bastards who had made him run like a coyote.

Lamas looked at the blue, cloudless sky. Apache, you have joined my roster for the dead. If the bluecoats do not get you first, I will have my turn with you. You have not long to live in my land.

Amused at his private thoughts, he laughed aloud. Then he slapped his palm on the pommel of his saddle. "You see any dust behind us? You have looked a thousand times. Is it the Apache you fear?"

Sanchez shook his head to dispel Lamas's concern. "I wondered who he was."

"Was he with the cowboy who took the woman away?" Lamas asked

"No. He is a scout for more Apaches or someone else. That cowboy did not know him."

"You were close enough to see that?"

"Plenty close."

"He was with a band of them?"

"I don't know. He was a Chiricahua."

Lamas glanced behind them. He was not afraid, but Chiricahuas were a bunch of bad marauders on both sides of the border. When he turned back in the saddle, he studied the hills ahead. He and Sanchez would spend the night in them. And soon he must do more planning.

In the late evening, Sam T. and his crew reached the place where the trail of the outlaws split. He stopped to hold a council. In the glow of sundown, Too-Gut and Sam squatted on their heels, while Da-yah wiped the horses' muzzles with a rag soaked in water from their canteens.

"Da-yah can follow the trail of the two men. Sam T., you ride with her. I will catch the one on the cripple horse and come back to join you," Too-Gut said.

"You think the horse is crippled?"

Too-Gut nodded. Sam studied the Apache's profile in the orange-red light. The small bump on his slender nose indicated that it had probably been broken at one time.

"All right. Da-yah and I will go slow. I want to surprise these outlaws. I have a pair of handcuffs in my saddlebags for you to use. Don't kill this man unless you have to."

Sam T. was not certain the ex-scout had heard his orders. Too-Gut took the pair of irons and grinned at him, then moved away to Da-yah's side.

He spoke curtly to her in his own language. Sam looked away to the distant mountains. He felt in his bones they were close to the outlaws. By this time Justine Stauffer must be safe. One day, he planned to look her up and see if the real woman matched the beauty in the tintype.

"We eat soon," Da-yah announced. Too-Gut had already left to follow the lame horse's trail. Sam moved by the small fire pit that she had fashioned earlier with her long-bladed knife. The beans were already beginning to steam and gave off a delicious aroma to his starved senses.

He realized if he had not been so hungry, he would not have appreciated the unsalted, half-cooked beans. But as it was, he was not going to complain about her frijoles.

"Moon come up soon, be better light," Da-yah said as they ate:

"Yeah." He used his tongue to dislodge a bean skin from between his teeth.

"You have a wife?" she asked. In her halting English, the words sounded like an accusation.

"No."

"White man crazy." She shrugged and used her fingers to scoop up more beans from the bowl. "White man cook own meals, sleep by himself, hold own horse. Stupid."

Sam chuckled softly. Here he was in a desert so vast that a man could ride for days in any direction and not see a soul, yet he was receiving a lecture.

"White woman no good for you!" she asserted severely.

"I suppose you're right. One wouldn't be much use out here." For a moment, he thought of Mrs. Stauffer and the murdered Indian girl who had been stranded in the desert.

Impatiently he shrugged the thought away. That part was over. He looked at Da-yah and forced a smile. "I guess I need an Apache wife."

"You need one when Da-yah not here to take care of you."

"Do you have a home?" he asked her curiously.

"Here is home," she said flatly. "Da-yah not like reservations."

He sympathized with her. She hated confinement as bad as he did.

When the moon rose they saddled up and rode the ridges. She halted often and dismounted. Then, satisfied by whatever tracks she found, she leaped back on her horse and waved at him to follow her.

A distant coyote yapped as the dark wall of the mountains drew closer. He rode with his right hand on the butt of his Colt. His ears strained to hear over the night insects' orchestration, and his eyes open wide to see as much as he could in the ivory light of the half moon.

At the mountains' base, Da-yah once again dismounted and handed him her reins. "You wait here. Two quail whistles means I am coming back."

"Yes." He watched her melt into the inky scrub desert.

After taking a drink of the tepid canteen water, he followed the woman's method of washing the horses' muzzles. Then he picketed them to a scrub brush and took his .44-caliber Winchester from his scabbard. He found a place to sit aside and wait for Da-yah's return. The moon arced westward, crawling towards the distant horizon.

The desert cooled and a gentle night wind touched his sun-baked face. Hours passed while he fought his heavy eyelids, which acted determined to close.

A quail's call jerked him to awareness. Again—two whistles came from north of his position.

It was Da-yah. She came into view almost silently.

"They are close. Sleep a few hours. When the sun rises, we can be in their camp."

"Two men?"

"One is wearing a fancy shirt. The other is a Yaqui."

"A mean one?" The term *Yaqui* was new to him, but he knew it meant an Indian tribe.

"He killed the Indian woman."

Sam tried to see her face in the dim light. "You saw that happen?"

"He is the one," she said obstinately.

He sighed. Her testimony would never hold up in court, but she was probably right. He considered both men mad-dog killers.

"Shouldn't we go up there now?" he asked.

"Bad luck at night. Apaches wait for light, so the bad spirits can't steal our souls."

He shrugged and rose stiffly. A few hours of sleep, even if on the hard ground, would be very welcome. He untied his roll and spread it out. Tomorrow, perhaps they would have the leader and his henchmen in custody. At last he felt better, as the noose closed in on the Border Gang.

In the early morning light, Sam T. crouched in the shoulder-high brush close to the outlaws' camp. He heard a horse stomping nearby. Stealthily he edged through the salt cedars toward the sound. Somewhere out there were two killers. His face was set in grim lines, the cocked Colt ready in his right hand.

On the other side of the canyon, Da-yah worked her way opposite him. She told him that if he heard one quail whistle it would mean to rush the killers. Two whistles would mean that she had them covered. The only problem with her plan was he could hear real quail far up in the canyon. He wasn't sure he would recognize Da-yah's call from theirs.

He stopped and surveyed the red walls above him. There was potential for an ambush high in this canyon. The fact that he could only hear one horse somewhere ahead bothered him.

Where was the other outlaw's mount? Had one of them circled around? He hoped not. Using his left hand, he wiped the back of it over his lower lip to remove the beads of perspiration.

Out of nowhere, someone jumped on his back; the force sent him stumbling to his knees. Taken down by the unexpected weight of his attacker, his gun hand flew up in reflex. The quick action deflected the blade of the powerful assailant's knife, but did not prevent injury. A sharp searing pain shot from Sam's forearm, causing him to drop his Colt. The man on his back tightened his vise-like grip on Sam's throat and moved the deadly knife closer despite Sam's grip on his wrist.

With his other hand, Sam T. grasped the sinewy arm locked around his neck. It was shutting off his air. His strength began to wane. He barely managed to hold the hand wielding the knife at bay with his injured one. The outlaw's other hold continued to squeeze off his wind-pipe, gripping harder and harder, cutting off his breathing. Sam twisted around in an effort to spill the man from his back, but the tenacious hold of the killer clung to him like a thick choking vine.

Hard huffing sounds rasped in Sam's ears as his assailant struggled wordlessly to end his life. Pain in his forearm became searing; he could feel his coat sleeve becoming soaked. The lock on Sam's throat threatened to defeat him.

An abrupt groan from the attacker sounded in Sam's ears. The man melted from his back. Sam T. made a dive forward for his gun and rolled over. He could see the Colt was not needed. Da-yah's knife was planted to the hilt in the man's back. The outlaw fell to his knees. Sam T. could see the look of death in his eyes. But even at the very gates of hell, the man's ratlike face held no remorse, only hatred. He must be the Yaqui she had spoken about the night before.

"Where's Lamas?" Sam T. demanded in a croaking voice

The man's hand flailed the air as he strived to reach back and pull Da-yah's knife out of his back. "Lamas will . . . kill you bastards. He will—" A strangled cough cut off the man's words.

Da-yah stood over the him. Hatred glazed her dark eyes. With a nod of satisfaction, she placed the toe of her leather boot against the Yaqui's spine and bent to pull the bloody knife from his back.

"He's not a bad one anymore."

Sam T. panted heavily and looked from the dead outlaw to the woman who had saved him. "Right," he agreed hoarsely. "I owe you my life, Da-yah."

She shrugged away his concern as nothing and wiped the bloody blade on the dead man's shirt.

Sam T. closed his eyes, then immediately opened them. Where was Lamas? Standing up with effort, Sam T. scanned the surrounding area, wondering if even at this moment Lamas had them in his sights.

"Any sign of Lamas?"

She shook her head in disapproval. A deep frown of concern drew her straight black brows together when she noted the blood dripping from Sam T.'s fingertips. A dark wet patch stained the ripped sleeve of his brown suit.

"You hurt bad?"

He slipped out of the coat and glanced at the bloody shirtsleeve.

"Only a scratch," he mumbled.

She clucked her teeth in disapproval. "Plenty blood. You sit down."

"No," he said irritably. He scowled at the sight of the cut. That outlaw leader was a damned slippery snake. Obviously he had expected the Indian to kill them.

"You stay here. I go get my things," she ordered and raced away.

Blood from the wound dripped off his fingers. He tried to find some solace in the knowledge that it was his forearm that had been cut and not his throat. But if it had not been for Da-yah . . .

She returned, carrying a leather pouch from her saddlebags.

"Lamas go north," she said with a toss of her head. "Maybe go last night. Leave him here." She made a curl of her lip and indicated the dead Yaqui.

"How much head start has he got?" He rose to his feet.

"No, you sit. I fix."

He glanced down at her stubbornly set face, then reluctantly agreed. The knife wound needed some attention. Fortunately he could still flex the fingers of his gun hand. He took a seat on a boulder with a sigh of resignation and held out his arm for her inspection.

From the leather pouch, she withdrew a curved needle and dark thread. Her hands were gentle as she folded the blood-soaked shirtsleeve up. Sam watched the canyon tops for a distraction while she began to stitch closed the gaping cut.

"Lamas plenty crazy," she muttered while she worked. "Wear out horses, ride all over like a crazy man."

A smile tugged at his pinched lips. She could fuss all she wanted as far as he was concerned. It was like music to his ears. He knew that, without her intervention, he would not be sitting there to listen.

She did an admirable job of stitching up his arm. But he'd sure bear a scar. The entire time she worked on him, she cursed the dead man in what he imagined was Apache.

"What do you want to do with his body?" he asked her when she cinched up the last knot with a hard tug.

"Huh! He make plenty good food for buzzards." She used her teeth to cut the thread. Then she wrapped the wound with a kerchief. Satisfied with her workmanship, she turned away and immediately began using her knife to dig a fire hole in the sandy wash.

Sam tried to find a comfortable position for his arm. He refused to put it in a sling as she suggested. A stab of irritation roiled in his stomach. He was no closer to capturing Lamas and now he was hampered with an injured gun arm. He looked at her.

"You said Lamas went north?"

"Yes." She glanced up from the pot she was stirring and pointed in a northerly direction. "You rest. I go after Lamas."

"No!" His voice rang harsh and he glared at her, trying to outstare her obstinate gaze. Things were in a big enough mess without sending her after the outlaw alone. Jesus would have no idea where Sam T. and Da-yah were. Too-Gut was off chasing another gang member. And his own arm was too sore to draw a pistol or shoot a rifle. Besides, it was now personal. He fully intended to bring the outlaw Lamas to justice.

"Sam T.," she said with a toss of her head. "Too-Gut is coming now."

He turned his ear and could hear the clop of a horse in the pass that led into the canyon. He rose stiffly to his feet and tried to see beyond the high brush. The return of his deputy would be a good thing, considering his throbbing injury. Had the Apache captured the outlaw?

When Too-Gut came into view, a smile twitched at Sam's mouth.

A hatless man in handcuffs trotted behind Too-Gut's horse, a rope around the outlaw's neck. The prisoner wore a scruffy-looking army uniform. This must be the Sarge whom Tagget spoke about. They were making progress.

"Beans about cooked," Da-yah announced.

Sam T. looked up at his Apache scout. "Good work." Too Gut released the lariat rope from his saddle horn, let it drop and bounded off his horse.

Sarge wearily dropped to the ground on his rear. Then he used his shackled, dirty hands to scrub his unshaven face and finally raised his eyes and frowned in puzzlement at Sam T. "Who the gawdamn hell are you?"

"An officer of the court," Sam T. said. "Did Too-Gut tell you that you were under arrest?"

Sarge ignored the question. "Are you a U.S. marshal or from the army or what?"

Sam T. expelled a deep breath. "Listen, Sarge, don't worry what I am. You have murder and kidnapping charges to face. I suggest you think about that."

"Hey, you kill Sanchez?" Sarge's gaze was on the prone body.

"No, I didn't kill him," Sam T. said flatly.

"He was a tough little bastard," Sarge grunted.

In silence, they sat around eating Da-yah's beans and drinking coffee. Too-Gut gave a head toss at the Yaqui's horse picketed close by. "Him plenty tired."

"Yeah, we all are, but he can carry Sarge. We need to get back to Nogales. Get some fresh horses and find Jesus." Sam T. looked to the north and wondered about Lamas. His plans included quickly overtaking the gang leader somewhere in the territory. With so many of his strongest henchmen in jail or dead, a portion of the rattler's fangs were gone. The one thing that niggled

Sam T. the most was the fact Lamas was going back north, leaving the sanctuary of Mexico. There had to be a reason.

No matter where the outlaw leader went, it was time for Sam and his posse to give up his tracks. Lamas was headed into Arizona; Sam T. felt certain they'd find him in a short while up there. But they were out of food and supplies, plus their horses were about done in, and would barely be able to make the ride back to Nogales. He wanted the sullen prisoner, Sarge, behind bars, and was anxious to know what Jesus had found out about Mrs. Stauffer. Besides, his damn arm throbbed worse than a bad tooth.

"We better turn east here and ride to Nogales," Sam T. said with a sigh of disgust.

"I can follow—" Too-Gut indicated the line of mountains to the north.

Sam T. waved the Apache's notion away with his good arm. "No, it's time to regroup and resupply. Find some fresh horses to ride."

Still engrossed in his concerns, Sam T. took the reins from Da-yah and smiled. Mounted and on their way to Nogales, he tried to protect his aching arm. But every bush and scrub along the way acted in a conspiracy to whip against it. Even Big Boy seemed out to deliberately jar him.

Justine Stauffer was still in shock when she realized she was to be locked up once again. The stuffy shed where Dan's men placed her was dark, except for a few shafts of daylight that sneaked through the boarded-over windows. At night, they rationed her a few candles, along with a lumpy mattress and a sour-smelling blanket.

She had been allowed to take a bath in a tinned tub

that two of Dan's men brought to the shed, and the water they hauled her was barely lukewarm. No matter the chill, she managed to wash off layers of dirt and grime that had felt permanently baked into her hair and skin.

Lamas's hacienda had better amenities, she decided. Then the memory of that confinement made her shudder. Her prison at the outlaw's home may have been more comfortable, but it had counted for little when she recalled the assaults on her body by that swarthy Mexican. At least at Dan's she had no cause for alarm on that score. He wasn't the least bit interested in resuming their affair. She cursed her own foolishness in believing that she had ever meant anything to Narrimore. How had she been so naive as to believe his glib tongue in the first place?

As if her thoughts had conjured him up, she watched the door open and Dan burst inside the dank shed. He moved toward her purposefully, then gripped her arms in a bruising vise.

"I don't have time to listen to any more of your excuses. I want to know what Tom's report said about the Silver Lady Mine."

She could not control her trembling mouth. Her vision blurred with tears. How long would he keep up the inquisition this time? she wondered. There was nothing she could tell him about the mining business. She simply had never been interested in Tom's work. As Dan's fingers tightened on her arms, Justine felt her temper rise.

Tilting up her head, she glared at him. "You used me. All you were ever interested in was what I might be able to tell you about it." The slight satisfaction at airing her deeply felt anger quickly faded under the hard look on his face.

He shoved her aside. She steadied herself and rubbed

her bruised arms. Without flinching, she met his look of contempt.

"Dan Narrimore, you are as big a snake as that dirty outlaw Lamas! At least he never pretended to be what he wasn't!"

His nostrils flared and his narrowed eyes bore into her. "You stupid woman! You don't know the first thing about me, do you?"

Justine blinked as she studied his face. His nose was too wide, his eyes too small and his lip curled sarcastically. She noticed for the first time his small, weak chin and already signs of self-indulgence showed on his flesh. What had she ever seen in him?

"You listen to me, Justine," he growled. "I only have a few days to make a decision on this mining stock. If that lardass sheriff over in Saguaro County knows something about that mine that I don't, I could stand to lose a lot of money." He paced the gritty floorboards, his head bent as if in deep concentration.

Abruptly he came to a halt, then slowly turned toward her. A smile tugged at his mouth, but it never reached his eyes. He held out a hand to her in a placating manner. He spoke again, but this time his voice held a coaxing note "Maybe I've been too hard on you, Justine. Now, just stop and think for a minute. What did Tom say about the mine?" he asked.

She sighed heavily and bowed her head. His actions never fooled her. He obviously changed his tactics in an effort to coax the information from her. The trouble was she had no knowledge to give him. But perhaps if she acted as though she were taken in by his persuasive manner, then maybe he would leave her alone for a while.

"Justine, honey," Dan said, "I have thousands of dollars riding on this mining deal. It's yours and my future. If I knew for certain that there's silver in the mines, then

I could buy that sheriff's stock. But if it's worthless, then I'll just tell him I changed my mind and he won't be the wiser. Do you see, Justine, why I need that information in Tom's report."

She listened silently and acted downcast. She was afraid he would know by the contempt in her eyes that she had seen through his charade. In defeat, she sank onto the bed and folded her hands in her lap, waiting for his next change in tactics.

Dan moved to her side and lightly touched her hair. She stiffened, but didn't flinch at his touch. "Justine, you don't have to stay in this place. I'll take you up to the house and . . ."

She frowned, wondering what she could possibly tell him that would convince him she was trying to think of something. "I—I'll try to remember, Dan," she said in a low voice. Chancing a look at his face, she paled at the scowl of impatience that blanketed his features.

Dan ran his fingers through her hair, then drew his hand back as if he would strike her. He expelled a sharp curse. "Gawdammit! All right, you stay here in this shed and you think hard. I'll be back and you damned well better have some answers. I'm sure if you're left here long enough your memory will improve, but I'm warning you: My patience is wearing pretty thin." Without waiting for a comment from her, he turned and stalked toward the door. Justine heard it being relocked. In defeat, she slumped back on the bed.

She peered at the cobwebbed ceiling in deep concentration. She could not recall Tom having said a word to her about the Silver Lady Mine. It seemed that all she could do was try to escape this hellhole they held her in. Sid had disappeared since he rescued her. And the other cowboys guarding her acted like a tough bunch. What were her chances of persuading one of them to let her go?

She ran a hand over her face and grimaced. Of course, her peeling face and cracked lips would hardly entice a man. It appeared to be a hopeless situation.

Somehow she would have to come up with a plausible story to tell Dan when he returned. Maybe if she racked her muddled brain, she could create some elusive details about the Silver Lady Mine.

Soon it would be night, and she was not looking forward to another restless evening spent in her prison. There had to be an answer, a way out of this mess.

Major Bowen stood in the shadows. He watched the young man from the telegraph office hike up the hill headed for the Harrington House. How did a telegrapher afford to go once a week to that expensive place? Good question. Bowen might not have been the wiser, but Town Marshall Abe Rutherford mentioned the same thing to him over a game of checkers. *Every Tuesday night, he goes up there,* Rutherford had said as he crowned his second king.

In the cooling night air, Bowen decided the young man needed to be interrogated. When the youth disappeared through the front door, Bowen turned on his heel. He felt satisfied that was the opposition's source of information. His ears still rang from Sterling's blistering oration about "how Green found out about the arrest in Nogales."

For a long while Bowen studied the lit windows and listened to the sound of a piano drifting from the Harrington House. He rubbed his chin thoughtfully with his fingertips. Perhaps he needed to speak to this Ella Devereaux. Somehow he suspected she might be at the root of his troubles.

His spying completed for the evening, he started for

home. One of the Border Gang was in jail, according to the telegram from Sam T. The news had elated him and Sterling both. His first territorial marshal must be getting close to the rest of the bandits by this time. Bowen glanced at the twinkling stars; he certainly hoped so.

CHAPTER 13

Late in the night, Sam T. parted with the Apaches, who went off to camp out of sight on the river. Sam T. booted Big Boy toward the twinkling lights of the Nogales ahead of them, winching at his throbbing arm when Sarge's sluggish horse jerked on the lead.

Half an hour later, with his prisoner locked in the jail and telegrams sent, Sam T. sat in a doctor's office, letting a whiskey-breathed physician examine his arm.

"Bad enough job of stitching. What the hell did they use, cat gut?" The man blinked his rheumy eyes under the lamplight. "Nothing I can do for it. Give you some pain medicine, so you can sleep. If you don't get an infection in it, you might save it. Otherwise we better amputate it quick-like. You understand?'

After the man redressed it, Sam T. pulled down his sleeve. He considered Da-yuh a better medical person than this old coot.

"If it ever gets infected—" the man whined.

Sam T. tossed down a dollar for the fee and headed for the office door. He had all the sorry advice he needed.

When he reached the base of the stairs, someone stepped from the shadows between the buildings.

"Sam T.?"

His heart quieted down when he realized it was Jesus. Without his gun hand, he considered himself defenseless. He straightened, looked around and the two of them moved back in the darkness between the two buildings to where they could watch the street and talk privately.

"I heard from the marshal that you were over here," Jesus said. "I was going to try to find you tomorrow if you didn't come to town."

"That's fine. What about Mrs. Stauffer?"

Jesus quickly explained the removal of Mrs. Stauffer by the back way of the hotel to Narrimore's ranch.

"She's alive, anyway," Sam T. said, perplexed by the matter.

They discussed Too-Gut's capture of Sarge and the demise of the Yaqui. Sam also explained the strange actions of Lamas heading north.

"He might hide in the barrio in Tucson, there are many bad men there."

"I've already sent a telegram to the Pima County sheriff to be on the lookout for him."

Jesus wrinkled his nose. "He hardly ever goes in that part of town."

"Well, we can't do much until daylight," Sam T. said. He flexed his sore arm to escape some of the pain. "Both of us need some rest, then in the morning you can take Too-Gut and get her some food and fresh horses. Big Boy gets a bait of grain in his belly, he'll be all right for me to ride."

Jesus nodded as Sam counted him out thirty-five dollars.

"Enough?"

"Plenty. I will meet you in the morning after I do that?" Jesus asked.

"Yes, I'll either be at the hotel or the livery. You tell them to be ready to ride. You better get some rest, too," Sam T. said, and they parted.

The next morning, dressed in his newly purchased brown suit coat and white shirt, Sam T. sat in a Nogales cafe eating a hot breakfast. Loud, heavy footsteps drew his gaze to the cafe door. The man who crossed the room toward him was a robust, red-faced individual wearing a tailored suit. His beady eyes seemed too small for his bloated face.

"You're Sam T. Mayes," the man greeted Sam in a gruff voice. "The name's Marcus Wainwright. Sheriff of Saguaro County."

"I've heard of you," Sam said tonelessly.

"Yeah, and I've sure heard plenty about you, Mayes. Where is this Stauffer woman?" Wainwright demanded as he pulled out a chair and sat down uninvited. "I want some answers, Mayes!"

Sam gritted his teeth and studied his fork in an effort to control his first impulse, which was to hit the obnoxious man in his big mouth. The dull ache in his arm and his scraped knuckles deterred Sam T. from action.

Raising his iron gaze to look in the man's face, he spoke with quiet, cold contempt. "This is not your territory. I don't have to answer one gawdamned question. Either you change your tone or get the hell out of here."

Wainwright's face reddened. He looked ready to explode. "Listen, you—"

"No, you listen! If you were in your district doing your job, I wouldn't be here."

"Bullshit! You're a damned bounty hunter. I know who you are."

"I've warned you twice," Sam T. said coldly.

"Warned me?" Wainwright scooted his great girth forward on his chair and abruptly changed his attitude to one of smiling persuasion. "Listen, Mayes, I'll pay you five hundred dollars to find that Justine Stauffer woman, but it better be fast."

Sam T. looked at his plate of congealing eggs. What in the hell made Justine Stauffer worth five hundred dollars to this man and worth a thousand to Narrimore? And what about Lamas? What was she worth to him? Sam knew there had to be an answer. Maybe there was even a connection between the three men, with Mrs. Stauffer providing the mysterious link.

"There, that made a difference," Wainwright said smugly, obviously mistaking Sam's silence for acceptance of his offer.

"What do you need from her?"

"The last report Tom Stauffer made on the Silver Lady Mine. That wife of his must have it."

"What if she doesn't?"

Wainwright cleared his throat and shrugged. "I'll still pay the money to get her, because she probably knows what that report said."

Sam T. studied the man's face for any change as he asked, "Are you Narrimore's partner?"

"Hell, no. What's he offering to pay you for the woman?"

"A thousand," Sam T. said without a blink.

Wainwright blew his breath out his nose like a snorting horse. "Oh, hell. All right, Mayes. I'll give you twelve hundred, but you only have two days. Where is she?"

"In a safe place," he lied blandly.

"Well, you heard what I said. You've only got two days to get her to me. After that, you can kiss the money goodbye." Wainwright rose awkwardly, grunting from the effort of moving his bulky body.

Sam T. watched him through narrowed eyes. "Is this report more important than the woman?" he asked.

Wainwright looked at him impatiently. "Of course. Why? Do you have it?"

Sam shook his head. "I'll see what I can do."

"You just remember—two days, that's all." He turned and went toward the door.

Sam pushed his plate away, his appetite gone. He recalled Taggett, the stage line manager, saying after the robbery that he had given a mine report to the deputy. The paperwork was probably sitting right in the man's office unless his man had thrown it away.

Sam rolled and smoked a cigarette while he considered his options. Maybe he should ride to Narrimore's ranch and find out for certain if Mrs. Stauffer was there. He knew her value to both men now. A damned mine report and one that meant more than the life of an innocent woman. What did all that have to do with Lamas?

Jesus mentioned the Tucson barrio was a hideout for thieves and cutthroats, but the Pima County sheriff did not patrol it. Lamas could be concealed in that area. Well, he'd sent the telegram anyway.

Inevitably, Sam's thoughts returned to Justine Stauffer. He considered Jesus' report of how Narrimore's men had whisked her out of Nogales. At the moment there did not seem to be any positive action Sam could take. Jesus should be back soon if he had no trouble finding Too-Gut and Da-yah's camp.

Sam T. paid for his breakfast and walked slowly back toward the jail. He kept his eyes on the riders in town, expecting to see Jesus among them.

"Mayes," the marshal greeted Sam as he ducked into the jailhouse. "Did Wainwright find you?"

Sam nodded and quickly changed the subject. "How far is this ranch Narrimore owns?"

"A day's ride east. Somewhere near those mines on Slide Creek. You thinking about riding over there?"

"Maybe. I keep thinking that Lamas is holed up in Tucson, but I'd like to ask Narrimore a few questions."

"About Lamas?"

"No. If they are in cahoots, he wouldn't have offered a reward for Justine—I mean Mrs. Stauffer. Any word on that other gang member, Black?"

The marshal shook his head. "No, he's denned up somewhere."

Sam T. tried to sort out all the puzzling facts of this case. Maybe if he rode over and checked on Narrimore and Mrs. Stauffer, there would be word of Lamas's whereabouts when he returned. Jesus seemed to have ideas of his own. Perhaps the two would put their heads together, if he ever got back to town.

Sam T. left the jailhouse and started toward his hotel. Down the end of the street, he noticed a figure wearing a familiar-looking sombrero. With a smile of pleasure, Sam T. stepped off the boardwalk and waited for his scout.

"Good morning, amigo," Jesus greeted Sam with a wide smile. "Our friends send their greetings."

Sam acknowledged the words with a curt nod. Now that his scout had returned, he was anxious for them to be on their way. "If you're ready to take off again, I'd like for us to get moving."

"*Sí.* I am ready. You have learned something more?"

"Maybe. Get my horse from the stable. We're going to Narrimore's to find Mrs. Stauffer. I'm concerned that she might be caught in a web between two ambitious bastards."

Jesus looked around, kept his voice lowered. "Should I get Too-Gut and Da-yah?"

"Yes. I don't know what we might find at Narrimore's. The woman might not even be there."

"No word of Lamas?"

"No, nor Black."

Jesus nodded thoughtfully. "I have heard that some-times Black stays at a *ranchería* north of here."

"How far from here?"

"Oh, a few hours."

Sam considered the idea of going after Black. "Can we swing by there on the way to Narrimore's?"

Jesus nodded. "It is not too far out of the way."

"Good. You get the horses and I'll get some more sup-plies. Oh, and watch out for Wainwright. He doesn't need to know our plans."

Jesus agree and spurred his horse onward. Sam watched him for a moment. He shook his head in dismay and hurried to the mercantile for supplies. Damn, this job was becoming more complicated by the minute.

Lamas exchanged his own clothes for a less conspicuous costume, including a peon serape and a weather-beaten sombrero. He left the Guiterez brothers' place on a sorry horse. Avoiding the main part of Tucson, he had ridden west, then south. He had sent word for Black to meet him at a small farm on the way to Narrimore's. The Guiterez brothers would bring four pistoleros and join them some-time during the day. Earlier, Franco had ridden out to pick up some fresh horses for the long ride.

So far hiring the brothers had cost Lamas almost a thousand dollars. The Guiterez brothers were not cheap, but they were very cunning and he needed them. Besides, the more he considered her body, the more he felt the white woman was worth the price. He had enormous riches from all the robberies and Don Marques would pay well for the rifles, so why should he be concerned about his costs?

In disguise and on his way out of town, Lamas jarred the dull horse with his heels. In a week he would be back in his hacienda with the gringo woman tied up in his bed. This time, he vowed, he would keep her chained up until he needed her supple body.

A smile cracked his lips as he rode past barking mongrel dogs and jeering children. If they only knew who they ridiculed, they would shrink away. He was satisfied that his disguise worked.

He arrived at the small farm in the late afternoon. He noted the big horse tied to a mesquite. Black's batwing chaps hung on the saddled horse. A quick glance around revealed Black squatted by the corral, a rifle across his knees.

"Well, amigo, have you heard all the news?" Lamas dismounted.

Black nodded. "I went out once and tried to find you."

"Much has happened, Ezra," Lamas said wearily. "We will ride tonight to this ranch of Narrimore's. The Stauffer woman is there. An informant told me also that the rifles that I ordered for my good amigo Don Marques are there too."

"How many will ride with us?"

"Six good men and you and I."

Black fell silent for a moment, digesting the information. He asked abruptly, "What about this man in the brown suit that I've heard so much about?"

"Ha! When he comes this time, we will set a trap and kill him."

At the sound of approaching horses, Lamas turned sharply, his hand on the butt of his gun. It was only Franco and the hired men. Lamas dried his palms on the sides of his pants. He felt better than he had in days. A new wave of confidence spread over him. Soon he and

his army would ride again and soon Señora Stauffer
would be back in his bed.

Justine smiled at the young cowboy who brought her supper to the shed. She tried to avoid staring at the handle
of his Colt. He acted obviously uncomfortable with his
task and avoided looking at her directly.

"Ma'am, you'd best eat before it gets cold." He cleared
his throat, shuffled his feet and searched around for a
place to put the tray down.

"Sorry about all this, ma'am." He gestured awkwardly
at the crude surroundings. "Me and the boys are just
doing our job. We ain't too sure why Mr. Narrimore has
you in this place."

Here was a perfect opportunity for her. She wished
she had the boldness of a whore. If she could pluck up
the nerve, she felt certain she could get close enough to the
cowboy to press her body against him. Then swiftly lift
the Colt out of his holster.

"Rudy!" the guard at the door shouted. "Get the hell
out here. You know the orders. The boss said not to talk
to her!"

"Yeah, all right." With a flushed, crestfallen face, the
cowboy turned. At the door he paused a moment, then
shook his head and shrugged.

She drove her fingernails into her palms and groaned
with frustration when the door closed after him. She
cursed her restraint. If only she had tried, she could have
seduced the cowboy.

No way. She could never degrade herself like that
again. A vivid scene flashed through her mind, the re-
volting image of her unbuttoning her dress to distract the
pockfaced gang member Jimmy. That vision was quickly
followed by another scene, one even more humiliating

than the last. She remembered all too clearly trying to be pliant and seductive in Lamas's arms. The sound of his amused, knowing laughter filled her ears and threatened to drive her to the breaking point.

Sam T. and his crew wound their way across the small pass in the black rock hills. Too-Gut rode in the front, then Sam and Da-Yah, with Jesus in the rear. The *ranchería*, where Black was reputed to stay, was deep in the catclaw brush ahead. Sam T. glanced back and could see over the Santa Cruz Valley far beyond and beneath them. When he turned in the saddle, through a veil of mesquite he could make out two broomtails standing hipshot in the corral. He released the thong that covered his pistol's hammer and tried to ignore the sharp twinge in his forearm as he did it.

No sign of Black. They rode abreast toward the low-walled cabin. Every muscle in Sam's body tingled. A woman appeared in the open doorway. In her thirties, she appeared to be white. Thin-built with slumped shoulders, she wore a wash-faded dress. Her steel blue eyes looked them over suspiciously. She spoke abruptly and shrilly in Spanish.

Jesus answered her, then rapped out a question. After listening to her spout a mouthful, the scout turned to Sam T. "She says Black left yesterday if we are looking for him."

"Ask her where he went."

In their vocal exchange, he heard the name *Lamas* several times. He wasn't surprised by Jesus' next words.

"Lamas sent for him."

Sam frowned in disgust. "Well, ask her where they were headed."

A translation wasn't necessary. The vehement shake

of the woman's head, her shrug and her uplifted palms
gave Sam his answer.

He tipped his fingers to his hat in thanks, then turned
Big Boy away. They rode back the way they had come.
Sam glanced back at the house and corrals. This was not
a grand place and the woman had been nothing special
to look at. Black had made his choice of lifestyle long ago
when he became an outlaw. Sam T. felt no sympathy for
him.

"Too-Gut," Sam called to his scout, who was riding
ahead. "Have you ever been to Narrimore's ranch?"

"Two times." The Apache held up his fingers. "The
army watered their horses at Narrimore's place while
chasing Geronimo into Mexico."

"How far from here?"

"Plenty of miles." Too-Gut pointed ahead with his
rifle.

"We better go there."

Too-Gut nodded.

Sam sighed and turned to check on Da-yah and Jesus.
He supposed if anyone saw his crew, they would think
them an odd-looking posse. Mayes's army of misfits, he
mocked himself silently. It seemed like they had to ride
all over the damned desert to pick up bits and pieces of
information.

Later, Sam and his assistants stopped to make camp
at a small spring. Da-yah went about her chores silently
while the men sat in deep thought.

"No word from the major, Sam T.?" Too-Gut asked,
in a tone devoid of expression.

"No, nothing," Sam said, unable to look at the Apache.
Surely Bowen with all his influence could come up with
a pardon for these Apaches. People like Wainwright and
his deputy were the ones who needed to be shipped out.

"Major big man," Too-Gut said confidently. "Him figure a way for us to stay with you."

Sam nodded, but did not comment. He couldn't believe a whole tribe of Indians were being punished because of one renegade known as Geronimo. The major needed to find some detail that would allow Too-Gut and Da-yah to stay off the reservation and help him.

Lamas and his outlaws headed south toward Narrimore's place. Franco's selection of horses proved excellent. They held a steady pace down the Santa Cruz Valley during the night. One of the men that the brothers hired, whose name was Checko, had been to Narrimore's ranch before. Lamas allowed the man to lead the way.

At dawn, they stopped at a friendly Mexican's place to rest and take care of the horses. Black stayed close to Lamas. Obviously he felt little kinship with the Guiterez brothers and the four hired men.

"Lamas," Black said in a low voice, "when this is over do you think those two brothers and their men will accept what you pay them?"

Lamas looked up at the taller man and frowned. "Why are you so suspicious of my amigos?"

"There's six of them and only two of us. I don't like those odds. They may act like they work for you, but I wouldn't like to count on it."

"So we should ride with our eyes open, no?"

Black nodded. "Exactly. That Stauffer woman is worth lots of money, and anyone in Mexico would buy the rifles."

Lamas had already thought of that, but he wasn't going to let Black know that he had any doubts about the brothers' loyalty. Having weighed his options, he had decided he had no choice but to trust the brothers and their hired men.

"Perhaps I am too trusting, but you, Ezra, are too suspicious," he said mildly.

"Maybe. But I'm still going to keep an eye on them," Black said with a grim frown.

Franco walked over to them. "Checko says the woman who lives here will give us food, and then we must ride. It is still many miles."

Lamas nodded in agreement. Then, to ease the tension that Black's disapproving silence was arousing, he clapped Franco on the back and laughed heartily. "It will be worth the ride, amigo. In Mexico we will have a big fiesta when we have finished with Señor Narrimore."

"*Sí.* That will be good." Franco laughed.

Good for what? Lamas wondered. Maybe Black was right. Was it possible that when Franco and Carlos saw Seora Stauffer, they would forget about such things as money and loyalty?

Lamas snapped his teeth together and muttered an oath. He had no choice but to use the Guiterez brothers. Otherwise he didn't stand a chance of getting the white woman back. And he must have her!

Justine looked up in surprise at the man entering her prison. It was Dan, but a haggard-looking Dan Narrimore, with bloodshot eyes.

"Well, Justine, have you remembered anything?" he asked, his voice tight with impatience.

What, she wondered frantically, could she say? Dejected, she sat on the bed. With her hands folded in her lap, she was hopelessly resigned to his repeated inquisition and prepared for him to become violent this time.

She wrung her fingers and swallowed nervously, then she suddenly recalled something that meek little Bailey had said.

"Wh-what does *'core sample'* mean?" she asked in a hoarse voice. Slowly she raised her head.

He stood completely still for a moment, his blood-shot eyes wide and unblinking. Then, in two quick strides he moved to her side. His hand gripped her shoulder hard.

"What? What about the core sample?" His fingers dug into her flesh.

Justine winced and ran her tongue over her parched lips. "B-Bailey said the core samples were very good. At least that's what I think he said," she mumbled uncertainly.

"With silver?" Dan was breathing heavily, looming over her like an oncoming locomotive.

Justine could not remember clearly, for the moment, but she felt there would be safety in a promising response.

"Yes. Silver. That's what he said."

"Ha! I knew it!" Dan boomed with a crack of laughter. He released her shoulder and began pacing the confines of the cramped shed.

Dust, stirred loose by his heavy boots, wafted up Justine's nostrils. Her nose twitched and a sneeze worked its way upward. Reminded vividly of the stagecoach ride when she had sneezed and nearly lost control of her bladder, Justine felt hysterical laughter building inside her. Clamping her jaws, she wiggled her nose, afraid of drawing Dan's preoccupied attention to her presence.

"I knew there was silver. Now I've got that stupid Wainwright right where I want him," Dan muttered.

Justine could no longer control the twitching of her nose. The involuntary sneeze came out in a short, sharp burst. Dan turned at the sound and looked at her through narrowed eyes. "Oh, yes, Justine, I had forgotten about you for a moment." He spoke softly, and she felt he was talking more to himself than to her. "I'll have to figure out something to do about you. You've become, should I say, an inconvenience." He moved toward the door.

Justine rose and impulsively followed him. In a moment of desperation, she clutched at his sleeve. "But Dan, you said if I—"

"Really, Justine, don't be so naive." He shook her hand off, scowling in disgust. "I have no further use for you. I plan to sell you to the highest bidder. They say those fancy bordellos in Mexico are all right." At her look of horror, he threw back his head and roared with laughter. "Don't run off anywhere, will you?" he said with amused sarcasm as he opened the door.

She could hear him chuckling as he bolted the lock on the other side of the door. A desolate groan escaped her lips. She had stupidly told him what he wanted to know, and by doing so, had sealed her own fate. One potentially even worse than Lamas.

Narrimore's ranch bustled with activity. Sam T. bellied down on a large boulder and studied the operation through his spyglass, sweeping it slowly over the buildings and corrals far beneath his perch on the mountainside. A large remuda of horses was being moved south by several wranglers. There were a couple of black-garbed women who were probably servants, but he could detect no sign of Justine Stauffer. He folded up the brass telescope and eased back off the boulder.

"Sam T.," Too-Gut said, squatting beside him on the hard-packed ground. "Riders are coming from the north."

Sam turned the glass in that direction. He could make out a faint wall of moving dust, but due to a ridge, saw nothing of horses or riders.

"Maybe it's more of Narrimore's men."

"He'll have plenty men," Too-Gut said, as if unconvinced.

"It'll be dark soon," Sam observed. "Tonight we'll check the place out. I can't risk the woman's life by going in there now with our guns blazing."

"Look there." Too-Gut pointed toward the ranch buildings.

Two men in a buckboard headed north. Sam trained the telescope on them. Either they were on their way to meet the riders in the north or perhaps they were unaware of the riders and were simply leaving the ranch. Sam judged by the mens' hats that one of them was a cowboy. The other man on the buggy seat wore a white flat-crowned hat; maybe he was Narrimore. Whoever they were, they were certainly in a big hurry.

Wincing from the strain on the taut muscles in his injured limb, Sam rose. His right forearm was still tender, but healing without any complications.

Checko, who rode in the lead, gave a signal to halt, and Lamas pulled up with the others.

"A buckboard is coming!" Franco shouted. His lathered horse pranced in a circle beneath him.

"Who is it?" Lamas asked. He squinted, trying to see the approaching rig.

The buckboard dropped under a rise, out of view, but the sounds of galloping horses did not diminish.

"Take them!" Lamas ordered, drawing his pistol. "They could warn the ranch we are coming."

When the team topped the rise, the driver stood up with his feet jammed on the dash and reined the team in a circle to head them back. Before he could utter a word, a shot rang out, striking him in the chest. The man fell over the side of the wagon, his body hitting the dry ground with a dull thud.

The startled team of horses bolted back toward the ranch house, but two of Guiterezes' hired men raced in and caught them by their bridles.

Narrimore remained seated, his face registering shock at their attack. He slowly raised his hands at their approach.

"Who in hell are you?" he asked Lamas, who urged his horse closer to the wagon.

Lamas ignored the question. "Where is the woman?"

Narrimore frowned in obvious puzzlement. "Oh, you mean Justine?" A wave of relief swept over his red face. "You want her?" he asked in disbelief.

"Yes, I want her."

Narrimore lowered his hands and grinned slyly. "Oh, you can have her." He dismissed Justine as though he were giving away a mangy dog. "Listen, I can pay you with gold."

"Where is she?"

Narrimore grimaced. "Back at the ranch. I'll take you there, but no shots, now. I'll call my boys off and no one else will get hurt. You can have Justine and a lot of gold."

"And the rifles?" Lamas asked.

"Yes. I have some new ones. You can have them too." He stopped and searched the bandits' faces for some sign of their intention.

"So, you are Narrimore?" Lamas questioned.

"Yes. Dan Narrimore. I'm a rich man. I have lots of powerful friends who would be very upset if anything happened to me."

Lamas reined his horse to the side and nodded at Black. "Kill him."

"No! You don't—"

The air became punctuated with pistol shots. Narrimore's body was torn to shreds as he fell back from the force of the bullets. The panicked horses screamed and reared on their hind legs. Acrid gun smoke created a cloud until the desert breeze swept it away.

Lamas moved away from the others. The bandits descended on Narrimore's corpse like children around a broken piñata. Lamas and Black watched the outlaws squabble over the gold pieces that they found in the man's pockets.

Franco looked to Lamas and laughed. "Now there is no leader at the ranch."

Lamas shrugged. "He wouldn't have given us the woman or the guns and gold."

"No," Franco agreed soberly. "Now we will take them." He reined his horse around and swore at his men. "Get on your horses!"

Checko grinned, his sombrero replaced by Narrimore's expensive white hat. "Bueno sombrero, no?" He rode on like some parading fool on horseback.

"Will there be horses there that we can sell in Mexico?" Franco asked Lamas quietly.

"Oh, yes. Many horses," Lamas assured him, forcing a smile that he was far from feeling. Perhaps the horses would satisfy the men. He wanted only the woman and the rifles. The bandits were welcome to the gold that Narrimore had mentioned. The extra bounty might prevent the confrontation that Black feared.

Still, the undisciplined way the hired men hoarded what they found on Narrimore worried Lamas. They were not his men, but perhaps their greed would play into his hands.

Sam T. thought he heard the sound of gunshots, but he couldn't be sure. With him and his crew positioned out of sight on a flat, high upon the mountain side above the ranch, his hearing was disoriented. He looked at Jesus busy cleaning his pistols; he had obviously heard nothing unusual. Da-yah stood holding the horses, her head cocked as though listening.

"Bandits!" Too-Gut shouted. He was coming down the slope behind Sam, his knee-high boots sending loose dirt down the hill. "Sam T., plenty of bandits are coming!" He pointed to the ranch below.

"What?"

"Big shooting down there." Too-Gut had reached Sam's side. He gestured with his rifle as he talked. "They must have stopped the buckboard."

"Oh, hell," Sam swore. "We better get down there fast."

Justine peered between the cracks in the shed. Something was going on outside. The whole ranch looked frantic with activity. She glimpsed several men brandishing rifles.

"Bandits are coming!"

The words filled her with dread. Bandits? It would be Lamas, of course. A quick check of her prison showed her there was no place to hide; he would surely find her in this shed, and when he did . . . She shuddered in horror and searched around frantically. There had to be a way out—she could not endure Lamas's touch again.

Taking several deep breaths, she tried to settle her rising hysteria. She had to think and plan; first she must calm down and be rational. With great effort she unclenched her fingers and wiped her damp palms on the sides of her skirt. Then she moved to the door and placed her ear against the rough boards.

There were no sounds from outside the door. A small ray of hope rose within her. The guards had deserted their post to get ready for the bandits. The opportunity to escape seemed to be upon her.

Almost whimpering with frustration, she darted a quick glance around the cramped room. Her eyes lingered on a three-legged chair propped against the back wall.

Quickly she crossed the room. The chair proved heavy and awkward to lift, but she managed, swaying slightly beneath the weight.

Fear gave her added strength as she smashed the stool against the boarded-up, waist-high window. Two boards separated under the force of the blow, but she knew it wasn't enough. Her arms ached and felt like leaden weights as she lifted the chair again. She staggered backward when the chair came into violent contact with the boards. The blows caused her arms to jerk in their sockets. A gasp escaped her throat when a bright stream of sunlight flooded through the opening.

Dropping the chair, she raced to the window and began pulling at the loose boards with trembling fingers. She ignored the sharp splinters and rusted nails that seemed intent on punishing her daring.

Finally the boards hung drunkenly at the side of the window frame. Glorious sunlight bathed Justine's face and she hoisted herself up on the window ledge. She cast a quick look around the area outside, but no one was looking her way.

She struggled out the empty window frame, her skirt caught on a nail. Cursing beneath her breath, she grabbed a handful of material and gave a vicious yank. Then, with her skirt hem clutched in her hand, she ran toward the barn.

Her breath came in painful gasps when she reached the relative safety of the sweet-smelling, hay-filled structure. When she slipped inside, a horse nickered to her. She heard the sounds of men's voices close by and hurriedly scuttled toward the harness room in the rear of the barn.

With her fist jammed in her mouth to keep from crying, Justine swept a glance over the small room. It was no larger than the shed had been, but it was clean and filled with oily-smelling harnesses and riding tack.

A sudden eruption of gunfire outside startled her into action. She threw herself on the straw-littered floor behind a stack of long, new-looking crates. A frenzy of activity began outside the barn. She tried to close her ears and mind to the gunfire, the horses' screams and the sound of men dying.

Lamas, the black-hearted outlaw, she knew, was out there somewhere. But this time she would not be taken alive; this time she would fight him until he was furious enough to shoot her. For the moment, all she could do was hide and wait.

Sam T. could hear them shooting. A serious fight had broken out on Narrimore's ranch. He had no choice but to descend down the mountain face and cross to the ranch in plain view. His only hope was that the fight between the bandits and Narrimore's men might be so distracting that he and his assistants would not be noticed until it was too late to stop them. The gunshots sounded like distant firecrackers in the high-walled canyon. When Sam forced his horse down the rocky mountainside, the shots became more distinct. The sorrel's hooves slid, causing Sam to lurch in the saddle. He did not draw his Colt yet, because he knew the weight of it in his hand would bring pain to his sore arm. When he got close enough to aim accurately, he would clench his teeth and fire the damn thing.

The Apaches were ahead of him about a hundred yards. He heard Jesus on his left, behind him, swearing in Spanish at his horse. Sam couldn't afford the luxury of looking at his assistants. If his attention was distracted for a moment, he was liable to be pitched off his horse in the wild descent straight down the hillside.

Lamas crouched behind a wagon, his pistol smoking. Black was beside him, reloading his pistol. The acrid smell

of gunpowder burned Lamas's nose. He raised his eyes
for a moment and peered through the smoke.

"Franco is hit," he hissed to Black. He watched Franco
trying to drag himself to safety. Carlos blazed his guns
at the ranch house and screamed at his brother to hurry.

Lamas noted a cowboy trying to run toward the house,
a smoking rifle at his hip. Raising his pistol, Lamas fired,
then smiled when the cowboy fell to the ground.

Checko lay pinned under his dead horse, his body
twisted grotesquely. Who else was down? Lamas knew
that two of the hired pistoleros were dead. A fresh round
of shots was fired in his direction. Lamas ducked low,
cursing the cowboys in the house.

"Let's get to the horses!" Carlos shouted. "Ride out!"

"No!" Lamas screamed. His eyes blazed in hatred. He
could see that Carlos had his wounded brother safely
behind an outbuilding. "Fight these gringos. Don't run
like dogs!" he screeched, the muscles in his neck bulging.

"What's he doing?" Black asked between shots.

"Turning coward. Shoot the bastard, Ezra."

Black's Colt blasted in rapid fire until the hammer
clicked on an empty. Carlos's screams were silenced;
there was no more gunfire from his position.

"Son of a bitch!" Black swore as he tried to reload.
"Lamas, we've got more company." He jerked his head,
indicating the men who were riding up behind them.

Lamas whirled. At the sight of the four riders approaching with blazing guns, his face paled and his heart
plummeted. He raised his Colt and aimed for the big man
in the brown suit This must be the gringo Sam T. Mayes.
The knowledge of who was closing in on him filled Lamas with a fiery rage. He squeezed off a shot, realizing
when the hammer struck the cartridge it was a dud. The
explosion muffled. He cocked the hammer, issuing
Spanish profanity with the trigger pull, when the next

round barely exploded. The big man drew closer. Frantically, Lamas began to punch out the shells.

Sam T. paced his own shots as he and his assistants drew closer. He kept his eyes on the two men, who were half hidden behind a wagon.

Black looked at Lamas, still reloading, then at the approaching riders. He shook his head, moved a few feet away from Lamas, then stood up.

"Hold your fire!" he shouted, raising his hands in the air.

From the description of the outlaws, Sam knew this must be Black. The shorter man beside him looked at his comrade in outrage, then quickly snapped off two shots at Sam that zinged by him. Abruptly the outlaw broke from his cover and raced across the yard toward the barn and corrals.

"Jesus," Sam shouted, "get the others; that one is mine!" He knew by his dress the fleeing man must be the leader, Lamas.

Urging his horse forward, Sam held his revolver ready, oblivious of the stinging pain in his arm.

Lamas reached the corral and looked around wildly for a horse. He could hear the hoofbeats of the gringo's horse getting nearer. But there was no route of escape, nowhere to hide now. Bracing himself against the side of the pens, Lamas swung up the barrel of his .44, ready to shoot the brown-suited bastard.

Sam rounded the corner of the barn, his eyes narrowed, his fist gripping the handle of his revolver. He aimed for Lamas's heart, just as the outlaw blasted in his direction. A bullet buzzed by Sam T.'s head like an angry hornet while the Colt in his fist belched acrid smoke and lead.

His bullet's force slammed Lamas into the corral rails. The outlaw tried to raise his gun arm, but could not find the strength. His vision blurred and he slumped to the ground. He had to say something to this hombre who had brought down the mighty Lamas.

Sam T. dismounted and stood over the outlaw. The look of approaching death on the man's face and the rapidly spreading stain of blood on his shirt gave Sam no sense of satisfaction.

Lamas forced his eyes open and peered up at the gringo, who seemed to be as tall as a mountain. "You are . . . Sam T. Mayes. . . . You have won, white man—" A wracking cough broke up the outlaw's words. "But I, Lamas . . . I had her white flesh first."

A smile, part smug and part sad, lifted Lamas's mouth as he slumped dead onto the ground. Sam T. frowned down at the gang leader. For an instant, searing anger whirled through him like a fire. He wanted to kick the man, jerk him up, beat his face to a bloody pulp, because even in death, the outlaw had no remorse. He remained a smug, cold-blooded animal.

Sam T. shook his head to clear it. The Border Gang was no more. He had done the job he was hired to do. Lamas had at last answered to the law of the Arizona Territory

With a tired sigh, he turned and walked back toward Jesus and Too-Gut. The two had rounded up the remaining men from both sides.

"Good job, Jesus. Go check inside the barn," Sam said, looking around at the wounded and dead. "Hey, you be careful. There might be one left in there."

Jesus waved to indicate he had heard and hurried off to the barn.

"Is Lamas dead?" Black asked flatly.

Sam T. holstered his Colt, wincing with pain. "He's dead." When he looked at Black, he was surprised by the expression of loss on the man's face.

"Lamas was a tough bastard," Black said quietly.

Sam shook his head in disbelief. How had such a vicious outlaw like Lamas inspired that much loyalty? It was a crazy damned world. Too-Gut and Da-yah guarded the prisoners, who were seated on the ground. Then it occurred to Sam: He had forgotten about Justine Stauffer. Surely she was there someplace.

The abrupt silence of the guns frightened Justine, who crouched behind a wooden barrel that smelled sharply of oats. Biting her lip, she lowered her hands from her ears and held her breath. Cautiously she peeked over the barrel she had hidden behind. The creaking of the wooden barn caused her heart to pound harder. Was it Lamas coming for her at last?

With that thought in mind, she rose and watched the alleyway through the open harness room door, awaiting her fate. A shaft of sunlight filtered through the front opening of the barn. A man stood framed in the light. He wore a sombrero and crossed belts of ammunition.

A scream rose to her throat. It was Lamas! She dropped down, huddled behind the barrels and chewed on her knuckles.

"Señora, do not scream," Jesus coaxed. "I am a friend. Please, I am here with the law. We are here to help you."

"You aren't Lamas?" Justine blinked her eyes, then ran her hand over her face. A shiver of relief ran through her entire body. Taking in her breath, she rose shakily and took a hard look at the man. "Oh, God, I thought you were Lamas coming for me."

"No, señora. Lamas is dead."

"Dead?" she repeated in shock. She couldn't believe it. Her tormentor and enemy dead? She cast her gaze at the loft floor; her prayers had been answered. A wave of relief washed over her. She hardly knew what to do next, but she needed to see for herself that Lamas was truly dead.

Cautiously she walked toward the man. "Where is Lamas? I want to see him."

"Señora, do you think that is wise?" At the stubborn expression on her face, Jesus relented. "Very well, but first I must be certain it is safe for you to come out." He turned toward the door.

"No! Don't leave me here alone." She rushed to be beside him.

Jesus sighed. "All right, Mrs. Stauffer, you will come with me," he said patiently. "We will go see Sam T."

A low whistle suddenly escaped Jesus' lips when he finally noticed the crates. "*Madre Dios!* Could those be the missing rifles?" He quietly moved forward and lifted the end of an opened crate. She stood beside him and blinked at the sight of the gleaming guns.

"This is a lucky day," Jesus said with a grin. "Sam T. will be happy."

Justine wondered about Sam T. Who was he? She was comforted somewhat by the knowledge that this Mexican, who looked like Lamas, knew her name. She looked into his face curiously. "What is your name, señor?"

"Jesus. Jesus Morales. Come, please." He held out a hand to help her over the threshold.

Outside, the setting sun was beginning to bathe everything with an orange glow. With this short man at her side, she felt reassured of her own safety. She clutched at his arm as she looked around. When they rounded the corrals, she discovered two Indians armed with rifles, guarding several cowboys seated on the ground.

"Who is that?" She indicated the Apaches.

"Ah, that is Too-Gut and his wife Da-yah. They work with us."

Justine blinked in confusion. First a man who looked

like a bandit rescued her. And now Indians had arrested
Dan's cowboys. What would this Sam T. look like?
And where was Lamas?

Sam T. handcuffed Black and put him with the other outlaws. There were a few loose ends left to tie up. When
he glanced across the yard, he noted Jesus escorting
a woman from the corrals. His first sight of Justine
Stauffer surprised him. Despite her dusty dress and dis-
orderly hair, she was beautiful. Much prettier even than
the tintype showed. A wave of relief filled Sam when he
realized the woman was alive and finally safe.

"Sam T.," Jesus said when he and Justine were a few
feet away from Sam. "The rifles are in the barn. I think
they are all there."

"Good job, Jesus," Sam said, feeling the woman's eyes
appraising him.

Justine studied the tall, broad shouldered man in his
dusty once-brown suit. He looked like a lawman, but
where on earth had he gathered such a strange posse?

Sam approached her with a smile, hat in hand.
"Mrs. Stauffer? I'm Sam T. Mayes, Territorial Marshal.
It's nice to meet you."

Justine extended her hand and noted the pain on his
face when he shook her hand. "Oh, you're hurt."

"An old injury," Sam T. said, feeling uncomfortable.
He engulfed her hand gently. "Mrs. Stauffer, could I ask
you some questions?"

She nodded; then, looking around nervously, she
rushed into her speech. "First, Mr. Mayes, I want to see
Lamas. I want to be sure he's dead!"

Sam T. stared into her strained face, then noticed
she was visibly trembling.

"I understand," he said quietly. Taking her arm in his

good one, he led her across the yard to the corral. When they reached the pens, he felt her fingers stiffen on his sleeve.

Justine looked at the outlaw lying prone on the ground about ten feet from them. Dark blood soaked the entire front of his silk shirt, his body lay twisted at an odd angle, but still she was not certain that he didn't have the power to hurt her again.

Pulling free, she hesitantly ventured toward Lamas. When she was within touching distance, she glanced back over her shoulder, her eyes pleading with Sam T.'s.

He reached her side quickly; then, dropping to his knee, he felt for a pulse at the outlaw's throat.

"He is dead, Mrs. Stauffer." And for a moment he recalled the outlaw's final words concerning the woman behind him, and his face grew grim.

"He can't hurt you anymore." He rose and placed an arm around her shoulders.

"Yes, yes, you're right. He can't hurt me ever again." Tears of relief welled in her eyes and trailed down her face. She allowed him to lead her away from the dead man, back toward the house.

"We'll have you home in no time," Sam T. said as he removed his hand and smiled down at her face. The skin had peeled in places on her cheeks and nose. It showed the hell she must have endured in the desert.

Justine used the back of her hand to wipe away her tears. Confidence seemed to radiate from this tall lawman and it warmed her. For the first time in days, a natural smile came to her crusted lips.

"I know you will, Mr. Mayes."

"Jesus, find that buckboard. Mrs. Stauffer is probably anxious to get away from here."

"Thank you," she said softly. She stared off at the

mountainside in the twilight. If she had only known he was coming to her rescue, she would not have worried so much. The idea brought a smile of genuine amusement to her face. Someday she would invite the impressive marshal to visit her home, when her life returned to normal.

"Wait," she said softly. "I can go with you and your men. What do I have to rush home for?" She waited for his answer.

"Be mighty kind of you, ma'am. You sure?" He looked at her hard.

"I am absolutely certain."

"Good. Then you call me Sam or Sam T."

"I certainly will."

"Good, you have a seat. I'm going hustle up a wagon to haul these prisoners back in."

Sam T., huh? She watched him rush off. Was he married? She hoped not, but anyway, she was pleased she'd thought of making the offer. Besides, it would give her more time to get to know him better. She closed her eyes and drew in a deep breath. It was finally over.

They loaded the prisoners in a ranch wagon, which Jesus drove. Too-Gut and Da-yah led the extra horses. Sam T. handled the buckboard and escorted Justine. The trip required two days and she found the time spent most interesting. This big man Sam T. had many interesting traits about him that showed his good taste. In due time she wanted to learn even more.

Near Tucson, Sam T. paid Too-Gut money out of his own pocket, promised him those passes from the major and told him to keep out of sight until Jesus came for them. They had lots more work to do. The Apaches loaded the remaining supplies on an extra horse to take with them.

"Sam T., we be ready to work plenty soon," Too-Gut said and waved his rifle.

Da-yah jumped off her horse, rushed up to him and rested her forehead on his chest. He hugged her until his sore arm hurt. Then she looked up and said, "You be careful." She ran to join her mate.

Her action caused a knot to form in his throat. He wet his lips and watched them ride away into the greasewood. Swallowing the lump down there, he just looked away for a long while.

"We better go," he said at last and climbed on the buckboard seat beside Justine. He was grateful when she didn't ask any questions. She obviously knew enough about the Apaches' plight from being around them the past two days.

Outside of Tucson, he prepared to part with Jesus.

"You can collect the reward for Lamas," Sam T. said. "And on these others. Turn them over to the Pima County Sheriff's Office. Don't talk about me or the Apaches to anyone. They ask you, simply say your friends helped you and they were concerned citizens who went back home. They were afraid these outlaws had friends who would see them."

"I will meet you at Tia's tonight?" Jesus smiled.

"Yes," Sam T. said with a confirming nod. "Get up there on that seat and take them in." He tied their extra horses on behind the buckboard.

Then he waited and watched the somber prisoners seated on the wagon floor, their arms and feet bound, as Jesus pulled out. It was about over. If his plan worked for Jesus to deliver them to the sheriff, the major should be happy. Best he could do under the circumstances.

He climbed on the seat and turned to Justine. "Time we took you home."

She reached over and hugged his arm, then impulsively laid her face on his left shoulder. "I'm being real brazen out here in this desert, aren't I?"

"I wouldn't call it that."

"Good. You will come by and see me when you return to Tucson?"

"Wild horses couldn't keep me away."

She raised her head and smiled at him, then leaned back against his shoulder and squeezed his arm. "Good."

When Sam T. arrived at Tia's, she drew him a bath while he explained about their success. How was Jesus? Fine. She beamed and told him to bathe while she hurried out to her ramada to make him some food. Grateful, he soaked away plenty of desert dirt and wondered about Jesus and how the encounter with the law went. After a while, he dried, dressed and went outside under the shade to enjoy some of her spicy food. After he ate, she hustled him off to take a nap. Jesus came in after dark and awoke him.

"What did they say?" Sam T. asked, combing his hair back and ready to pull his boots on.

"The sheriff, he says, 'You expect us to believe that Black is the only member of the whole Border Gang left alive?'"

"What happened next?"

"Black said he was the last one."

Both men laughed.

"The rewards are coming. The sheriff, he asked me if I wanted to go to work for him."

"And?" Sam T. paused before pulling on his last boot.

"I told him I had to spend that reward money first, huh?" Jesus grinned with pride.

"He never asked any more questions?"

"Oh, plenty more, and some boy from the newspaper asked me a thousand things." Jesus shook his head as if the ordeal had been tiring.

"What did you tell him?"

"Lots of lies."

"Did they believe you?" Sam T. snickered, envisioning the man doing it.

Jesus shrugged. "What else could they do?"

"Nothing."

"I have some more good news. A Texas sheriff is coming to take Jimmy back to Texas to stand trial for murder. And the one they call Sarge that you left in the Nogales jail: the army already has him under arrest for murder and much more. They say he will hang."

"That settles the whole thing. Let's go get us some food." Sam T. reached for his hat. "Tia can come along too. You ready?" he asked Jesus, who stood with her under his arm.

"I am ready. It has been a long time."

Sam T. slipped on his hat. It had been a long time, but he did enjoy it. Beat working in a city like Denver. He stepped outside into the night and studied the spray of stars. This marshal business wasn't so bad after all, especially with Lamas and his gang taken care of.

The next morning Sam T. parted with Jesus and climbed on the Prescott stage. It was all arranged for Jesus to keep his profile low, collect his rewards, make certain the horses were reshod and ready and watch for the mail. Tia would read it to him.

A day later, in Prescott, Sam T.—stiff and sore from his long coach ride—hiked up the hill to Bowen's house in the early morning hours to explain the results.

When he finished his report, the major, who sat across the dining table, beamed at him. "It worked. The governor is excited as can be. He's convinced this marshal business is the answer. How much rest do you need?"

"Enough time to get passes for two Apaches."

There—he'd put his cards on the table. What would the major do about it?

Bowen wiped his face with his hands, then looked hard at him. "By gawd, Sterling will just have to arrange for them."

"Good." The matter, for Sam, was settled.

"I've got this deal for you," Bowen began. "One of Quantrel's chief men, Terrel Martin, is living the high life in Mexico. Sterling wants him brought back to the States and tried for his war crimes."

"He's in Mexico. No extradition, is there?" Sam knew the answer before he asked. Whew. He closed his eyes.

"Mary, bring that whiskey," Bowen said and rambled on about the details of the case. Sam settled back in the chair and listened.

Ella Devereaux stood at her upstairs front window behind the lace curtains. Earlier that morning, she learned from a teary-eyed Lily that her plant in the telegraph office, Brad Townsend, under some sort of duress from the law, had fled Prescott. The notion did not make her any happier. That boy had been her source of much useful information.

In her hand was the latest telegram from Senator Green:

LEARN ALL YOU CAN ABOUT THESE BOUNTY MEN STERLING HAS HIRED— GREEN.

Deeply engrossed in the contents, she frowned at Abraham's shouting in the house. Why, he'd wake up all the girls. Whatever did he want? She could hear his big feet pounding down the hallway. Out of breath, he rushed